The

The Vigilante Life of Scott McKenzie

Chapter One

1958

Ten-year-old Scott McKenzie put his arm around his little sister Cheryl. They were hunkered down in the closet of Scott's room in their home in Middle Falls, Oregon. Even hidden away, the sounds of the fight in the living room still echoed loudly in their ears. His closet had been their sanctuary for the endless series of fights his parents had.

This particular set-to had started like many before it. It had begun with their father coming home late and drunk. It escalated from accusations of infidelity to the sounds of slapping, punching, and furniture being knocked over.

Scott held Cheryl's face in his hands, willing her to meet his eyes. "What do mares eat?"

"Oats," the little girl said, a waver in her voice.

"And what about does?"

"Oats."

"And how about little lambs?"

"Little lambs eat ivy."

"A kid'll eat ivy, too. Wouldn't you?"

Scott had used this game to distract Cheryl from the terrible happenings in their home on dozens of occasions, but tonight, *Mairzy Doats* wasn't doing the trick. She did her best to look at

Scott, but her eyes continually darted to the slats in the closet door. He felt her tremble under his protective arm.

Things went deathly quiet in the living room. Scott hoped that meant that the fight was over and the cleanup was in progress. *If it's not that, then things are about to get a lot worse. I need to go and see if Mom needs help, but I don't want to leave Cheryl all alone in here.*

He held Cheryl tightly against him. This quiet in the eye of the storm unnerved both of them. He strained his ears, but couldn't pick up any sound.

I need to go check. He might be killing Mom.

He whispered in Cheryl's ear. "Come on. I think it's over." He acted as though he had a brand new idea. "Hey, it's still warm outside." It wasn't, but the cold was an easier problem to deal with than whatever was happening in the house. "Maybe we can go for a walk around the neighborhood. We'll be safe out there." His mind's eye went to the playground down the street, lit by the soft glow of a streetlight. "There won't be anyone at the park. Would you like me to push you on the swings?"

Cheryl nodded, but the look in her eyes showed she was scared to the point of not thinking.

Scott pushed the closet door open. Slowly. It made the barest of creaks and he paused, waiting. There was still no sound from the other room.

Scott grabbed Cheryl's small hand and led her out of the closet. They were both in stocking-feet. There was no time to think about tenny runners. Scott was focused on one thing.

Distance.

Distance from the fear, the fighting, the violence that hung over the house like a dark cloud.

They crept past Scott's bed. Past the open *Curious George* book turned face down on the floor. Past the Howdy Doody marionette that laid crumpled beside the toy box.

The door to his room was closed. Scott laid his hand on the knob for two beats while he labored to hear anything that might indicate whether they were walking into either safety or danger. The house was still bathed in eerie quiet.

I should be able to hear them talking by now. What are they doing?

Scott and Cheryl walked on cat's feet, down the hall. Past the bathroom, and their parents' bedroom. The light from the living room cut like a knife's blade across the deep shadows of the hall. Scott put his toes as close to the light as he could and slowly leaned forward to peek around the corner.

A gunshot filled the house and echoed down the hallway. It was made all the louder, all the more terrible, by the deafening silence that had preceded it.

Scott cried out and jumped instinctively back. His cry was lost in the echoing reverberation of the shot.

He turned and looked at Cheryl. Her eyes were thrown wide, her mouth a perfect circle of fear. He reached for her, but she had lost her small reserve of courage. She turned and skittered down the hall, not caring how much noise she made.

Scott nodded. *Good. I don't want her to see whatever I am about to see.*

With the echoing explosion of the gun gone, deep silence returned to the house.

His heart beat a pounding rhythm in his throat, but he forced his leaden feet to take another step toward the living room. *Maybe he shot the gun to scare her. To scare us. But why can't I hear her?*

He forced himself to look around the corner.

What he saw remained in his memory for many lives.

His mother was on one end of the sofa, his father on the other. Her head was thrown back and her right arm was laid across the back of the couch. She looked as though she had braced herself for a long laugh. The blood spatter on the wall behind her told a different story.

Scott stared at his mother while the realization of what he was seeing sank into his brain.

He finally tore his eyes away from her and slowly turned his head toward his father.

Mark McKenzie sat staring directly at his son. With his violence discharged, he was calm. Dead calm. His eyes never moved from Scott.

Scott looked at his father with wide eyes. A gun sat on the sofa cushion next to him.

Mark McKenzie picked the pistol up and looked at it as though seeing it for the first time. He pointed it directly at Scott, considering. There was no shake in his hand.

Scott wanted to turn and run like Cheryl had, but he stood rooted to the spot.

With exquisite slowness, Mark McKenzie moved the gun in an arc until it was pointing directly at his own face. He continued to stare directly at Scott. He let his jaw fall open, pushed the barrel of the gun against the top of his mouth. He blinked once.

Pulled the trigger.

Chapter Two

Twenty-year-old Scott McKenzie dried the last of the night's dishes and put the casserole dish and plates away.

From the living room, his grandfather called, "Hurry along, Scotty, it's almost time."

It was December 1, 1969. Scott and Cheryl McKenzie had been living with their grandparents for ten and a half years—ever since the day their father had shot their mother and then himself. Earl and Cora—Gramps and Gram to Scott and Cheryl—had flown into Portland the next day. They drove to Middle Falls and brought the siblings home.

Scott was glad to have the opportunity to move to Indiana. In Evansville, he was only "the new guy." Back in Middle Falls, he would have been "the kid whose dad shot his mom."

His parents' murder-suicide had changed his life in a thousand different ways. Where he finished school was only one. Certain images from that night would never leave his memory, no matter how much time passed, or how he tried to forget them. It was almost impossible for him to think of his mother without seeing the image of her stretched out on that sofa.

Cheryl still jumped and cried at sudden, loud noises. Scott's nightmares eventually lessened, but still awakened him, sweating and shaking, from time to time.

Even the most horrific wounds eventually heal over and fade into scars. Their grandparents provided them with many things they had missed while their parents were alive—primary among them, safety and a sense of calm.

Scott finally felt like he had his life under control. In eight months, he would turn twenty-one, and could finally enroll in the academy for the Evansville, Indiana police force. He had graduated from high school two years earlier with grades that were good enough to get him into college, but Scott had never considered it—he was going to be a cop.

The night his parents had died, his first instinct was to run out the front door and never look back. He knew he could not leave his sister behind, though, and there was no way to get her out of the house without seeing the horror show their living room had become.

Instead, he had looked up the number, called the police and told them what had happened. The first responder on the scene had been a large man in full uniform. He had been an awe-inspiring sight to the frightened ten-year-old boy. He had brought such a sense of calm and order to the scene, that Scott knew that was the job for him.

The summer after his senior year, he had taken a job at the local Chevy dealer. He washed cars, ran errands, and worked as a general-purpose gofer at the dealership, working and saving until he was old enough to get into the academy.

While working at the dealership, he met Sherry Dickenson, a pretty brunette girl with a friendly smile who liked to wear miniskirts to her job as the front desk receptionist. It was hard to say which of those traits attracted Scott more. Before he knew it, he was in love.

At the tender age of twenty, then, he had his life planned out. Enroll in the academy, become a police officer, then ask Sherry to marry him and live happily ever after. As simple as one, two, three.

The only potential monkey wrench in his plan was the Selective Service Draft, which was going to be televised on CBS that very night in place of a new episode of *Mayberry RFD.*

The newspaper that morning had said that if your birthdate was drawn in the first third of the selection, you were almost certain to be drafted. In the last third, you were almost certain not to be. If you were in the middle, it could go either way. This was one lottery that no one wanted to win.

Scott dried his hands on a dishtowel and walked into the small living room. His grandparents were already in their favorite chairs. His grandfather had that day's *Evansville Courier & Press* open on his lap. His grandmother was knitting an afghan she intended as a Christmas present for one of the ladies at church. Cheryl, who was in high school now, was in her room, ostensibly studying. In reality, she was laying on her bed, staring at a poster of Bobby Sherman and talking on the princess phone she had gotten for her birthday.

CBS correspondent Roger Mudd, reporting on the low-tech affair, sat in the front row, like a witness to an execution. He turned in his seat, looked directly into the camera and in hushed tones, explained that the United States hadn't held a draft in twenty-seven years, since World War II.

Scott sat on the edge of the couch.

They're not gonna show them draw all three hundred and sixty-six numbers, are they? That'll take all night.

In a stroke of almost unbelievable anticlimax, Mudd intoned, "The famous first number drawn for this draft is September 14. That will be number zero-zero-one. If that's your birthday, it's time to start packing."

His grandfather dropped his paper into his lap. "Shit."

"Earl!" Cora said. "Language." She cocked her head and looked at Scott. "Oh, Scotty, I'm so sorry. This is so awful."

Scott leaned back into the couch, stunned. He had been anticipating this night for weeks, and before it even started, it was all over for him.

"The famous first number drawn for this draft is September 14."

Of course. My birthday. Am I never going to catch a break?

Scott glanced at his grandfather, whose mouth was set in a thin line as he shook his head. "Damned war. There's no way we're going to win over there. Nixon keeps saying he's going to end it, but instead, he's throwing more and more of our young men into the fire."

Scott tried to find a smile to flash at his grandparents, but he couldn't manage it. Instead, he said, "I think I'm going to go for a little drive."

"Oh, honey," his grandmother said, soothingly. "Why don't you stay here with us? We don't need to watch this. I'm sure there's a movie on one of the other channels. I can make some popcorn."

"Thanks, Grandma. I just want to go for a little drive and clear my head. I'll be all right. I've got to think things through."

He kissed his grandmother on the cheek, grabbed his keys off the hall table and hurried outside. His old Chevy Apache pickup sat in the driveway, and he climbed in. Five minutes later, he was outside the city limits of Evansville and driving through the countryside.

Now what. Wait it out? I don't think it will be much of a wait. How long until they send Draft Notices to those first few numbers?

He rolled the driver's window down and a cold blast of air filled the cab.

Go to Canada? Can't do it. I don't have it in me, and I can't leave everyone behind anyway. That doesn't leave many options.

He shook his head at the unfairness of it all. He realized he was trapped.

Chapter Three

Scott asked for, and got, the next afternoon off from work at the dealership. He drove to the Army Recruiting office, which was in a small storefront in downtown Evansville. It was a modest affair—just two desks, a few chairs against the front wall, and an American flag in one corner of the room.

One desk was empty, but a barrel-chested man in a crisp U.S. Army uniform sat behind the other. When Scott walked in, the man jumped to his feet, his posture erect, a small smile on his face. For a moment, Scott thought he was going to salute him, but he extended his hand instead.

Scott shook it, firmly.

"Good handshake, son. That's a good sign." The man gestured to a chair in front of his desk. "Sit down, and we can talk. I'm Sgt. Berkman. What brings you into the office today? Looking for information?"

Soft sell. I'm sure they pick these recruiters based on their personalities.

"I guess so. My birthday is September 14."

Sgt. Berkman didn't wince, or commiserate. He didn't need to look at a sheet of paper to see what that birthday signified. He nodded and said, "Oh-oh-one. So, I guess the die is cast for you, then, isn't it?"

"Seems that way."

"With that birthday, you're going to be in the first group called. It might be better if you just signed up now."

"When will the first group of draftees be called?"

"No way to know. I don't expect it will be too long, though. Likely right after the first of the year. You'll be better situated if you volunteer."

Scott nodded glumly, but didn't ask exactly *how* he would be better situated.

Sgt. Berkman nodded sympathetically. "Last night wasn't good news for you, eh?"

"No, sir. I was planning on joining the police academy as soon as I turned twenty-one. Now, I won't be able to do that."

"Well, hold on, there. Don't get too far ahead of yourself." He paused, reached for a pen, and made a note on a pad of paper. "What's your name, son?"

"Scott McKenzie." Scott braced himself, ready in case the sergeant asked him about the song, *San Francisco (Be Sure to Wear Flowers in Your Hair)* by the "other" Scott McKenzie. It often came up when he told people his name. If Berkman had ever heard it, though, he made no comment.

Berkman made another note on his pad, nodded to himself. He leaned forward, conspiratorially. "I think I can help you out, here. You want to be a cop, right?"

Scott nodded. "Yes, sir."

"Well, you could *maybe* get into the academy next year, but if they have too many applicants, you'll get pushed out a year, or even two. Often, if it comes down to the last three or four candidates, they'll go with the older person, figuring they have more experience." He said this as if he had a pipeline directly into the people who ran the academy. In sales, confidence is more than half the battle. "But, what if your application to the academy stated that you were a United States Army veteran, with a few years of being a Military Police officer already under your belt. Do you think they'd turn you away then?"

"Isn't that kind of the luck of the draw, though, if I get picked to be an MP or not?"

Berkman shook his head. "That's the advantage of signing up before you get drafted. I can attach a note that says you want to be an MP, and I recommend you for the job. There's no guarantee, of course. I'm not allowed to promise you that you'll get it, but my experience is, they listen to us most of the time. I think that if you want to be a cop when you get back, that's probably your best bet."

Scott considered. *Don't know if I can trust this guy. Maybe I should go talk to gramps and come back tomorrow. But, what real choice do I have? This guy is better than what I've got going for me now, which is absolutely nothing.*

Berkman leaned back in his chair, as though it didn't matter what Scott did, one way or the other. After a few moments of silence, he opened a drawer and withdrew a thick sheaf of papers.

"What do you say? Want to get started on the paperwork?"

Two hours later, Scott walked out of the recruiting office with his enlistment papers tucked into the back pocket of his jeans. He was the United States Army's newest recruit.

In exchange for enlisting, Scott was allowed to stay home through Christmas, but was scheduled to leave for basic training in Fort Dix, New Jersey on December 27.

Scott didn't want to leave his grandparents, sister, and girlfriend behind, but it was the only option he could live with. Since the moment his birthday was pulled, the draft felt like a sword hanging over his head. Try as he might, he couldn't seriously think about running to Canada. He felt like that would be just as bad as enlisting, since he would be away from everyone he loved, and he would be a draft dodger, to boot.

He and Sherry grew even closer in the weeks leading up to his departure. The night before he got on the bus for basic training, he picked her up from work and they went for burgers at Artie's Drive-In. The two young lovers sat in Scott's truck, had hamburgers and chocolate shakes, and listened to KMFR play *Fortunate Son* by Credence Clearwater Revival, and *And When I Die,* by Blood, Sweat & Tears. The irony of those songs escaped the young couple. They were busy eating and trying hard to pretend that one of them wasn't about to leave for a very long time.

As they pulled out of Artie's parking lot, the KMFR disc jockey announced, "Be sure to listen to our Top Forty Countdown this Saturday night from eight to midnight, hosted by our own Scott Patrick. I can't say exactly where, but this song will be on there somewhere." The opening violins of The Supremes' *Someday We'll be Together* filled the pickup.

Sherry snuggled closer to Scott and said, "Let's go somewhere a little more private."

Scott kissed the top of her head and said, "You know, I believe this. I believe that someday, we'll be together."

Sherry turned her face upward and her brown eyes had a sparkle in them. She laid a hand against his leg. "Me too."

That night, parked under a grove of elm trees, Sherry gave Scott the send-off that women have given their soldiers as they left for battle for thousands of years.

Later that night, sitting in front of her parents' house, Scott pulled Sherry close.

"I'm sorry. I didn't plan this very well. I don't have a ring. But, Sherry Dickenson, will you marry me?"

"Oh, Scotty! Of course I will! I can't wait to tell Mom and Dad!"

The porchlight flipped off and on, off and on.

"That's my signal. I've got to go in. Oh, you've made me so happy!" Her face grew momentarily serious. "You be careful, wherever they send you. Come back to me."

She jumped out of the pickup, then stopped halfway up the walkway to her house. She gifted him with a dazzling smile and blew him a kiss, then bounced inside.

Scott never saw her again.

Chapter Four

Basic training at Fort Dix lasted eight weeks. Those two months went by in a blur of five-mile runs, 5 a.m. reveilles, and his introduction to army food. It did not compare favorably to what his grandmother made.

Scott's training was more thorough than he had anticipated. His drill instructors were a little salty, but nothing like what would eventually be portrayed in movies like *Full Metal Jacket.* Fort Dix was one of the largest training camps in the country. It even had a replica village built to resemble a Vietnamese community. It was designed so that the rawest recruits would not be caught completely unawares when they landed *in country*, as the veterans called it. Its true effectiveness was debatable, but it did make the young soldiers feel somewhat more equipped for the challenges ahead.

After his initial eight weeks of training, he went through another two months of AIT, or Advanced Infantry Training. At the beginning of this advanced training, Scott asked his sergeant when he would be eligible to go into training for the Military Police.

The sergeant, a short, wiry man, took Scott in with a glance. "Recruiting promise you that?"

Scott shook his head. "He didn't promise it. He just said it was likely."

"Good. I hate to break promises. Now, get your ass out to the rifle range."

Scott was smart enough to not mention it again, and no one ever mentioned it to him.

It turned out that Scott had an excellent eye. After the initial rounds of testing, he was trained to be a sharpshooter. That made his eventual assignment easy. He was an infantryman, destined for the front lines of a country he couldn't have picked out on a map.

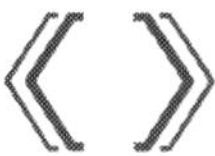

BACK HOME IN EVANSVILLE, Scott's grandparents and sister watched Walter Cronkite and the CBS Evening News religiously. Many nights, the news featured a graphic of that day's reported number of American deaths and wounded. Often, the report included how many North Vietnamese soldiers were reported killed as well—as though if that number was higher than the American number, the U.S. was winning the war.

The number of those "killed in action" had peaked in 1968 and had fallen substantially by the time Scott first put his boots on the steamy, muddy ground of Southeast Asia. Declining death tolls or not, American soldiers, especially poor and black American soldiers, were still dying there every day.

Scott had always been a fast learner. Within the first few months in country, he learned that even with the might of the U.S. military behind them, this was a frustrating and nearly impossible war to wage. They were fighting an enemy that appeared then faded back into the jungle at will. He also learned that those above the rank of Sergeant often risked the lives of their men based on orders from those higher up, without asking questions. More than anything, he learned there was a brotherhood with his fellow grunts. They believed they had the guy on their left and the guy on their right, and that was all they needed.

Each of them had been plucked from their homes and dropped into an unknowable war zone ten thousand miles away. They lived in constantly shifting, temporary conditions, and all knew that they were not guaranteed another sunrise. They had no one but each other to rely on, so that's what they did.

In April 1970, just a few weeks after being deployed, Scott was part of an advance patrol, walking along the razor's edge between rice fields and jungle. All was quiet, which was rarely a good sign. Scott never saw the soldier whose shot hit him just above the right collarbone. He was jerked around by the impact and was hit twice more before he could manage to fall to the ground. His M16 went one way, his helmet another. He crumpled like a string-cut marionette.

Around him, the chaos of a brief but intense firefight reigned. Scott felt removed from it. He lay mostly on his back, blinked up at gray skies and felt warm drops of rain hit his face. An explosion of pain raced through him and destroyed his ability to think. He gasped for breath, but couldn't get oxygen into his lungs.

I thought if I got hit, I would be numb. Goddamn, this hurts.

He blinked the raindrops away, which were mixing with his own tears.

I don't want to die.

Scott McKenzie laid in the mud and muck and waited to see if he would live.

The ambush ended as quickly as it had begun. After one final burst of smoke and gunfire, quiet settled in. Seconds later, Private First Class Bruce Teller leaned over him.

Of course. The one guy I had an argument with. Sorry, Teller. I didn't mean it when I called you an SOB during that card game.

Teller pulled out his knife and cut Scott's shirt off. A year earlier, Teller had been driving a forklift in a warehouse, now he was doing field triage.

He leaned into Scott's face. "It's okay, brother. You're hit, but you're going to be okay. We'll get you out of here. Congratulations. You got your ticket out of this shithole." He pulled two doses of morphine out of his kit and jabbed them into the fleshy part of Scott's arm.

Tears leaked from the corners of Scott's eyes.

Brother. Thank you, brother. I don't want to die.

They were less than a mile from their encampment, so Teller and Jepson stood guard over Scott while Abramson and Sawyer ran back to get a medic and a litter. Two other men in the patrol had been hit, but there was no need to hurry, not for morphine or a medic. They would only need stretchers to return their bodies.

While Jepson stood watch, Teller pulled the dead men close to Scott. Their race was over and they both looked peaceful in death. One man's glassy eyes stared straight at Scott.

The field medic arrived and dusted him with powder designed to keep infection at bay and dosed him again with morphine. At that moment, as shot up and ragged as he was, he felt fine. Ninety minutes later, Scott was back in camp.

Teller's words cycled through his brain over and over.

Congratulations. You got your ticket out of this shithole.

The moment the bullets tore into and through Scott's body, he started on a nightmare journey that lasted longer than he could have imagined. In many ways, it was a journey that began in this lifetime and finished in another.

First lying in the muck, and then later, while being treated back at camp, he focused on the idea that he was done. He had survived. His experience in the Vietnam War had been brief, but the echoes would last for many lifetimes.

Scott's journey started on a stretcher, then moved to a small riverboat, which picked up half a dozen other wounded men while they floated downstream to a landing zone. There, he was picked up by a Huey medical evacuation helicopter. Many areas of the U.S. military operated inefficiently in Vietnam. Two areas where it excelled were moving fresh bodies in the front door while dropping the wounded men onto an assembly line out the back door.

The Huey dropped into a tent hospital in Da Nang, where Scott was finally looked at by a doctor. The surgical team talked about Scott like he wasn't there. The first doctor who looked at him said, "This one's not going back out there. Get him into surgery."

An unseen hand placed a mask over Scott's face.

Mercifully, he was finally out.

When he came to, many hours later, he was once again on a Huey, this time being flown to rendezvous with the *USS Sanctuary.* The *Sanctuary* was a floating hospital, filled with a minimal crew, wounded men, and a medical staff charged with keeping the men alive during the voyage.

The trip from South Vietnam to the USA took fourteen days. Rough seas added seasickness to the ghastly wounds many men had suffered. Despite the efforts of the staff, blood and vomit pooled underfoot. The smell was so bad that Scott longed for the funk of living in a tent with a dozen unwashed men.

For fourteen days, Scott told himself that he just had to hang on. As soon as they got to port, he was sure life would be better.

This showed both Scott's optimism, which hadn't been completely beaten out of him yet, and his penchant for being wrong.

Life would not be better for Scott McKenzie for much longer than the length of the voyage.

Chapter Five

While he was still at sea, Scott received his Purple Heart, as did every wounded man on board. It was presented to him, then tucked away with his comb and toothbrush—his few remaining personal possessions.

The *Sanctuary* docked in San Francisco on May 1, 1969. It was exactly six months since he had sat in his grandparent's living room and watched his birthday jump up as the first number called in the draft.

In San Francisco, he was transferred to a VA hospital. Aside from lacking the constant threat of seasickness, it was not an improvement over conditions on the *Sanctuary*. The doctors and nurses did their best to treat and rehabilitate the wounded men. It was a case of too many men wounded too badly, and too few medical professionals to properly deal with it all. The overall cleanliness of the hospital was subpar, and although they weren't professional healers, the orderlies performed many of the medical duties. The orderlies were like any of the guys in the infantry—putting their time in, waiting to get back to their real lives. Of course, serving stateside, they had the advantage of not being shot at on a regular basis.

Scott was still in terrible condition when he arrived at the hospital. His wounds had become infected on the voyage, despite the best efforts of the nurses and doctors. There was some doubt as to whether he would pull through or not, as well as whether his damaged right leg could be saved. He did and it was, but the infection set his recovery back by six months.

Once his wounds began to heal, he was tormented every day by physical therapy. He was never going to be the strong young man he had been when he walked into the recruitment center. His goals were more modest now. Push yourself in a wheelchair. Walk with crutches. Walk unaided. Feed yourself.

There were volunteers from the local community who came to visit and help the wounded vets. Sometimes they snuck food—real food—in. If Scott had thought that army food was bad, and Meals Ready to Eat were even worse, he found the bottom of the culinary scale in the veteran's hospital. Salt was apparently rationed carefully, because none of it—or any other seasoning—ever seemed to make it into the food.

Thus, the food brought in by the volunteers—cookies, pastries, real fruit from the Farmer's Market—were highly prized and the most valuable trading commodity, above even cigarettes. Scott hadn't taken up smoking like most everyone else in his platoon, but he still collected and traded cigarettes. They were the currency of the day.

The most popular volunteer was a young man who came in twice a week and wrote letters home for those who were unable to hold a pen themselves, which included most of the patients at one point or another.

The first week he was there, Scott dictated letters, one to his grandparents and sister, and another to Sherry.

Scott found it simple to tell the man what to write in the letter to his family. It was much harder to say the words he wanted to say to Sherry out loud.

The man, who looked to be about twenty, leaned in close and in a soft voice, said, "Pretend I'm not even here. Act like you're speaking directly to her."

Scott tried, but he couldn't do it. Through long nights in Vietnam, he had thought of nothing but her. How soft her hair was. The smell of her perfume. More than anything, he thought of their last night together before he left for basic training. With the earnest young man sitting in front of him, Scott couldn't find a way to put his feelings into words. He did the best he could, and the young man, whose name was Kevin, added a bit here and there for him.

He heard back from his family less than a week later.

"*Oh, Scotty,*" the letter began, in his grandmother's familiar scrawl, "*we've been so, so worried about you. We found out you'd been wounded, but could never get any information about how badly. We are so thankful that you are alive and will be home soon. Grampa and I have moved into the upstairs bedroom, so you won't have to go up and down the stairs. Please come home as soon as you can. Doctors are fine, but my chicken soup will fix you right up.*"

Tears filled Scott's eyes. *So typical of them. Almost eighty years old, and they're the ones doing the stairs every day so that I don't have to. Cheryl and I lost the lifetime lottery when it came to a father, but they almost make up for it all by themselves.*

As happy as he was to get the letter from home, he waited ever more anxiously for some word from Sherry. With help from Kevin, Scott sent her two more letters. Finally, after he had been in the hospital almost four months and had despaired of ever hearing from her again, a small, thin letter arrived.

It had been sent to the correct APO, or Army Post Office, but the letter had bounced around the globe from there. It had been sent to his unit, but arrived after he had been wounded. It chased him to the hospital in Da Nang, but was by then several weeks behind him. For reasons evident to no one, it had been sent first to Germany, then back to the original APO, before it was finally dispatched correctly to him in the hospital in San Francisco.

Scott's right arm was still not functioning, and he found that it was nearly impossible to open an envelope with one hand. He held the envelope tight between sweating fingers for long minutes. Finally, he flagged down a young nurse and asked her if she would read it to him.

"Of course," she said with a smile. She looked at the handwriting on the envelope. "Girl back home?"

Scott nodded. "Fiancée. I hope we can get married as soon as I get home."

The nurse, a little on the heavy side and no one's idea of beautiful, nodded.

"She's a lucky girl." She neatly tore the end of the envelope off and a single page of stationary slipped out. As it did, the smell of Sherry's perfume wafted toward Scott. He breathed it in.

"I'm going to want to keep that."

"Of course. Okay, let's see. 'Dear Scott, I hate to put this in a letter, but I don't have any other way to reach you. I...' The nurse stopped and looked at Scott. His smile was frozen, but slowly melting away.

The nurse read through the next few paragraphs and pity spread across her face. "I have met someone else, and he has asked me to marry him—"

"—That's enough." Scott looked away.

"I'll leave it here for you on your table."

"No, please don't do that. Take it away."

She glanced at the page, read the rest, and then tucked it away in the pocket of her uniform. "I sure will. Private McKenzie, is there anything else I can do for you?"

Scott couldn't make eye contact with her. Couldn't speak. Couldn't even move to acknowledge her question.

The nurse left him alone.

Chapter Six

Two years to the day after he had enlisted, Scott McKenzie was released from the hospital in San Francisco. He didn't precisely receive a clean bill of health, because he was never likely to achieve that. He had regained most of his normal functions, though, and that was the victory the Army was looking for.

He received an honorable discharge. Because his wounds were considered severe and the army judged he was unlikely to be able to find work, Scott was eligible for the upper end of the Veteran Disability Compensation. It would pay him monthly for as long as he was alive.

He was issued a sturdy cane, but he felt like an old man when he used it. As soon as he was outside the hospital, he leaned it against the wall and walked away. He wasn't steady on his feet, but he didn't fall over.

If I start using that damn cane, it feels like I'll always be using it. I don't want to spend the rest of my life hobbling along if I don't have to.

Johnny Johnson, one of the orderlies that Scott had come to know well enough to call a friend, loaded him into his beat up 1962 Cadillac convertible and gave him a lift to the bus station. Johnny carried Scott's bag, helped him buy his ticket, and did what he could to transition Scott back into the real world.

Scott got on a Greyhound headed east. Evansville was the only place he knew to go. Home is where your family is, where they have to take you in. He had called ahead and talked to Cheryl, who was midway through her senior year in high school. He let her know he would be home before Christmas.

He settled into a seat toward the back of the bus and hoped that no one would sit beside him. He didn't object to people, but he was still awkward standing and walking, especially on a bus. He didn't want to have to hold his bladder through each leg of the trip, but also didn't want to step all over someone to get to the cramped facilities.

Scott didn't have a book, and he didn't buy a newspaper. He leaned his head against the cool, tinted window and watched America roll by one mile, one billboard, one tiny town at a time. After seeing nothing but the inside of a hospital for so long, the changing view was a blessing. He dozed off and on, changed buses four times, and ate a lot of vending machine and small-town diner food. All of it was a marked improvement on his diet of the previous two years.

When he was half a day away from Evansville, he called home from a payphone to let them know what time he would be in, barring any breakdowns, traffic, or major storms.

When the bus finally rolled into Evansville, Scott was glad to get off the bus. It had gotten him there, but sitting in one position for that long didn't agree with his injured body. He limped off the bus and looked left and right, expecting someone might be there to greet him. He turned up the collar of his green army-issued coat against the wind and spitting snow. He didn't recognize anyone. He tipped the driver a buck to haul his suitcase inside the depot for him, then sat and waited.

The inside was like every other bus depot across America in the early 70s—dingy, with dirty tile floors, molded-plastic seats attached to each other, and a sense of despair that hung in the air. Bus stations were the dropping off point of the lower middle class and poor. In large cities, hustlers flocked to them to find marks who were literally fresh off the bus from Kansas, or Iowa, or any of the other flyover states. Evansville wasn't big enough to attract any of that. It just smelled of too many weary travelers and too little disinfectant.

Scott took all this in, then fixed his eyes on the two sets of double doors that led inside and waited.

I talked to both Cheryl and Gram. There's no way they'd forget about me. I could call them again, but I think instead, I'll just wait.

Snow was swirling in tiny cyclones on the ground, but not so much that the roads would be difficult. If he had learned anything in his two years in the army, though, it was how to wait patiently.

When he first sat down, the neon clock over the doors had read 3:22. By the time it read 5:15, it was almost dark outside.

Suddenly, Cheryl burst through the doors, looking frantically for Scott. He raised his hand to wave, but she had already spotted him and before he could get up out of his seat, she had crossed the room and threw her arms around him.

Her words came in a rush. "Oh, Scotty, I'm so sorry. Today was all about you. Gramps and I painted your room and were getting it ready for you, but just when we were coming to get you, Gram fell. She didn't slip and fall. She was walking across the kitchen, then she was down. She wasn't unconscious, exactly, but she wasn't making sense, either. We called the ambulance, and then followed it to the hospital. That's where we've been, trying to find out if she's going to be okay. I'm so sorry we weren't here to get you..." Hot tears spilled and ran down her cheeks. "Oh, Scotty, look at you. You're so thin. Haven't they been feeding you?"

Scott ignored the question and tried to process the speech his sister had delivered. Trying to slow Cheryl down a little, he said, "Help me with my duffel, will you? If I carry it, it throws me off balance. I'm not walking too great yet."

She tilted her head and a look of profound sadness passed over her face as the reality of her wounded brother sank in. Scott had always been her warrior, her protector. Now he was frail and broken.

Intellectually, she had known how badly he had been injured. Now it sank into her heart. She brushed her tears away and did her best to smile at Scott. "Right. Come on, let's get back to the hospital."

She picked up his duffel bag, which wasn't heavy, then slipped her other arm around Scott's waist. Scott did better with his walking when left alone, but it felt so nice, he didn't say a word.

Outside, the snow had picked up and they drove to the hospital in a kaleidoscope of oncoming flakes.

Scott glanced at Cheryl as she drove. *When I left, she was still a girl. Now, she's definitely a young woman. She didn't even have her license yet then. Now look at her, driving through a snowstorm like a pro.*

"I know you probably won't want to talk about it when Gram and Gramps are around, but how bad was it?"

I don't want to talk about it when anyone is around, sis. I can't tell you that, though, because we always told each other everything.

"The war is hell, but being in a veteran's hospital is so much worse. I'd rather die than go back there."

"Scotty!"

Scott shrugged. "I didn't say I'm ready to jump off a bridge. I just could never go through that again. You know when you go to the pound and see all the abandoned cats and dogs? It's a little like that, but it smells worse."

Cheryl wrinkled her nose. "I'm so sorry this happened to you. We'll get Gran patched up and nurse both of you back to health. Everything will be good again."

It doesn't feel like it will ever be good again.

They found a spot inside the parking garage, which Scott was grateful for. He hadn't been forced to try out his newfound balance on slippery walkways yet.

Inside the hospital, they hurried as best they could down the long corridors and into a shared room.

Scott leaned over and kissed his grandmother's cheek. Her eyes fluttered open, a mixture of fear and surprise in her eyes.

"Oh, Scotty, oh my boy. Give me a hug!"

Scott did his best. Between his partially functioning arms, and her palsied, shaking hands, they wrapped each other in an awkward embrace.

Gran held Scott's face and looked deep into his eyes for long moments. She looked past his eyes and into his soul. Finally she said, "Oh. Oh, Scotty, I am so sorry."

When she released him, Scott walked to his grandfather, who appeared unchanged from the last time he had seen him, and hugged him, too. The old man held Scott out at arm's length, then shook his head. "You look like you've been drug through a knothole backwards."

Scott could only nod in agreement.

"We'll get him home and get some good food in him," Cheryl said.

Scott looked at his grandmother, expecting her to chime in with how she would be up and around in no time, making her chicken and dumplings and beef stew for him. Instead, she remained quiet.

Scott leaned over her again and whispered in her ear. "You okay?"

She didn't answer, but gave the slightest shake of her head.

Chapter Seven

Cora Bell, born Cora Lee Newsome, known as Gran to Scott and Cheryl, never left that hospital. She had suffered a stroke while waiting for Scott's arrival. The next morning, she had a heart attack and died. She was surrounded by those who knew and loved her best.

Scott's homecoming, which was never destined to be a happy occasion because of the extent of his wounds, became even more somber and muted. When they finally got home after Cora had died, Cheryl parked her grandparents' Plymouth in the driveway. Scott saw a handmade banner above the front porch. It read, "We're glad you're home, Scotty!" The snow of the previous day had turned to rain, and the words were smeared and running. One corner of the banner hung down and flapped in the breeze.

Cheryl followed Scott's gaze and shrugged. "It looked a lot better yesterday." She helped Scott out of the car and up the slippery walkway and steps, then went back for Earl, who was also a little unsteady on his feet.

It had only been two years since Scott had called the story-and-a-half house home, but it seemed to have shrunk in his absence. In his memory, it was lit by a warm fire in the stove and the smell of something delicious coming from the kitchen. When he walked in, the house was cold and walls seemed to have moved inward several feet. The absence of his grandmother hit him hard.

Earl immediately went to the woodpile out back so he could get a fire started. Cheryl bustled around in the kitchen, trying to throw together a lunch for them. She wasn't Cora, but she had learned at Cora's apron strings. Scott, meanwhile, sat on the couch, watching the rain and feeling like a stranger in this familiar land. Before lunch could be served, he drifted off.

Cheryl and Earl let him sleep, and when he woke up, darkness was gathering outside. He had laid over in his sleep, and Cheryl had covered him with a quilt.

"Guess I needed some sleep."

"Guess we all do. You just got a head start on it. Good for you," Earl said.

Now that Scott wasn't so bowled over by everything that had happened, he took a longer look at his grandfather. His first idea that he hadn't changed was either wrong, or he had aged a decade in the preceding twenty-four hours. His cheeks were sunken and he seemed to be melting into himself.

Cheryl made dinner and they ate on TV trays, silently watching the news.

The house was often silent over the next few weeks. Cheryl was gone to school during the day, finishing up the last few days before Christmas vacation. Earl, who typically spent his days in his basement shop happily messing with one woodworking project or another, mostly sat in his chair doing nothing.

The American Psychiatric Association wouldn't list Post Traumatic Stress Disorder until 1980, but that didn't mean it didn't exist. In World War I, it was called "shell shock." In World War II, it was "combat fatigue." During the Vietnam War, it was typically called "Post-Vietnam Syndrome."

Whatever it was called, tens of thousands of broken and damaged soldiers brought it home with them. Many thought that when they returned home, it would take a few months to reintegrate into a society where someone wasn't trying to kill you every day. Scott was one of those. He believed that a few weeks or months of quiet life back in Evansville would cure the depression, the nightmares and flashbacks, and the overall numbness he felt.

Scott was wrong.

The longer he sat in his grandparents' house, the more anxious and fidgety he became, and the more prevalent his nightmares became. It wasn't unusual for him to awaken the house with his screams.

Earl and Cheryl did their best to treat his injured psyche with love and understanding. They knew where he had been and what he had been through. What they didn't know, was what they could do to help heal him.

Scott did what he could to exorcise his demons. He tried helping Earl with his projects in the basement. He did his best to read books, but found he couldn't focus for more than thirty seconds at a time.

He got rid of everything from his army days except for his Purple Heart, which he gave to his grandfather. He ceremoniously burned the army jacket he had worn home from the war. It was tough and built to withstand a lot, but he poured half a gallon of gasoline on it and let that soak in, then dropped it in the burning barrel. That did the trick.

Finally, by the spring of 1973, Scott's mood swings and anxiety drove him to take a bus downtown, where he found a bar called The Rusty Bucket that was frequented by other vets and blue-collar workers. The clinking of glasses, the softly playing jukebox, and the crack of a cue ball breaking a fresh rack soothed his soul. The beer, and later in the day, the whiskey, helped him self-medicate and hold his inner demons at bay.

Time passed. Earl eventually returned to his woodworking. Cheryl graduated from high school and got a job working as a receptionist at a veterinary clinic. Scott contributed part of his monthly check to the household and spent the rest at the Rusty Bucket.

The three of them moved in different directions.

As the months passed, Earl got thinner and thinner. He had never been a heavy man, but since Cora had died, he had become whippet-thin. By the time he went in for his annual checkup and the cancer was discovered, it was too late. He was gone by Halloween.

For the second time in less than a year, Scott and Cheryl buried a grandparent. It wasn't as traumatic as when they lost both parents at once, but when Cora and Earl passed so close together, it felt like they were orphaned all over again.

Scott's drinking had progressed to a point that a few glasses of beer and whiskey at the bar were no longer sufficient to dull his pain, and he began to stop at the liquor store each day to bridge the hours between closing time and when it reopened the next morning.

He had reached that tipping point where one drink was too much, but one hundred wasn't enough.

Cheryl worried and fussed about Scott's drinking, but it was like trying to hold the tide back with your hands.

By the time Scott had been home for a year, he knew he wanted to leave. He wanted to go to the open road, stick his thumb out, and see where fate took him. The only thing that stopped him from doing so was that he couldn't imagine abandoning Cheryl, even though he was effectively no help to her.

Cheryl had begun dating Mike, a man who had brought his cat into the vet clinic a few months earlier. He had taken to spending most evenings at the house, which helped Scott feel less guilty about staying later at the bar.

On Christmas morning, Cheryl made biscuits and gravy for breakfast, and she and Scott exchanged their gifts. A new watch for Scott, and new seat covers for Cheryl's Pinto. By noon, Scott was on his way to celebrate the day with his other family at the Rusty Bucket and Cheryl went to dinner at Mike's house.

The next morning, she sat Scott down and showed him an engagement ring on her left hand.

Scott was as present as he ever was, because he'd already had a few nips off the flask he kept in his bedside table. His motto had become, *If you never sober up, you'll never have a hangover.*

Scott smiled.

Cheryl said, "I think that's the first honest-to-God smile I've seen on your face in I can't remember how long."

"I know, I know. I'm not doing too good, am I?"

Cheryl didn't contradict him, or bother to correct his grammar.

"So, aren't you guys moving pretty fast? You've only known each other, what, a couple of months?"

"Yes, but when you know, you know. You and I need to talk, though. What do you think is best? Mike's sharing an apartment with two friends, but he's thinking we should get a place of our own. I don't want to leave you here all alone, though."

Scott shook his head. "No. That doesn't make any sense. I've been thinking about taking a little trip, anyway. You and Mike should move in here. If you don't mind keeping my bedroom open until you fill this place up with kids, you two stay here. I'll come back and stay when I'm not on the road."

"What does that mean, 'on the road,' anyway? You gonna become a hobo or something?"

"I don't know what it means. That's what I want to find out."

Chapter Eight

Cheryl and Mike's wedding was at the end of April. By then, Scott was antsy and itching to get out onto the open road. He agreed to stay in Evansville and watch the house while the newlyweds went to Florida on their honeymoon. As soon as they returned, he was off.

He traveled light. Everything he needed fit into a canvas knapsack on his back.

He hadn't continued with his physical rehabilitation once he had gotten home, but he had begun to move little by little, and by May of 1974, he walked almost without a hitch in his step. He wasn't strong yet, but he was upright, and that let him get moving.

He shouldered his pack, walked to Interstate 69 and stuck out his thumb. He didn't have a specific destination in mind, but several of the vets in the Rusty Bucket had talked about a place in Mexico that was welcoming to veterans of all wars. Even better, their monthly checks stretched a lot farther there.

With that in mind as an eventual destination, Scott rode his thumb first south, then west, then south again. He crossed the US-Mexico border at Tijuana. He had hoped to lose himself in a different country, but soon found himself hanging out at a bar that, aside from the fact that it sold a lot more tequila and had more colorful decorations, was a lot like the Rusty Bucket back in Indiana. Different location, same concept—drink yourself into oblivion.

He found an inexpensive second floor room and set out to drink his life away, one day at a time. When that proved to be too slow, he branched out with his self-medication.

In less than a year, he was living a life he never could have imagined when he was a young man with clear eyes and a full heart. The little boy who had vowed to become a police officer because he wanted to help others was a strung-out junky, living in a three-dollars a night flophouse in Tijuana, injecting every bit of his government check into his veins.

Scott McKenzie was as lost as any human being could be.

Seeking the final oblivion, he blew his remaining bankroll on two double barrels of heroin, went into his cramped, fetid apartment, and sought the solace of the final darkness. He went through the ritual he had come to know so well, injected himself, and laid on his bed, waiting for death.

It came.

Chapter Nine

Scott McKenzie opened his eyes. He felt warm, and there was a pain in the shoulder where he had been shot. He hadn't felt that particular pain in a long time. In fact, he discovered that he hurt almost everywhere.

He was on his grandparents' couch, in the living room in Evansville, Indiana. He sat up and threw the heavy quilt off of him.

What the hell? Where am I? Gram and Gramps' place? No way. Nope. I've had a lot of tripped-out dreams and nightmares, but they all had that feeling of unreality. This feels like I'm here, which is impossible.

Down the hall, the toilet flushed and his grandfather emerged from the bathroom.

"You all right, Scott? You look like you've seen a ghost."

Yeah, but which one of us is the ghost? Pretty sure both of us are dead, so does that make it you, me, or us?

"Gramps?" Scott said. His voice was weak and tremulous.

"Of course. Who else? There's just me and Cheryl here."

Hold on. How did I get here? If someone found me before I died, I should be waking up in a hospital in Mexico. Not here. And, especially, not having a conversation with a man who died more than a year ago.

"Gramps, how did I get here?"

Concerned flashed in Earl's eyes. "You got out of the hospital and rode the bus here, remember?"

"Right. Of course. Uhh... how you feeling, Gramps?"

Earl gave Scott a look that tried to ask *Are you Stupid?* but the words he spoke said, "Your grandmother died this morning. How do you think I'm feeling?"

Okay. So, I'm dreaming I am back in Evansville on the day Gram died. It's so realistic, though. I can smell food cooking in the kitchen, and it's too damn stuffy in here, with a fire going and this quilt over me.

Scott attempted to throw the quilt off, but his arm didn't function correctly, and he gave a small gasp of pain.

"Hey, Hey!" Cheryl said, running in from the kitchen, spatula still in hand. "Take it easy. I'm sure the doctors told you not to exert yourself too much, right?"

"Right," Scott agreed. "I think I'm going to go lay down for a little while."

"Good idea. Dinner will be ready in about half an hour. I'll come get you."

Scott limped across the living room.

This is too damned real. I haven't felt like this in years. What the hell is going on?

He made it to his bedroom, which smelled of a fresh coat of paint, and collapsed on the twin bed.

None of this makes sense. I've already lived this once before.

Scott wracked his brain, trying to logically figure out the impossibility he was living. He was still chasing one idea after another with no solution in sight, when Cheryl knocked on his door and poked her head in.

"Come on, dinner's ready and Gramps has Cronkite on. Let's eat."

As they had done the first time through this moment, the three of them ate in silence. This time, though, Cheryl and Gramps exchanged worried looks first at Scott, then at each other. Scott pretended not to notice.

When he had eaten as much as his stomach would allow—which wasn't much—Scott stood up to take his dish into the kitchen. Cheryl jumped up and took it from him.

"I don't want to be cleaning peas and casserole out of the living room carpet. I've got it."

Scott nodded and said, "I'm gonna head to bed. I'm still tired."

"Of course you are," Cheryl said, kissing him on the cheek. "Sorry, Scotty. This isn't the homecoming any of us envisioned."

I thought this day was odd the first time I lived through it. Repeating it hasn't smoothed out any of the wrinkles.

Slowly, Scott undressed, pulled the covers back, and climbed into bed. He slipped between the cool, clean sheets—a marked improvement over what had passed for a bed in Tijuana.

I can't believe I'm back here, but even if I am, so what? Nothing's changed. Life still sucks. I don't feel the need to go running out into the streets for my next fix, so I guess that's good. Nothing else has changed, though. Doesn't matter. I'll probably go to sleep and wake up in some other place. Please don't let it be back in the jungle or in the hospital. I can't live through that again.

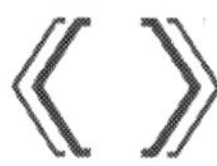

AS SOON AS THE FIRST rays of light filtered through the curtains the next morning, Scott's eyes flew open.

Still here. Shit. What's next, then?

He swung his feet onto the floor and tried to stand up. He made it most of the way, but lost his balance and fell back onto the bed. *And this sucks, too. I'd gotten a lot better, at least in some ways. Now I'm back here again.*

He walked into the living room and saw his grandfather sitting there, looking out the window at nothing in particular.

Wait a minute. Gramps is still alive. I can make a difference with him at least.

"Morning, Gramps. I want to ask you a favor."

Earl pulled his eyes away from the deep nothing he had been staring at and focused on Scott. "Cheryl's already gone to school."

"Okay, I figured." Scott stood between the old man and the window. "I want you to do me a favor."

"What do you need?"

"I want you to go to the doctor for a checkup."

"My next checkup isn't for six months yet."

"Right. That's why I said I want you to do me a favor. I had a bad dream about you last night. It will put my mind at ease if you'll get in to see someone."

"Likely caused by your Gran's passing." He sighed. "Sure, why not? No harm in it."

This lifetime, then, the cancer was discovered earlier. It was more treatable. Earl went through the painful treatments with a stoic cynicism.

He died a few weeks after Halloween, this time.

Scott realized that all that he had accomplished was to cause Earl more suffering.

The rest of Scott's life played out to a similar drumbeat.

He hung out at the Rusty Bucket and waited for Cheryl to announce that she and Mike were engaged, which she did right on schedule. By then, he was drinking heavily again, but hadn't progressed to the drugs he had used, the drugs which had killed him in his first life.

When Cheryl and Mike's wedding was in the rearview mirror for the second time, he hit the road again. He ended up in a different town, this time—Oceanside, California, instead of Tijuana, Mexico, but the end result was the same.

He found the drugs, or maybe the drugs found him. At this point in his lives, there was no difference.

He died the same way he did in his first life, albeit in a somewhat nicer place. He chose a deserted stretch of beach for his overdose this life.

He woke up back on the couch in his grandparents' house, with Cheryl cooking dinner and his grandfather coming out of the bathroom.

He played through this life in this way so many times that if he had been asked, he couldn't have told you the number.

Finally, after a particularly rough departure, thanks to a poisoned batch of black tar heroin, taken in a men's restroom in Amarillo, Texas, he awoke as he had so many times, on the couch, covered by the quilt, in his grandparents' house.

He sat up, looked around the empty living room and said one word.

"Enough."

Chapter Ten

E*nough.*

A single word, but one that represented a decision. Scott McKenzie had finally had enough of that endless, debilitating cycle of life, death, life, death.

Making a decision is often easier than following through with it, especially when it comes to breaking well-worn habits.

When he opened his eyes—again—under the heavy quilt in his grandparents' house, he knew that if he had truly had enough, he was going to have to do the most difficult thing a human being can do.

Change.

Change his mindset, change his attitude, change his habits.

After so many trips through this moment, he was used to waking up feeling weak and unsure of his balance. He sat up carefully, acclimating to his surroundings. He folded the quilt and put it on the back of the couch.

He heard the toilet flush and turned to see Earl coming out of the bathroom.

"Gramps? I know this is bad timing, but can I ask you a favor?"

Earl sat down in his favorite chair and said, "Of course."

"I think it would be easy for us to sit around and mope about losing Gran, but I'm pretty sure that's not what she would want for any of us. I'm going to call my VA rep today and see if I can get a physical therapist assigned to me. That will help. But, I'm wondering if maybe tomorrow, we can go down to the basement and start working on a few projects that will help me?"

Earl's watery blue eyes considered Scott for several long moments. Finally, he nodded. "You're right, of course. If she was here, she would be kicking me in the butt and asking why I was just sitting around." He turned his head and stared at a picture of the two of them taken decades earlier. "I never thought I'd have to live without her, but here we are. First thing tomorrow, we can head down to the basement and see what we can come up with."

Cheryl had emerged from the kitchen and listened in. She crossed over to Scott and kissed him on the cheek. "I love you, Scotty."

And I have a hunch I'm going to need every bit of that love and support to turn things around.

"I love you, too. Right at this moment, I'm glad Gran taught you how to cook. I'm hungry."

SCOTT SLEPT LONG AND deep that night. He woke up late and wandered into the empty living room. For the first time in more than a dozen lifetimes, he took the time to drink in his surroundings. The house was not large, but it was homey. Signs of Cora's presence were everywhere. Doilies she had made covered most flat surfaces. Inexpensive paintings of vases with flowers or sunsets hung in the living room. Shelves in the kitchen were filled with jars of her canned peaches, pickles, and apple butter.

To everyone else, you died yesterday, Gran. For me, you've been gone a long time. I still miss you.

The basement door was open and Scott could hear Earl scuffling around. The occasional mild cuss word floated up the stairs.

Scott shouted down, "Permission to come aboard, captain?"

"Come ahead, soldier."

Scott made his way down the stairs, but it wasn't easy. There was no handrail and his balance was still tentative.

Earl glanced up at him. "That's my first project." He held up a length of steel pipe. "I'm building us a set of handholds going up and down those damn stairs. It's only by the grace of God I haven't killed myself yet."

"Good idea, Gramps. Let me help you."

They worked on the project mostly in silence for quite some time. While they were absorbed in their work, Earl began to tell Scott stories.

"Did I ever tell you about my first date with your Gran? It didn't go so well."

Scott smiled and shook his head. *I don't think you've ever told me anything about when you two were young. You've always seemed old to me. Hard to imagine you in the old days.*

Earl told Scott a story about a disastrous date where things went from bad—him spilling a coke all over her pretty new dress—to worse—running out of gas on a lonely country highway and having to walk almost three miles to get her home.

"And there was still a second date, huh?"

"Cora was a forgiving woman. Plus, she had the ability to look inside people and see them for who they were. She was that way with your father, too. She warned your mother, but it was too late at that point. Your mother was in love."

What's gotten into you? Cheryl slip a truth serum into your oatmeal this morning?

"I don't remember much of anything about Mom and Dad. Just the fights, really."

"We never knew anything about those. If we had, I suppose we would have come and got you and your mother and brought you here. We didn't find out until it was too late."

"I knew that I should have told you, but I was scared of what would happen."

"It wasn't your job to tell us. It was our job to know. It's the biggest regret of our lives."

By the time Cheryl got home from school that afternoon, they had hand grips built to make the stairs easier for both of them, and had cleared out one corner of the basement. That was where they were going to build Scott's rehabilitation center.

Over the next few weeks, it took shape. They were even able to use all the odds and ends that Earl had been keeping "just in case" for decades.

The work of building things was therapy for Scott in different ways. He got to know Earl more as a human being, instead of just as his grandfather. Plus, even before he got to start the physical therapy, the work helped him with his fine motor control and balance.

He faced a dilemma each day as he watched Earl work. He knew that every day, the cancer inside him was growing. But, he also knew that getting him to go to the doctor and discovering it earlier had only heightened his suffering and in the end, prolonged his life for a few weeks.

He made the decision to not say anything, but it tore at him.

Once they had built that everything Earl had sketched out, Scott spent a few hours every day in the basement, going through the exercises his physical therapist had given him and listening to Earl tell him stories about what life had been like in the period between the two World Wars.

Earl had been a little too young to fight in WWI, and too old to fight in WWII. He had enlisted anyway, and had spent four years working in the motor pool at Fort Lewis, Washington. Four years was enough time to be away from the girl he loved, so after his honorable discharge, he returned home.

While Earl told stories and worked on other projects, Scott sweated. Six months after he woke up in this life, he was in better shape than he had been since the fateful day he had gone on patrol in Vietnam.

Emotionally, he was doing better, although he wouldn't have said he was cured of what ailed him. Unexpected noises still made him jump and break out in a sweat. The nightmares and crying out in the night still happened, but the intervals between them grew farther apart.

He realized that in each life, he had awakened with a fresh start. Each time he had opened his eyes back in his grandparents' home, he didn't have the physical craving of an addiction to drugs or alcohol. It was the emotional pain inside him that had driven him to seek them out and become addicted again and again. This life, he vowed to stay away from both.

His first goal was to get in good enough shape that he could still apply at the academy and pursue the dream of becoming a police officer.

In June, he watched Cheryl graduate from high school for the twentieth time.

I think I deserve a medal for listening to all these speeches once, let alone this many damn times.

He was tempted to sneak a transistor radio and an earpiece into the ceremony so he could listen to the Cubs play the Cardinals, but he refrained.

He applied to the academy the next day. Sergeant Berkman had been right about at least one thing. Having the U.S. Army on his resume did help him get accepted, even if he didn't have the promised MP training.

Scott applied himself to the classes more than he ever had in high school, and he excelled.

In the end, his physical limitations were simply too much. There were certain standards that every graduate of the academy had to meet—the ability to lift and carry weight, completing an obstacle course—and he couldn't do it. What was worse, he had to be honest with himself and realize that no matter how hard he worked, he would never be able to.

He would have to find another avenue to fulfill his dreams.

Chapter Eleven

It was mid-October, 1973. Earl Bell had received his cancer diagnosis and knew that he was dying. He was doing everything he could to get things in order. As he had done in previous lives, he met with his attorney and went over his will to make sure that Scott and Cheryl would receive the house and whatever money he had.

He sat in the living room drinking coffee and watching the winds of autumn blow in. The leaves had already turned amber and orange and quite a few had taken the plunge to the ground. He watched Scott on the ladder outside, putting the storm windows up. It was a job he and Scott had always done together. He was too weak to help this year, though, and sat watching instead.

When the job was finished, Scott came in, sniffed the air and said, "Coffee in the afternoon, huh? What are we rich folks or something?" He poured himself a cup.

Earl snorted a small laugh at the idea of them being rich folks, but it died quickly. Scott joined him in the living room and they sat for a few minutes, watching the weather.

Finally, Earl said, "So what's next, then?"

"Oh, I suppose I need to get up on the roof and make sure all the flashing is ready for another winter."

Earl shook his head. "No. I mean, what's next for you?"

"Oh. Well, that question's a lot harder."

"It always is."

"I guess I don't have a real plan yet. All my life, I wanted to be a police officer. Now that I know that's out, I haven't figured out what I'm going to do."

"I know you'll be okay financially. You two will have the house, and it's paid off. You've got your benefits from the army, too. So, you'll never starve. Still, a man needs something to do. A reason to get out of bed in the morning."

"Any ideas for me?" Scott was genuinely curious.

"None that are of much use. Have you thought of going to college for something? You've got your GI Bill to help you out with that."

"I was never much of a student. I know I need something, though, you're right."

"Find something you love. Me, I loved working with my hands. I enjoyed going to work every day, finding new challenges. If you're lucky enough to find something like that and someone you look forward to coming home to every night, you've got the world beat. That's what I had."

Scott noticed a book open on Earl's lap, in place of his usual newspaper. "What are you reading?"

"Not much. Just picking up a few of the books I've read over the years and looking at them again. This one is *In Cold Blood,* by Truman Capote."

"Never heard of it."

"You're young. There's a whole lot of things you've never heard of. Doesn't mean they're not worthwhile."

TWO WEEKS LATER, EARL Bell was dead. At the very end, he smiled at Cheryl and Scott and said, "I'll miss you both, but don't fret about me. This is good. I'm ready to go."

For many previous lives, that time period between Earl dying and Christmas was a waiting game. Scott was letting time pass so that Cheryl could tell him she was getting married and he could tell her that he was moving on. Now, he wasn't sure what he wanted to do. He could let the two of them move out into their own place while he stayed in this house, but that felt wrong. Three bedrooms called out for a family, not a young bachelor.

By the time the inevitable Christmas conversation came, he had decided to move out and start fresh. Cheryl argued with him and asked him to stay, but he had no interest in sharing a house with newlyweds.

He moved into a small apartment on the edge of town while they were on their honeymoon. He picked up a few sticks of old furniture and some dishes at Goodwill and was mostly settled in before they returned. The only thing he took from the house was his clothes, his Purple Heart, which Earl had given back to him just before he passed, and the stack of books sitting on the table next to Earl's chair.

If they were good enough for him, they're damn sure good enough for me. Can't see much of a reason to get a television set, so I've gotta have something to pass the time.

His first night in his new place, he wandered around, lost despite the cramped surroundings. He finally settled on the couch and plucked the top book off the stack he had brought with him. Again, it was *In Cold Blood.*

He cracked the book open and realized it was the first thing he had read since he had graduated from high school years earlier. The next time he looked up, two hours had passed. The story of the destruction of the Clutter family resonated with him—the randomness, the loss of an entire family, all done for almost no reason at all.

When Scott glanced at the clock again, he saw it was after midnight. He hadn't even bothered to make up his bed yet. Stretching out on the ugly green couch he had just bought, he slept.

When he woke up, Scott realized how unequipped he was. He may have had a frying pan, but he didn't have eggs. He had a battered old coffee pot, but no coffee.

Better go to the store first thing.

Then, his mind drifted to where he had left off in the book the night before. When he had stopped reading, the two killers had just been apprehended and brought back to Kansas to stand trial.

If only the Clutters had known it was coming, or if someone had been there to protect them, none of it would have happened.

A sudden thought hit Scott, and it stopped him dead in his tracks.

Someone who knew what was coming. Maybe someone like me.

The idea hit him so strongly, he had to sit down.

Nothing I can do for the Clutters, of course. They've been dead since I was a little kid. But what if someone that kept starting their life over and over again knew when something was going to happen? I could stop those bad things before they happened.

Chapter Twelve

As Scott wheeled a cart down the aisle of the grocery store, he turned things over in his mind.

Not too much I can do in this life. I never managed to live past 1975, and I wasn't paying attention to what happened in the world. Hell, I wasn't paying attention to anything except where my next fix was coming from. But, what if I did pay attention this lifetime? Took notes. Did research. Taught myself to remember things. Then, when I started over again, I could be ready.

Scott didn't watch where he was going and his cart clipped the edge of a toilet paper display, sending it tumbling to the ground. Embarrassed, he began restocking them haphazardly back on the shelf.

He didn't want any other mishaps while he was on this trip so he focused on his grocery shopping, then his driving. But as soon as he got home and got the shopping put away, he focused on the idea once more.

I could live a normal life, but keep tabs on bad things that happen. I could read more books, magazines and newspapers. I could put together a list of horrible things that happen over the next several decades. Maybe I can change them. If someone had done that for us, maybe Mom would still be alive.

For the first time since he had been wounded, Scott felt excitement, anticipation—a purpose.

It's just a question of where I want to spend this life. Here? It would be nice to be close to Cheryl. Maybe be here when she has kids and be Uncle Scott to them.

He tried to picture that, but failed.

Of course, I could always come back for visits. That's probably better. Cheryl's got Mike and her own life now. It would be good to get out and see the country a little, without trying to kill myself.

As soon as the six-month lease on his apartment was up, Scott donated all the furniture he had bought back to the same thrift store.

He stored a few belongings in Earl's old workshop and once again limited himself to what he could carry in his backpack.

Hitting the road this time was different from the twenty or so times he had done it before. Then, he was trying to lose himself. Now, he was looking for a home. He rode his thumb south, but soon found that the Carolinas, Georgia, and Florida were too humid for his tastes. Still, he didn't give up easily and made it as far south as he could. He caught a ride in Miami that took him across the Florida Keys all the way to Key West, home to Hemingway and the occasional tropical storm. He loved the sunsets, being on the water, and the laid back attitude everyone had. But in the end, he had to admit he wasn't cut out for waking up to temperatures pushing ninety every day.

Hitchhiking north again, Scott caught a ride on an empty freight car heading west. He hopped off in Texas and spent a few months wandering around cowboy country.

He was in no hurry and was happy watching the calendar pages flip as he explored the country.

Texas was a big state with friendly people. Eventually, he realized he wasn't going to find a place in Texas that felt like home and he moved on again.

Southern California had perfect weather, but he didn't recognize the people there as his own tribe. After a year of doing oil changes and minor tune ups for a small garage, the steady drumbeat of cloudless, warm weather wore on him. He discovered he liked a little variety to his seasons.

He trekked north and wandered the Pacific Northwest. He chose to bypass Middle Falls—which wasn't hard to do—because he wasn't ready to face the accompanying memories. Eventually, he crossed into Washington State and settled for a season in a nice town on a plateau that called itself *The Gateway to Mt. Rainier*. That season turned out to be the rainy one, which the locals joked started in early September and ended in late August. Those few days in between were glorious, but they weren't enough for Scott. He moved on again.

Eastern Washington was as desolate as the western side of the state was green. Living among rolling, endlessly brown hills held no appeal.

He set his sights on the Dakotas. North Dakota, in particular, is a state that is easy to miss. It's not an easy state to pass through on your way to somewhere else, unless you're heading for the Canadian border. Aside from that, you've got to plan to go there. There were things he loved about North Dakota. It was an easy state to get lost in. Again, the people were wonderful and everyone respected your privacy. One of the books he had read from Earl's stash told the story of the Norwegian settlers who had homesteaded the area. Having seen the area first hand, he developed a new respect for anyone who could scratch a living from that inhospitable land without modern equipment.

He kept moving.

Scott arrived in the upper peninsula of Michigan during the bicentennial celebration of 1976. He thought he might have found his place to settle down. It had the green beauty he had seen in Washington, Oregon, and Idaho, but didn't rain nearly as much.

The Upper Peninsula took up almost a third of the land area of Michigan, but had only three percent of the population. That suited Scott fine. The Great Lakes were a bonus. There was never a shortage of things to do—hunting, fishing, hiking, and snowmobiling. He loved his time there in August, September, and October.

One long winter's stay in the hamlet of Iron River convinced him it was not where he wanted to put down roots. Three hundred inches of snowfall that year encouraged him to move on again.

At that point, he had been on the road for three years, so he took a side trip back to Evansville. Where Scott's roots were shallow, Cheryl was putting her own roots deep in Indiana soil. She was pregnant with her first baby.

Scott spent the summer in Evansville. He worked on projects in Earl's basement woodshop. He was able to be at the hospital when Cheryl and Mike welcomed Andrea Nicole into the world. By fall, he had grown antsy again.

He got his grandfather's old atlas out and laid it on the kitchen table. He traced his finger along the route he had followed the previous three years. It formed a large oval around the USA, but had skipped one part—the northeast.

Scott hated goodbyes, so he woke up one morning before the sun was up, left a note on the dining room table, and started walking. He walked to the bus depot, which felt like it completed a cycle in his life. He rode the Greyhound east and then north. The Finger Lakes region of upstate New York were tempting, but he was enjoying being on the move once more.

Continuing east, Scott finally stepped off the bus in the little town of Waitsfield, Vermont.

It feels like I've walked onto the set of a Hollywood movie.

It was a picturesque New England town, with a covered bridge, a quaint downtown area, and charm by the truckload.

I can't put my finger on it, but this feels like home.

Chapter Thirteen

Before long, Scott discovered that Waitsfield had lots of snow, cold temperatures and limited daylight during the winter months. These were things that had bothered him elsewhere, but as his sister had once told him, "when you know, you know." He never regretted the decision.

He rented a furnished room in a boarding house on his second day in town and stayed there temporarily. Eventually, his newfound love of reading led him to something more permanent. He had been haunting a used bookstore called *Twice Told Tales* most every day, when the lady behind the counter said, "You must love to read."

"I do now. Never did much of it until the last few years. My grandfather got me started again."

"I haven't seen you around until the last few weeks. New in town?"

This was a standard small-town question. *Are you from away?*

"I've been traveling around since I got out of the service. Looking for a place to settle. I think this is it."

"Found a place already?"

Scott looked at the woman. She appeared to be somewhere in her forties. Short, a little round, with hair gone mostly to gray. Her expression wasn't unfriendly, but it wasn't cheerful, either.

"Just staying at Mrs. Carvill's boarding house until I can find something more permanent. Places to rent seem to be hard to find."

"You've just got to know people. Here, put your books on the counter and follow me." She locked the front door and flipped the paper sign over to read, "Closed," then led Scott through a curtained area at the back of the shop. "There's two ways up, including a door from the outside."

She took a key ring out of her pocket and unlocked the door at the top of the stairs. It opened into a studio apartment with a small kitchen off to one side and an equally small bathroom at the back. The front of the apartment was made up of windows that let in plenty of ambient light.

"Just had my last tenant move out a few days ago. If you don't mind living above a bookstore..."

"I'll take it."

"I'm Greta. I'll be your landlady, then." She twisted the key off the ring and placed it in Scott's open palm. "Seventy-five dollars a month. You can bring it to me in the shop when you move in."

Scott had an urge to hug her, but she was not an easily-hugged woman. Instead, he offered her his hand and said, "I'm Scott McKenzie. Thank you, Greta. Do you want me to fill out an application?"

She shook her head. "No, you pass my eye test. It's never let me down. Don't be the first."

Scott smiled and said, "I'll go settle up with Mrs. Carvill and be back here soon. Thank you so much."

If he had been physically able, he might have skipped down the stairs to the street. For the first time in longer than he could remember, he had begun to feel at home.

Scott spent a happy six months living above the bookstore. He loved how light the apartment was, and the fact that the entire building smelled like old books. Waitsfield was a small town—a population of less than two thousand people in 1977—but living right in town still felt a little too close quarters for him. In the fall leaf-peepers and other tourists made the place feel more crowded than it was.

In the early spring of 1978, he was sitting in an old armchair in front of the bank of windows reading a book about the flora and fauna of New England when there was a knock on his door.

He opened the door and said, "Hello, Greta, what's brought you up from the store?"

Greta Gnagy looked at him shrewdly. "I like you, Scott."

Her straightforwardness made him laugh a little. "I like you too, Greta!"

"I have someone else down in the shop, looking for a place to live."

Scott tried to guess where she was going with this line of conversation, but failed.

"They want a little place in town, just like this."

"You're not kicking me out, are you?"

"I'd no more kick you out than bite off the end of my nose. But, you mentioned once that you would like to find a place a little ways out of town if you could, didn't you?"

"Yes, but those places aren't easy to find. Everyone wants to come to this part of Vermont and live like Thoreau."

"They'd have to get on I-93 and drive south a few hours to do that, but I understand what you mean."

Mental note: Don't make a literary joke with a woman who owns a bookstore.

"Here's why I'm asking. My brother passed away a few months back."

"My condolences."

"Thank you. He is missed. He left his little house out in the woods to me, and I haven't decided what to do with it. I thought about selling it, but I think I'd need to put too much into fixing it up to make it worth it. So, I'm wondering if you'd like to trade your little place here for that little cabin in the woods."

"Yes. I'll take it."

"Don't be so hasty. It needs a lot of work."

"I understand. I'll take it."

"It's only a small place, one bedroom. My brother was old and infirm for quite some time, so he hadn't been able to maintain it."

"How many different ways are you going to make me say I'll take it?"

"Good enough. It's still got all Henry's furnishings in it. Would you be willing to move in as-is? If you would, I'll rent it to you for the same amount I'm renting you this place."

"Please don't make me say I'll take it again. If you've got a few boxes in your storeroom, I can be packed and ready to move this evening. Would you be willing to give me a lift in your truck and show me where it is?"

"Come on and get those boxes. I'll tell the young woman she can have this place tomorrow. I'll close the shop at five, and give you a ride. You can sleep out there tonight, if you want."

Greta hadn't oversold the place. It was truly a bachelor's house in the woods and it needed work. The whole structure seemed to be canting at a slight angle. The forest was in the process of reclaiming the building for its own, with plants, bushes, and trees encroaching on the walls and porch. The roof was so old that it looked like moss might be the only thing holding it together. Inside, the furniture was old and there was a layer of dust on everything. The door creaked loudly when Greta opened it.

She closed one eye and said, "I didn't remember it being quite this bad. Are you sure you want it?"

Scott laughed and said, "I love it. It's perfect. Thank you, Greta. I'll get to work on it right away."

Standing in the doorway, Scott could see almost all of it. One room constituted the kitchen, dining room, and living room. There was a small bedroom and bath off the back of the house. It sat in a small clearing ringed by trees. Beyond the sound of birds in the trees and a small brook that ran through the back of the property, it was completely quiet. For Scott, the best feature of the place was a covered front porch with a solid old rocking chair. He could envision many happy nights sitting there, reading and watching the world pass him by.

Chapter Fourteen

Scott cut and stacked enough firewood to get him through a long Vermont winter. He sharpened an old scythe he found in a back shed and cut back the encroaching vegetation. He reclaimed the area around the house as his own.

It'll never get a spread in a magazine like House Beautiful, *but I can't imagine a more perfect place for me.*

His new home was miles out of town, located off an old logging road, so he didn't get a lot of drive by traffic. When someone did drive by, they were typically looking to get away from the world as well and left him alone. He couldn't see much use in buying a vehicle, but he did buy a used bicycle at a yard sale. It was equipped with a basket big enough for a few groceries or a stack of books.

The rent that Greta charged him was so cheap that he didn't need to work—his benefits gave him more than he needed for the simple life he led. He did take odd jobs around town from time to time, mostly to get himself out in polite company so he didn't become a complete hermit.

When it became obvious to the denizens of Waitsfield that he wasn't just passing through, he made a number of friends, including Louise, who ran the Waitsfield library. Like much of Waitsfield, the library was small, but it was a completely charming brick building with white columns in the front. He found out what day the out-of-town newspapers arrived and became familiar with the microfiche system. The small town library's acquisition budget for non-local newspapers wasn't large, but Scott subscribed to dozens and had them all sent to the library. Soon enough, their collection was the envy of all other library systems in Vermont.

Scott got in the habit of spending most of the day on Tuesdays and Fridays in the library. He designed a process where he scanned every out-of-town newspaper that came in for lurid stories of death and destruction. Each of those stories went into a notebook marked with the year. He knew he couldn't stop all of them—there wasn't much he could do about an airplane crash or a tornado touching down. He spent his evenings with a map of the United States, planning out where and how he could make a difference and how he could make it from one to another in time.

About a year after he started his research, Louise asked him, "What in the world are you doing, reading all those newspapers every week? Isn't it the same news everywhere?"

He'd known that question was coming eventually and had an answer prepared.

"You'd be surprised how much difference there is. I'm thinking of writing a book about how different newspapers report the same story. That's why I'm always sifting through the newspapers, looking for different angles."

"Well, you're certainly diligent about it. You're my best customer!"

From experience, Scott knew that when he woke up again, he would only have whatever he'd had with him the day he had fallen asleep on his grandparents' sofa.

That, and his memories.

He took a mail order course that taught him a number of tricks to improve his memory. The more he practiced, the better his memory got. After a few years, his memory become prodigious, and he filled it with a litany of dates, times, and names. A Hall of Fame for serial killers, rapists, murderers, and all-around awful people. He continually sorted and updated his list with the latest information that became available to him. It wasn't unusual for a serial killer to emerge and Scott had to go back to a previous year's notebook to make notes about where he had begun killing.

He found that true crime books, which were often deeply and impeccably researched, often provided the best insight into when and where would be the best place to stop a perpetrator. When Ann Rule began publishing her books in 1980, she became a go to source for him and he had a standing order with Greta for each new book.

Scott also knew that when he woke up, he would once again be in a weakened state, not yet recovered from his war wounds.

He wanted to have time to rest, rehabilitate and get strong, so he started researching events and bad happenings starting in the summer of 1974. That would give him time to get healthier, watch Cheryl and Mike get married—again—and get to wherever he needed to be to stop it.

He constantly battled with himself. One day he was anxious to get started on this new life, and the next he felt so happy with his quiet life in Vermont that he never wanted to leave it. He wanted to begin helping people and stop bad things from happening, but the longer he lived in this life, the more he would know.

Scott watched the seasons and years pass and he fell into a routine. He spent his two days each week in the Waitsfield library. He filled in for Greta at the used bookstore every fall so she could visit her children in Maine. There was something comforting about sitting among the dusty stacks, reading a new book and not knowing or caring if another customer would come in or not. Once each year, he made the trip back to Evansville to see Cheryl, Mark, and their brood of children, which had grown to include two new brothers for Andrea. They had named their oldest boy Scott.

Each time he visited, Cheryl and Mark both tried to convince him to move back to Evansville, but Scott never considered it. His home was in Vermont now.

In December, 1980, Scott was as shocked as the rest of the world to read about the murder of John Lennon. In picking out which cases he could do something about, Scott had typically tried to avoid high profile incidents. He didn't want to become famous, or do anything that would put a crimp in his ability to move anonymously around the country. He knew he couldn't let the murder of John Lennon pass unchanged, though.

Once he started making his list, the problem was in limiting it. He was initially shocked at how many bad things happened to good people. Over time, he realized that is the way of the world—part of the human condition.

His list grew. As the 1970s passed into the 1980s, serial killers became more prominent in the news. He followed their trails and researched their kills after they were captured to see if he could find an opportunity where he could have found and stopped them from killing early on. The more research he did, the more he wondered if he would actually be able to do what needed doing when the time came.

Can I really kill someone before they do something awful? But, what if I don't? In a way, would that make me just as responsible?

It was a question he chased round and round in his brain as he drifted off to sleep each night.

The years passed quietly and easily for Scott. In the early spring of 2002, just a few months before his fifty-fourth birthday, he experienced a new pain. After all these years, he was used to pain flare-ups from his old war wounds, but this was something new. He did his best to put it out of his mind and concentrate on his work.

Soon after, he began to have a hard time urinating. He read up on home remedies and drank lots of cranberry juice. He found himself making more nighttime visits to the bathroom, which he explained away as his body getting older and from drinking all that cranberry juice.

As the months passed, the pain increased. Finally, when the worst of the snows had melted and he wasn't so housebound, he made an appointment to visit Dr. Jasper. Jasper was the only doctor in town, and Scott knew him from seeing him in the bookstore.

Dr. Jasper gave him a full physical. A few days later, Scott returned to his office for the results. When he did, Jasper referred him to a specialist thirty miles northeast in Montpelier.

Scott planned to hitchhike the distance. He hadn't owned a vehicle since he had moved to Vermont and he knew enough people in town that he was sure he wouldn't be stranded for long. Dr. Jasper tipped off Greta, who was now a robust eighty years old, about Scott's appointment. She insisted on driving Scott to Montpelier.

As they rode, Scott watched the scenery roll by and reflected on what he was about to learn.

I suppose if I'd only had one life to live, this would be a frightening moment. Preparing to face the unknown. Heaven, hell, or the abyss of total oblivion. It's not like that, though. Unless something has changed, I'll wake up in Evansville in 1972 again. Cheryl will be cooking dinner and Gramps will flush the toilet and come walking down the hall. It'll be good to see him again, when the time comes. It's been too long.

Greta glanced across at Scott and saw the faraway look in his eyes. She reached a hand out and gently laid it on his for a moment, then put it back on the steering wheel. It was the only vaguely maternal gesture she had ever made to him.

"It's going to be all right, Scott."

"It's always all right in the end. If it's not all right, it's not the end, right?"

"True words."

Montpelier is the state capitol of Vermont, but it's really just a small town with a big title. When Greta and Scott rolled into town, there were only 8,200 souls living there. Still, there were some great shops and restaurants there that Waitsfield didn't have. Greta dropped Scott off at the entrance to the medical center and promised to be back in a few hours to pick him up.

The oncologist that Dr. Jasper had referred Scott to was Dr. Gardner. He gave Scott another thorough exam, drew blood, and spent quite some time sitting opposite him, reviewing Dr. Jasper's reports.

"I see you were in the army. Vietnam?"

"Yes, sir."

Gardner nodded. "I am going to refer you to a VA hospital. They're going to want to take care of you."

"I don't understand. How could what I have now be related to something that happened almost thirty years ago?"

"Agent Orange. Virtually everyone who was in Vietnam was exposed to it. There are a number of diseases associated with that exposure, including Hodgkin's disease, multiple myeloma, and various other cancers, including prostate cancer."

"Is that what you're saying I've got? Prostate cancer?"

That makes sense. Guess I shouldn't have been so stubborn and gotten the tests earlier.

Dr. Gardner didn't answer, but instead said, "On your reports, it says that you've been feeling certain levels of discomfort for some time. How long would you say?"

Scott squirmed. Sitting alone in his cabin, dealing with the pain himself had seemed like the right thing to do. Here, sitting in this doctor's office, he felt more than a little foolish.

"Probably a year, now. Maybe a little longer."

Gardner didn't scold him. He didn't need to. "Prostate cancer, when caught early, is highly treatable. If it's allowed to grow unchecked for long, treatment becomes more difficult. As I say, though, I'm going to give you a recommendation to the VA hospital in New York. I think that's our best option.

Scott nodded and shook Gardner's hand. "Thank you, doctor."

"My nurse will be in touch."

Scott didn't bother to tell him that he didn't have a phone in his little cabin in the woods. He already knew what he needed to do.

Chapter Fifteen

On the ride back, Scott could tell that Greta was fighting within herself. Her normal reserve was trying to hold off her curiosity, but he could see she desperately wanted to ask what he had found out. Finally, Scott took pity on her.

"Nothing to worry about. It's good news. Just need to get on some antibiotics for a few weeks and I'll be right as rain."

Greta glanced at him, trying to ascertain if he was being honest. After a few seconds, she said, "Oh, that's lovely, Scott. I didn't want to have to try to find someone else to rent out that old cabin." She did her best but couldn't hold back a mischievous smile.

"You're all heart, Greta."

Back in his cabin, Scott made his preparations. Over the years and decades, his research had filled enough notebooks that they took up an entire shelf in his living room. Some of it was organized, some was not. He'd always thought he had plenty of time.

I always thought I'd get organized when I got old. I never thought about what might happen if I didn't get the chance to get old.

He opened a fresh notebook and began to jot down the key elements from each crime or incident that he would need. He organized them first by date, then location, then any details he would need.

When he was done, he had ten pages of notes written out.

That's a whole helluva lot to remember. Not sure I can do it. Should I pare it down a bit?

He leafed through the notes, glancing at each notation.

Sure. Let's pare it down. Who on this list doesn't deserve to be rescued? The children Susan Smith drowned? Or how about Lawrence Singleton's victims, or Westley Allen Dodd's?

He continued flipping through his notes.

Nope. Gotta find a way to remember all this. I know I can do it.

Scott didn't know if it was getting the diagnosis, or if his cancer took that moment to announce itself more forcefully, but he didn't have another pain-free moment in that lifetime.

Instead of distracting him, the pain galvanized him. He knew whatever pain he might be feeling paled next to the people who he intended to rescue.

He stopped eating for the most part. The pain simply took his appetite away. Like his maternal grandfather, he had never been heavy, but now the pounds fell off him. He had to punch new holes in his belt and his cheeks rapidly became sunken. He knew he couldn't go into town or people would know he was not long for this lifetime.

As he studied, a new thought came to haunt him.

I don't know how all this works. What if the rules are different than I know? What if I die of natural causes? Do I go on to whatever is next, instead of starting over?

The thought stunned him for a moment and he sat back in his chair.

Have I been starting over because I've been essentially killing myself every damn life? If I live it through to the end, I might get an entirely different result.

With an effort, he stood and walked shakily to the front porch. He sat with a grunt in the rocker and looked out at the setting sun.

Would that be better? To finally live to the end of a life and get out of this infernal loop I'm in? No. That would mean this was a wasted life. I'm going to help these people. I shouldn't take any chances, though. Better study fast.

Scott barely took time out to sleep the next three days. He hunched over his notes until his back ached and his mind felt like it would shut down. He used every memory trick he had. Formed associations with people and places. Created mnemonic devices. Created keywords for each crime. More than anything, he read and reread his final master list.

After those days of intense study, he had to admit that he couldn't imagine forgetting any of what he had stuffed into his memory.

Like a man waking from a long nap, he looked around his cozy home.

I loved this place. I will miss it.

He grabbed the pistol from the drawer where he had kept it for the past ten years. He had only fired it once—the day he got it, to make sure it worked. At the time he bought it, he hadn't been sure why he had. It made sense, living out in the middle of the woods.

Now. Where? Not in here. Don't want to do that to Greta. If I had the strength, I'd dig my own grave and lay in it, so all they had to do was throw the dirt in on me. I don't have that strength, though. I feel this cancer eating at me, spreading. Cancer lives by killing its host, which then kills it. Stupid cancer.

Scott walked out to the forest that ringed his house. There was a small seasonal stream twenty yards further on, but he was failing fast and couldn't make it that far. He had expended the last of his strength.

Finding the old red maple tree that he had always loved, Scott half-sat, half-fell against its base. He dropped the pistol, but was able to retrieve it.

In an unconscious mimicry of his father, he opened his mouth and put the barrel against the roof of his mouth.

Pulled the trigger.

Chapter Sixteen

Scott McKenzie opened his eyes and sat bolt upright.

"Gah!"

A wordless exclamation that, loosely translated, means, "I never want to do that again."

His hand reached up and patted the top of his head. Logic told him that his scalp was there, just where it should be, but he wanted to confirm that fact.

Okay. My head is all in one piece. And damn, every time I wake up back here, I forget how much it hurts to do anything.

Adrenaline coursed through him. He broke out in a sweat. His heart pounded as if he had run up three flights of stairs.

He took a deep, cleansing breath and threw back the comforter. Pain wracked his body, from his surgically repaired shoulder to the wound in his leg that would take several more years to fully heal.

I hope this will be the last time through this life. It's going to take a little more getting used to this time—it's been so long since I've been here. At least I never got addicted to having all the luxuries of what is now the future, so I won't miss cell phones, GPS systems, and computers. I knew I was going to feel this crappy, but knowing it and actually feeling it are two different damn things.

He heard the toilet flush and his grandfather emerged from the bathroom.

Hello, Gramps. So good to see you.

Unexpectedly, he felt his throat tighten and tears spring to his eyes.

It's been so long. I know you said you were ready to die, but I sure do miss you when you leave. Gotta remember that for you, Gram just died. You're devastated, of course.

Scott gently swung his feet of the couch and sat up.

"Glad you got some sleep. I know you needed it," Earl said as he eased into his chair. "Cheryl's working on some dinner for us."

And just like that, here I am once again.

A moment of panic filled him.

Wait. Can I remember everything?

There was a momentary void where all his memories about his studies had been. Then, the first page of his notes appeared in his mind and everything was there.

I made it. I've got everything I need. It took a lifetime to get here, but now I can get started.

SCOTT HAD METICULOUSLY planned for what he would do when he woke up again in this life. But he had dreamed it so often that actually living this life again felt slightly surreal.

The first eighteen months played out almost exactly as it had the last time through. He asked Earl to help him build a place to do his rehabilitation and spent many happy hours in the basement with his grandfather. Scott listened to him whistle tunelessly and tell him the same stories he had before. He didn't mind hearing them a second time at all. Getting to spend more time with Gramps was a gift, and he recognized it as such.

Scott had a lot of other preparations to make in order to be ready. He knew he would want weapons with him as he went about his newfound vocation, but he wanted to avoid guns if at all possible.

Guns were loud. No silencer ever worked like it did in television and movies. Plus, they left more information behind than he was comfortable with. He wanted to be as untraceable as he could be.

Finding a mail order supply house catalog for police departments, he ordered a collapsible steel baton. Small enough to easily be hidden on his body, but able to do serious damage when it was extended.

He also purchased a karambit, a weapon he had learned about in Vietnam. It was a short, curved knife with a finger ring on the end of the handle. That grip made it difficult for an opponent to dislodge the weapon during combat. Perfect for close combat, and potentially lethal.

The one question Scott couldn't answer was, when faced with the opportunity, would he be able to actually do this thing? Could he kill someone even though they hadn't committed the crime yet? Did he have enough faith in the way things had played out in his previous lives to actually put someone in a grave? He believed so, but he suspected that was something he wouldn't actually know until he was faced with the decision.

In all his previous lives, he had burned his green canvas army jacket while he was rehabilitating himself—a way to forcibly separate his past. He chose not to do that this time, thinking that the jacket might allow him to blend in better in certain situations.

When his grandfather died once again, Scott knew his moment was almost at hand. While he waited for Cheryl to once again announce her engagement, he worked on getting into the best shape possible.

He bought a set of weights, set them up in Earl's old workshop and spent several hours each day working on building up his muscles and improving his sense of balance. He also focused on his stamina. He started by walking a mile each time he went out, but by the time the wedding rolled around again in April, he was able to jog a few miles at a time.

He prepared Cheryl and Mike for the idea that he would be going on a walkabout when they returned from their honeymoon. They were once again planning the trip to Florida. The fact that their lives played out almost exactly the same, time after time, showed him how little impact he and his changing lives had on them.

Scott had taken the time to write down all the notes he had memorized. He knew they were hardwired into his brain by now, but it made it easier to sort through and plan when he could look at the specifics on the page.

For most of his previous life, he had known what his first mission was going to be.

Brock Allen Jenkins had murdered his wife and children in Waterville, Maine, on the 4th of July, 1974. It had been a horrific crime that had made headlines around the country at the time. Jenkins had gone drinking with friends at a barbecue earlier that day. He had arrived home to find his wife Sylvia and their three children sitting in the front yard.

No one ever knew what set Jenkins off, or why he did what he did, but he had killed his entire family. The medical examiner, upon examining the victims, had theorized that the deaths didn't occur at the same time, but were spread out over a period of five or more hours.

When Scott thought of what each of the children or his wife had been thinking as they watched the rest of their family be murdered, it sickened him. In some ways, it was a carbon copy of what he had gone through when he was ten years old.

By the first week of May, 1974, he was packed and ready to hit the road. He had eight weeks to get from Indiana to Maine.

Chapter Seventeen

Scott knew that one of the keys to his long-term success would be the ability to travel anonymously. He decided that meant growing his hair out. That would help him fit in with the times.

One more long-haired guy wearing an old army jacket riding his thumb or the bus through an area wouldn't be particularly interesting or memorable to most people.

Scott made his way on Interstate 69 north to Indianapolis. There, he turned east. He managed to pick up a ride with a sales rep at a truck stop outside of Indianapolis that took him across Ohio and into Pennsylvania.

His previous trip through Pennsylvania, he had barely nicked through the northwest corner of the state on the way to New York. This time, he caught a number of short rides that took him right through the heart of the state.

As he worked his way across Pennsylvania, he wondered how he had missed it while wandering in his previous lifetime. It was lovely—filled with small towns and a tremendous amount of history.

Scott knew he had plenty of time to arrive in Maine, so he allowed himself to take a few days off when he reached Gettysburg. He stayed in an inexpensive motel and took a guided tour of the battlefields.

While passing the time in Vermont, he had made a study of military history, reading as many books on strategy and wars as Greta had in stock at Twice Told Tales. Somehow, reading about many centuries of war helped him put his own brief battle experience into perspective.

His guided tour ended with a visit to the hill where Pickett had made his charge. As the sun set, Scott stood in the last rays of light, lost in contemplation, trying to picture the life and death struggle that had happened in that very place. Twelve thousand Confederate soldiers had run, crawled, and bled over three-quarters of a mile of empty field while the Union army rained hellfire down on them. The Confederacy breached the Union lines in a few places, but couldn't hold their position. Eventually they were forced to retreat, with nearly fifty percent casualties. The Civil War continued to play out for several more years, but that marked the high-water mark for the South.

Years later, when a reporter asked General Pickett why his charge had failed, he answered, "I always thought the Yankees had something to do with it."

Scott shielded his eyes against the dying rays.

There haven't been many times in our history when we weren't sending our young men off to fight in a battle somewhere or another. Almost eight thousand people killed right here. Forty thousand badly wounded, all in a single battle.

The next day, Scott caught a bus out of Gettysburg and rode it up through the verdant farmland of New York and across the border into Vermont. The closer he got to Waitsfield, the more he felt like he was coming home.

By the time he arrived there, it was the third week of May. Hitchhiking is the most economical form of travel, but it's good to not be on a tight schedule. For the uninitiated, hitchers live by what is widely known as *The Rules of Thumb.* Those rules weren't written down anywhere, but if you stepped outside of one of them, any experienced hitcher will let you know.

Rule number one was, *if you arrive at a spot and there's another hitcher already there, you sit and wait.*

That means you don't go back up the road half a mile and try to steal their ride before it gets to them. It means you don't stand with them while they hitch. It means that you take a seat on the grass or dirt a sufficient distance away and read a book or soak up the sun until the person or persons ahead of you get their rides.

If there were two or three people all trying to catch a ride out of town at the same time, that meant Scott often sat under a shade tree reading for the better part of a day.

His ride from Montpelier dropped him off right in downtown Waitsfield. He didn't want to spend too long there. He knew he had to get to Maine and still have time to scout out the area there. Still, he couldn't pass up the opportunity to visit what he had come to think of as his hometown.

His first stop was Twice Told Tales. Greta sat in her normal spot behind the counter, thumbing through a book about train travel through Europe.

Greta, you look a bit younger than that first day I met you. Still formidable, but younger.

"Hello," Scott said.

"Hello, is there anything in particular you are looking for, or do you just want to look?"

"I think today is a just looking sort of day."

"That's what old used bookstores are good for. You never know what treasure might be lurking around the next stack. Feel free to look around. Fiction is mostly here on the main floor. Nonfiction and reference books are up in the little loft."

It's so strange to see you like this, Greta. I know you so well, but I am a complete stranger to you.

Scott browsed the true crime section out of old habit. Nothing there was new to him. He picked up a Sydney Sheldon paperback and a few *True Detective* magazines to read in case he got stranded on the roadside somewhere.

He paid for his books, said goodbye to Greta again and strolled outside. Vermont did have a hot season. The temps in July and August often reached above 80 degrees. But here, in late May, the afternoon temperature was only fifty-eight degrees. The clean air and towering trees of the forest beckoned him to go for a walk.

Without a conscious thought, he walked the road that he had traversed for decades in his last life. The sun filtered through the trees, the birds chattered and he felt both at home and at peace. Before he knew it, he saw his old cabin dead ahead. A white haired man sat in the rocking chair on the front porch, watching him come up the road.

Scott intended to pass by with a wave, but the old man said, "Just out for a walk?"

Greta's brother, Kurt. Of course he would be here.

Scott stopped and said, "Out to see what I might see."

The man waved his arm in an all-encompassing gesture and said, "What you're seeing is about all you're going to get down that road. It dead ends into the old quarry in another half mile or so. This old place of mine isn't much, but it's the last sign of civilization."

"Good to know. Guess I'll turn back toward town, then."

I envy your place, Kurt. It was a simple life, but so good.

"Whatever you please. Just wanted to let you know." Kurt Gnagy stood up with an ease that belied his advanced years, spit a long ribbon of saliva off the porch and went inside.

For a few long moments, Scott stood looking at what had been his hideaway home. With a sigh, he turned back toward town.

Enough of a trip down memory lane. Time to get to the task at hand.

Chapter Eighteen

Scott arrived in Waterville, Maine, on June 2nd. He clambered down from the delivery truck that had given him a ride for the last fifty miles and yelled "Thanks!" to the driver. He stepped onto the sidewalk and tried to get his bearings.

He had expected Waterville to be a little smaller, a little more rural, but it was a bustling, busy town of eighteen thousand people. The downtown corridor, which would be hit hard in a few decades, when the suburbs and big box stores drew people away, was still the center of commerce in 1974.

Scott stopped at a drug store and inquired where the library was—that was his planned first stop at each new town. He knew you could learn a lot about a town from the library and the local newspaper. It was easy to combine both at once. The clerk behind the counter gave him directions to a location a quarter mile away.

After a short walk, he saw the library. It sat off by itself and was an impressive brick building with a turret and three arched doorways that led to a small covered area. He liked it immediately.

If a town's personality shows in its library, then I like Waterville already.

Scott jogged across the street but saw that the library was dark inside. He glanced at his watch and saw that it was a bit after six o'clock, but he had no idea what day of the week it was. Keeping track of days and dates hadn't mattered to him for a very long time. He knew that now, and for the foreseeable future, he would be on some sort of schedule and made a mental note to grab a tiny calendar for his pack.

He turned back toward a small motel he had seen on his walk and rented a room. He planned to spend a month in Waterville, but he wouldn't want to spend it all in a hotel. He had some cash saved up, but didn't want to drain it staying in a motel that long. He vowed to find a longer-term place to stay in the next few days. For tonight, the King's Arms Motel would do.

Checked into his modest room, Scott sat on his bed and went over the notes he had on both Waterville and the murders themselves. His notes on the city reminded him that there was a small liberal arts college in town.

That's the answer. There will be houses around the college that rent to students. Semester probably ended a week or two ago. There's gotta be room vacancies.

He took a long hot shower and thought of the task that lay ahead of him.

Everything has been theoretical so far, but it's going to be real very soon. Am I ready? Have I done everything I can to prepare for this?

By noon the next day, he had managed to rent a room with kitchen and bathroom privileges. Almost all of the other rooms in the house had been vacated for the summer. He had a cover story ready to tell the landlady, but she didn't care. She was just glad to see a warm body with cash in hand.

The next morning, he was waiting at the library when the librarian unlocked the door. After reviewing his notes, he realized that he had a fair amount of information about the murder, but none on the family before the crime, and not much on Waterville itself.

He didn't want to make a lot of inquiries about the Jenkins family around town. It wouldn't be good if Brock Jenkins suddenly disappeared and it came to light that a stranger had been nosing around, asking questions about him.

The first thing Scott did was wander around the library and familiarize himself with the layout. Next, he found a local phone book. He looked through the Js until he came to *Jenkins, Brock and Sylvia.* He jotted their name and address in his notebook.

Gotta remember to burn these notes before I leave town. Don't want to get pulled over at some later date and be carrying around a list of people who have been found dead or missing.

He found a table at the edge of the library where the sun shone through the filtered glass. He found the previous months' worth of copies of the local newspaper, *The Morning Sentinel.* Scott had hoped that the paper would be a weekly, but found it was published seven days a week.

Damn. Weekly papers are a lot more concise with their reporting. Gotta cram a whole week's worth of news into one issue. Daily papers like this have a lot more filler. I don't even know what I'm looking for, but I guess I'll know it when I see it.

He developed a system. He scanned the first section of the paper, which had a mix of local, regional, and national news. He skipped the Sports and Classified sections, but looked carefully through the Local section. That was where the police blotter was, and small stories like car accidents and break-ins were reported.

By noon, he had scanned through three months' worth of papers without finding a mention of any member of the Jenkins family. He stood, stretched the kinks out of his back and returned the papers.

For his three hours of effort, he had written exactly one note—the Jenkins' address and phone number.

He walked to a café downtown for lunch, then went into the Chamber of Commerce Visitor's Center. He wasn't interested in the Colby Museum of Art, or the Fort Halifax State Historic Site, but he got what he *was* interested in—a map of the local area.

Scott found where he was on the map, then located the Jenkins' address, which was on Greenbrier Lane. Initially, he thought that

Greenbrier wasn't on the map, but then he saw it—a small street in a wooded area northwest of the city proper.

It was hard to judge distances on the map, which didn't seem to be drawn to an accurate scale. He guessed it might be three or four miles to get to the street they lived on. He decided to put that trip off until the next morning and returned to the library for more searching.

He made it through another three months' worth of *The Morning Sentinel* that afternoon. He still didn't find any mention of the Jenkins family.

I guess that's not too unusual. How often does a family get their name in the paper, anyway? Besides, I'm not even sure what I was looking for. Maybe something to convince me that I need to do this. Sitting in the library an entire lifetime ago, this all seemed so black and white. A bad man in Maine killed his family. I should kill him, so his family can live. It was easier then.

He picked up the stack of papers and returned them to their proper place. The young librarian behind the desk smiled at him for being a good citizen, but Scott didn't notice.

I know I can kill someone. I did it before. But, that was with a rifle, at a great distance, or with my handgun, when they were rushing at me, intending to kill me first. Can I be the instigator of violence? Can I look someone in the eyes and kill them?

Scott walked out of the library and toward his new home in a residential neighborhood half a mile away.

He looked around as he walked, soaking in the feel of the town.

Just another All-American town. Feels like it could be the setting for a Jimmy Stewart movie, not a Stephen King novel.

Chapter Nineteen

The next morning, Scott woke up, grabbed a coffee and donut from the bakery downtown, and set off to walk to Greenbrier Lane. It was a perfect summer day in Maine, with a few wispy clouds and temperatures heading for a high near eighty.

Scott had a tough time deciding what to take with him on his exploratory jaunt to the Jenkins place. He would have been more comfortable with his collapsible baton and karambit with him. At the same time, he knew that walking through strange neighborhoods with weapons was not a great idea. Sometimes local cops like to have conversations with guys they see walking through a residential area they have no business being in. In the end, he left his backpack and jacket in his motel room and set out wearing nothing but his Levi's, walking boots, and a light shirt.

He tucked his hands into his pockets and whistled as tunelessly as his Gramps ever had as he walked through one comfortable neighborhood after another. As he got further away from the downtown area, the houses were more spread out and tended to sit on larger lots.

By the time Scott finally found Greenbrier, the sun was high in the sky and he had beads of sweat on his forehead. It was the most rural area he had walked through yet. All the houses sat on acre-plus lots, and most of them had long driveways with the house well back from the road. His only chance to figure out the address of the house was by checking the numbers on the mailbox.

He walked along the opposite side of the road he knew the Jenkins house would be on, doing his best to look like just another guy out for a stroll on a sunny day. After walking half a mile along Greenbrier, he saw the house he had been looking for. It turned out he didn't need the address after all.

He had read about the Jenkins murders in a book that featured shorter compilations of famous crimes. Stuck in the middle of the book were a few pages of black and white photos. The Jenkins family murders were famous enough to have warranted a book of their own, but the lack of drama in the capture of Brock Jenkins and the overwhelming lack of motive, relegated it to a smaller story.

One of the pictures in that book, which Scott had dissected like it was the Zapruder film, was a medium-distance shot of the house that was now in front of him in living color.

That photo had shown a conventional two story home with a series of objects neatly lined up in the front yard. Those objects were four tarps covering Sylvia Jenkins and her children. The oldest two children were girls—Brenda and Alicia. The youngest was a boy, Danny. The kids had ranged in age from twelve to only two years old.

It's generally established that when family members kill someone close to them, they often arrange or cover them in a lifelike pose, hoping to minimize the damage they've done. Not Brock Jenkins. After taking hours to kill his whole family, he had stacked them like cordwood in his front yard.

After he committed the murder, he had run. Because he had left his family's bodies out in the open, it wasn't long before a horrified neighbor saw them and reported it to the Waterville Police. An all-points bulletin was put out for Brock Jenkins and his green 1970 Dodge pickup.

He was taken into custody at a rest area fifteen miles short of the state line by an alert Vermont State Policeman, trolling license plates for numbers he recognized. He was literally arrested with his pants around his ankles in the bathroom.

Vermont had eliminated the death penalty in 1972, so Jenkins had been sentenced to life in prison. He had originally been sent to Windsor Prison, the oldest prison in Vermont. That old pile of rocks was closed two years later, but he was transferred a few miles away to the new Windsor prison. He had still been there the last time Scott had checked on him in his previous life.

He never accepted visitors, and never gave a reason for why madness overtook him and he killed his entire family. By all reports he was a model prisoner.

And now, that same house was in front of Scott. He walked past it, trying not to be too obvious about paying attention to it. There was a neighbor on one side, an open field behind the house, and a stand of trees that ringed the property on the other.

Fifty yards past the house, Scott sat and rested his back against a telephone pole. The Jenkins house was quiet and dark. There were no vehicles in the driveway. There was no sign of kids at the house at all—no blow up pool to wade in, no swing set, no bikes leaned against the garage or tricycles left in the middle of the sidewalk. If he had just glanced at the house, he might have guessed a childless couple lived there.

There were no survivors that day, and no one saw him do it, so I don't know for sure what time it happened. The question is, can I afford to wait until that day and stake this place out? I'm sure I can find a stealthy place in those trees. I could hide there and wait for him to come home. Or, I could try and find a time when he's home alone and do it then. If I have the guts to do it that way. The problem is, things don't always happen the same way. Do I have a right to kill him before he's done anything?

Just then, a light green Dodge pickup rolled up the road and turned into the driveway. The driver's head turned toward Scott.

I know it's probably not possible, but it feels like he's watching me, all the way up the road and into his driveway. I'm probably just freaking myself out.

The pickup sat quietly for a few long moments with the engine turned off. Finally, the driver's door opened and Brock Jenkins stepped out. He wore blue jeans, a denim shirt, and a trucker's hat. He carried a black lunch box in his right hand. He walked slowly to the bed of the truck and leaned against it. He didn't seem perturbed, but he stared steadily in Scott's direction.

It made Scott's skin crawl. He had to fight the urge to stand up and walk away.

Jenkins finally turned away and went inside.

This is probably my shot. Looks like no one else is home. And I don't have my baton or knife. Even if I wanted to, could I get into hand to hand combat with him and subdue him? Likely not. And, if I did, how would I handle it from there? I've got to get a better plan put together.

Scott stood up, brushed the dirt off his jeans and walked back up the road the way he had come. He passed the Jenkins house on his right. He forced himself to keep his eyes straight ahead and to keep his pace casual. He even attempted a soft whistle, but his mouth was too dry to pull it off.

If he had looked, he wouldn't have seen anything inside the house. It was still dark behind the sunlit glare of the window and the curtains were pulled. Standing behind those curtains, holding them a few inches to the side, Brock Jenkins watched Scott until he was out of sight.

Chapter Twenty

The month of June dragged a bit for Scott. He made a mental note that for most events, he wouldn't need so much lead time to do his research and get set up. He realized he had been a little overly cautious on this first time.

He still went by the library most mornings, but he mostly gave up on reading the local paper, looking for mentions of the Jenkins family. He drifted into the books section and got lost there instead.

He chose not to go back to Greenbrier Lane again. There was no sense in tempting fate, and his silent run-in with Brock Jenkins had unnerved Scott a bit.

I don't want to give him credit for some kind of supernatural powers, but it almost felt like he knew who I was and why I was there. That's ridiculous, of course. How could he?

Brock Jenkins worked as a mailman and Scott considered tailing him on his route. Again, he chose to keep his distance. He didn't want to raise his suspicions.

On the 4th of July, Scott woke up with a nervous stomach. He sat on his bed in his small rented room, going over his notes again and again.

I've been pointing to this day for so long, it seemed like it would never arrive. Now it's here and I feel so uncertain about what I'm doing.

The week before, Scott had decided he wouldn't be able to kill someone before they had shown they were still going to carry through with their crime. His plan, then, was to leave his room in the boarding house with no intention of ever returning. He would throw everything he owned into his pack and retrace his steps out to the Jenkins house, save the family, then hit the road.

He remembered that Brock Jenkins had gone to a barbecue at a friend's house before returning home. To Scott's mind, that meant that the attack must have happened sometime in the afternoon or later. His plan was to walk past the house and get far enough away that he wouldn't be seen by anyone inside. Then, as casually as possible, he intended to slink off into the woods and work his way back to a point where he could scout the Jenkins house unobserved.

If I stay alert, I'll be close enough to stop anything from happening. First sign of trouble, I jump out and put him down however I can. Hopefully, I can slip away before the police are called. If not, I'll just be a passing stranger who saw trouble breaking out and came to the aid of a woman and her children. It might be a little tougher to explain why I was armed with a baton and knife, but hey, it's a tough world out there, right, officer?

Scott stopped at the grocery store and bought some Gatorade and beef jerky to get him through the long hot day. He tucked it into the top of his pack and began the walk toward Greenbrier Lane. As he walked through the downtown area, he saw flyers stapled to telephone poles advertising the 4th of July Extravaganza. A community picnic was scheduled to start at 6:00, and fireworks were set to go off a little after 10:00.

With any luck, I'll have this behind me and I'll be well out of town by the time the first boom happens. I just want to get off the beaten path somewhere. I can lie up in some farmer's field for the night and put some real miles under my boots tomorrow.

Scott walked by the Jenkins house a few minutes before noon. On this day, there was plenty of activity. A pretty young woman sat on the front steps with a chubby baby boy on her lap. The older girls were spread out in the yard around her. The woman caught Scott's eye as he walked by. She smiled and raised a casual hand in greeting.

Scott gave a small wave back, but didn't slow his pace.

Looks like she doesn't have a care in the world.

Scott's heart beat a little faster.

He walked on past the house a full quarter mile, then turned and walked slowly back. His head swiveled left and right, doing his best to see if anyone was watching him. He didn't see anyone anywhere, so when he approached the tree line that ran alongside the Jenkins house, he dropped into the ditch. He eased his way into the trees, which were sparse near the road, but thickened the farther in he walked.

There was no trail through the woods, so Scott picked his way slowly.

Don't need to sound like there's a moose loose in here. There was no pickup truck at the house, so he's off to the barbecue. Feels like things are lining up exactly the same way they did last life.

Scott hiked through the trees until he estimated he was approximately as far back as the Jenkins house. As quietly as possible, he moved toward their yard. As the greenery started to thin out, he was able to push a small sapling aside and saw that he had overshot the house by a few yards.

Good enough. From here, I can see them, but I don't think there's any way they can see me.

He glanced around, hoping for a friendly stump he could sit on to pass the time. No such luck.

He maneuvered himself around a bit and found a spot in the shade where he was perfectly hidden, but had a small opening he could look through to see where the kids were playing. He shucked off his pack and set it softly on the ground. He unzipped the top of the pack and removed his Gatorade, jerky, and his two weapons. The karambit was in a sheath that he hooked through his belt. He left the steel baton shut and slipped it into his back pocket.

He drew a deep breath.

Ready.

Scott may have been ready, but any drama that was going to unfold in front of him was not. He stood still for the better part of an hour, waiting, waiting. The only part of the scene that changed in front of him was what game the kids were playing. Sylvia Jenkins went in and out of the house several times but was never gone for long.

Eventually, she carried a rolled up Slip 'n Slide out from the house and laid it out in the yard. She unrolled the hose and connected it. By the time she had turned the water on, the kids were jumping up and down, ready to slide.

Scott had lived a long time without television, internet, or any distraction other than a book, so he was used to patiently watching and thinking. He did that for the next few hours while the Jenkins kids slipped and slid, jumped and laughed. Sylvia Jenkins even rolled her pants legs up and scooted the toddler along for a turn or two.

Scott shifted in place, stretched his back, touched his toes, and did everything he could to stay limber. He had made tremendous progress since being wounded, but he still stiffened up easier than he would have liked.

Finally, a little after five, the green Dodge pickup that Scott had been waiting all day for rolled down the road and turned into the driveway.

Sylvia Jenkins hustled around the yard, picking up a stray tennis shoe, a thrown ball, a dropped dolly. She smiled at her husband, but even from a distance, Scott thought there was strain behind it.

Scott focused in on Brock Jenkins.

Is he steady on his feet? The theory was that he had been drinking heavily at the barbecue.

If he was drunk, he showed no sign of it. He was dressed much as he had been the last time Scott had seen him. His trucker's hat was pulled low over his mirrored sunglasses. At one point, he turned and stared directly in the direction Scott was standing.

There is absolutely no way he can see me. Right?

Brock Jenkins took three deliberate steps toward Scott.

Chapter Twenty-One

Scott stopped breathing. He had to will himself not to twitch nervously.

Brock Jenkins stopped, but continued to look directly into the woods. Slowly, he rolled his shoulders, as if releasing tension. After a few more long, breathless moments, he turned back toward the front of the house.

Sylvia Jenkins opened the garage door and set two webbed lawn chairs out. While Brock sat in one, she went in the house. She was back moments later with a beer for him. She sat in the chair next to him.

The children, who had been so childishly playful all day, settled down. The two older girls sat off to the side holding onto a dolly each and talking between themselves. The toddler moved a Tonka truck back and forth.

Brock Jenkins stood and went to his pickup. He reached inside and pulled out a package of sparklers. He sat back and pulled a lighter from his pocket.

Brock flicked three sparklers out of the box, held them together and lit them with his lighter. The girls stood around with their hands at their sides. He handed each of them a sparkler, then gave the last one to Sylvia, who slowly waved it in front of her, entrancing the toddler on her lap.

Scott's stomach lurched.

Glad I haven't eaten much today. Not sure if I could hold it down. Why does this feel like it has the weight of inevitability behind it? Nothing here is inevitable. I can change anything.

When the sparklers were almost burned down, Brock waved the kids back over. He shook out three more and lit them off the dying embers of the ones in their hands.

Scott took half a step forward without realizing it. He focused his entire being on the tableau before him.

Is this it? Is it time? I can't go charging out into this happy little domestic scene, swinging a metal baton and wielding a knife, can I? I feel like I am staring into the abyss, and the abyss is staring back.

Sylvia Jenkins stood and watched the girls run around the yard, using their sparklers to paint designs in the air. She walked into the house but returned a minute later with a glass filled with ice cubes and liquid.

Brock Jenkins stood up and for the first time Scott saw how he towered over his wife. He was more than a head taller.

The two of them put their heads together in a whispered conversation that Scott couldn't begin to hear or imagine.

Brock took one step backward and with a sudden explosion of coiled violence, he balled up his right hand and swung a roundhouse. Sylvia never had a chance to react or move. The fist connected above her left eye and she crumpled in a heap.

Things evolved quickly.

Sylvia Jenkins crumpled to the ground.

The girls, caught off guard, continued playing in the yard for the moment. The boy immediately began to cry. Brock grabbed the back of the boy's t-shirt, lifted him in the air, and threw him across the yard.

Scott McKenzie jolted into action. He surged forward as fast as he could. He took two steps then stumbled and nearly fell. His legs were wooden, having nearly fallen asleep after hours of standing unmoving. He regained his balance, but his next few steps resembled a marionette with a drunken puppet master.

His stumble caused the baton in his back pocket to jar loose and fall to the ground.

He closed the distance. His legs were pistoning, finally acting more like legs instead of logs. As he ran he pulled the karambit from its sheath.

Behind Brock Jenkins, the girls had realized what was going on. They had dropped their sparklers and were rushing to their mother. The young boy lay unmoving on the lawn.

Scott had no plan. He only had momentum.

When he reached Brock Jenkins, he slashed out with the knife, aiming at his midsection.

Jenkins turned sideways, took a half step to his left and easily avoided the thrust. As Scott's momentum carried him by, Jenkins unleashed a vicious kick at Scott's legs. Scott fell, but did his best to roll with the momentum, focusing on not dropping the knife.

Scott scrambled to his feet and turned back toward Jenkins. The other man was moving fast, going away, retreating. Scott pushed up onto one knee, then got on his feet. By then, Jenkins had reached his pickup truck and opened the door. He reached inside and when he turned around, he held a pistol in his hand.

He strode toward Scott and slowed only when there was only a few feet separating them. Scott's chest was heaving, his face flush. Jenkins seemed to possess an otherworldly calm.

"Who are you? What are you doing here?"

Scott shifted the karambit in his hand, prepared to lunge.

Jenkins saw the shift in his balance.

He raised the pistol.

Pulled the trigger.

Chapter Twenty-Two
Universal Life Center

A young woman with long, dark hair and a confused expression sat at a desk in an impossibly long row of identical desks. They sat side by side, each with a space just wide enough to walk in between them.

In front of the woman was a milky cylinder called a pyxis. Inside the cylinder was an image of a young man, sleeping under a heavy quilt on a couch.

The woman sighed. "I am never going to get the hang of this job. Just when I think I am figuring something out, I find out that I am not."

"Frustrated, Semolina?"

It was Carrie, the head of the department. She always seemed to pop up when Semolina, or any of the other Watchers, had a problem. There was a rumor that had spread that said there were actually a hundred identical Carries. Like most rumors, it was both fun to think about and completely untrue. There was only one Carrie, but she was efficient at being exactly where she was most needed.

"Frustrated with myself, I guess," Semolina answered. "I thought I knew what was going on, but then something like this happens, and I know I still don't have a clue."

Time didn't exist in the standard sense in the Universal Life Center, so there was no way for Semolina to know how long she had been serving as a Watcher. However, she knew she was among the least experienced. All around her, other Watchers deftly handled their pyxis, using it to scoop emotions and feed The Machine. Semolina watched far fewer people's lives and still ran into difficulty.

Carrie touched Semolina's pyxis, then dragged the image inside it to her own, identical cylinder. She pulled the image up, so that it floated in the air between them. She moved her pyxis counterclockwise. As she did, the image moved backward. She saw a man running toward another man. A brief scuffle ensued, then the other man walked to his vehicle, grabbed a gun, and shot the first man. The scene shifted to the man who had been shot, now sleeping on the couch.

"Tell me what is confusing you."

"He didn't kill himself."

"I agree. He acted rashly, and those actions resulted in his death, but he didn't kill himself."

"Then why did he go back to his starting point? I thought once he lived his life to completion, he got to go on."

Carrie nodded and smiled. "I understand your confusion. Would it help if I told you that I once made exactly the same mistake?"

Semolina met Carrie's kind eyes. "I suppose. So, why was he forced to start over?"

"Because he hasn't solved the dilemma he was restarted to solve yet. He was started over to give himself a chance to work through the things he needed to. He's making progress on that, but he doesn't appear to be there yet. That's why The Machine restarted him. I know it's frustrating, and hard to understand, but I have come to accept that The Machine and its algorithms are never wrong."

"So, the fact that he lived what appeared to be a complete life cycle isn't enough?"

"Sometimes it is. My last life, I was stuck in a horrible cycle. I was eligible to move on, but I was so stuck in a well-worn path that I couldn't find my way out of it. One of my own True Family members had to come and kill me to set me free."

"I'm never going to understand all this."

"I said the same thing, and look at me now." Carrie laughed at how ridiculous that sounded. "When I woke up in the white room, I was so confused. I expected to wake up back on my parent's couch, like I had done thirteen times before. If not that, then I expected to be in line for judgment. Heaven, Hell, all that."

"Quite a shock, then."

"It was. In a secret part of myself, I held on to those ideas long past the time I knew they couldn't be true. I found comfort in them."

"That's true, isn't it," Semolina said. "There's comfort in the old beliefs, even when we have every evidence that they are wrong."

"It's another way we work on ourselves, I suppose. The sanding off of our rough edges."

Semolina nodded at the image of the sleeping man in her pyxis. "So, everything is fine here, then."

"All is as it should be. It will be all right in the end..."

"If it's not all right, it's not the end," Semolina finished for her.

Chapter Twenty-Three

Scott McKenzie woke with a jolt. A wordless scream escaped his lips. He threw the heavy quilt away and winced at the pain in his shoulder. He looked around the living room in a daze.

Hot tears coursed down his cheeks. Tears of fear, frustration, anger.

Cheryl rushed in from the kitchen. She saw Scott in distress and rushed to him. She sat on the couch and held him to her. He nestled his head into the comforting nook of her shoulder.

"Shh, it's okay, Scotty. It's better that she's not suffering anymore."

Of course. She thinks I'm upset because Gran just died. For her, that was only a few hours ago. For me, she's been dead for more than fifty years.

Down the hall, the toilet flushed and Earl walked back into the living room. He glanced at Cheryl holding Scott, comforting him, but didn't say anything. He sat in his chair and looked out the window.

Cheryl held Scott's face in her hands. There were tears in her eyes. "You okay, Scotty? That's silly, isn't it? None of us are okay right now, are we? How could we be?" She hugged him to her. "But, we've still got to eat, and dinner is on the stove."

She stood, wiped at the corners of her eyes with her apron, and hurried back into the kitchen.

Holy God, I don't think I can do this again. I've lived this life too many times. I'm tired.

Many people, at one time or another, think *I can't do this anymore.* Typically, for those people, they have a choice. If it's about a job, or a relationship, they can make a change in those things. For someone in Scott's unusual position, it's a different matter. If he couldn't do it any more, what option did he have? If he killed himself, he knew he would simply start over in the same place.

Scott spent the first month after he woke up in 1972 sad, depressed, and moping. He had spent an entire lifetime planning, studying, memorizing, *and preparing* for a life when he could fix many of the world's wrongs. On his very first assignment, he had failed.

He had failed to take care of a killer. He had failed that killer's victims. He had failed himself.

Again.

Cheryl and Earl watched Scott lay and limp around the house. They had never had to deal with someone in his position before—someone just returned from the service so obviously broken in mind and body. The truth of the situation was, they didn't have any real idea what his situation was. They saw him as a wounded warrior, broken by a war and returned home to find his own path.

The truth was, he was all of that, and more.

It's possible Scott would have followed the path of misery and self-pity for a long time—perhaps a lifetime.

Earl Bell was not the kind of man to stand by and watch that.

Mid-January days in Evansville, Indiana tend to melt together. Overcast skies and rain were the order of the day, unless a stray snowstorm blew through.

One of those gray days, sitting in the living room with Scott, Earl blew on his coffee. The television was on in the corner and Scott was half-heartedly watching it. Earl had noticed that Scott did everything in low gear these days.

"Scott, I need to talk to you."

Scott stood up and hobbled to the television and switched it off. He may have been depressed, but he still gave his grandfather the attention and respect he deserved.

"Yes, sir. What is it?"

"I know this life has dealt you a lousy blow."

Change that to lives, *and I agree with you, Gramps.*

"So, you can dig yourself a hole and pull it in after you, if you want, but that leads to nothing good. Hiding from the world only feels good for so long."

In a way, I guess, that's what I've been doing since I woke up here the second time around. First, it was booze and drugs that helped me hide away. I got rid of those, but then I went and hid in my little cabin. In a way, that was digging my hole and disappearing into it, too. In my own way, I was hiding from the world. As always, you're right, Gramps.

"Will Rogers said, 'When you find yourself in a hole, stop digging.' I always found that he knew what he was talking about. It seems to me, you might still be digging your hole."

If anyone else had said that to Scott, even Cheryl, he would have shot back with an angry comment. Not to his grandfather, though.

"I know you're right, Gramps."

"There's nothing we can do about what's got us in this predicament. Our government sent you off to war and used you up, then sent you home with a little money in your pocket so they could forget about you with a clear conscience. That's done. But, we need to make the best of the situation. I love you, Scotty, and I know what potential you have. I don't want to see you waste it sitting around here with this broken down old man. I couldn't stand that."

Scott absorbed that.

"This isn't something we can fix in a day, or a week, or a month. But we need to both get back in the swing of life. Sitting around feeling sorry for ourselves only means we have more to feel sorry about. So, I got us both a membership at the YMCA here in town. I figure maybe you can drive us there. If nothing else, it's warm in there, and they've got a pool and an indoor walking track. That'll get us moving."

"When?"

"What do you mean, 'When?' There is only one best time to start on a project."

Scott smiled, which felt odd on his face. "Right. Now. I'll get the keys."

Chapter Twenty-Four

In the movies, someone who is depressed gets a real talking to, or listens to a happy song, and the shackles of their depression fall away in an instant—or during a song montage. In real life, of course, it isn't like that. Crawling out of the darkness happens one small step at a time.

Scott McKenzie took many of those small steps with his grandfather.

Going to the "Y" every day was too much for Earl, so he only went twice a week. Scott found that the increased exercise—swimming, walking miles on the indoor track, joining callisthenic classes—helped him more than anything.

His head slowly cleared and he got some perspective on his previous life.

He found that he thought best while he was swimming laps. At first, swimming was painful, as his war injuries were still fresh. Over a few months, though, and with the assistance of a swim instructor, he figured out the strokes that helped him build up his stamina without hurting himself. He worked his way up from swimming a single, agonizing lap from one end to the other, to eventually swimming fifty laps per day.

While he swam, he considered where he had gone wrong.

I thought I was ready, but I wasn't. Not even close. First time I got into a hand-to-hand situation with someone, I found out how unpre-

pared I was. Make a mistake like that with the people I'm facing off with, and there's only one outcome. Exactly what I got.

He wasn't able to do a fancy swimmer's underwater kick, but he tagged the deep end of the pool and pushed off.

I still want to do this. There are too many people out there, alive and depending on me, whether they know it or not. I can't let them down.

He finished his laps, climbed out of the pool and toweled off. His body was scarred by the bullets and the surgeries. Adults usually noticed and looked away, but the kids often stared. Scott didn't mind, and did his best to set their minds at ease.

Today, the "Y" was nearly empty. He changed back into his street clothes and was heading toward the exit when he saw a new notice up on the bulletin board.

It was printed on bright orange paper. At the top was a hand-drawn graphic of a man in a karate gi throwing another man to the ground. In bold letters beneath that, it read, "Self Defense Classes, right here at the YMCA, Monday, Wednesday and Friday at 10:00 a.m."

Below that, in smaller print: "Isshin-Ryu Karate taught by sensei Jerry Werbeloff."

Scott stood in front of the notice, contemplating.

This will help. I have no idea what Isshin-Ryu is, but I'll bet it will help with my balance. It will help me defend myself. It won't stop me from getting shot like I did by Brock Jenkins, but maybe it would have helped me from getting my ass kicked by him in the first place.

There was a signup sheet on a clipboard that hung on a nail. Scott signed up.

THE FOLLOWING MONDAY, Scott showed up early enough to get a swim in before the self-defense class. After his laps, he changed into a sweat suit and reported to the room where classes were held.

"Looks like I'm early," Scott said, to the man laying mats out. He was wearing a loose-fitting karate gi and had a friendly smile on his face.

"Five minutes early is right on time."

Scott tried to hide his surprise. He had expected someone older to be teaching the class, but this was a good-looking kid who appeared to be no more than eighteen.

"Jerry. Good to meet you." He offered his hand, and Scott shook it.

Jerry cast an appraising eye over Scott. "Leaning a little. Slight limp. What're your injuries?"

Scott was off-balance. No one had ever spoken to him so frankly about his wounds.

"Vietnam. Shot here, here, and here," Scott said, pointing to his right collarbone, right thigh, and left ankle.

Werbeloff nodded. "Good to know. We'll make some special exercises for you that will help offset those injuries. I'll draw up a list of stretches for you, too."

"I don't want to hold the class back."

The door opened and two middle-aged ladies walked in, holding gym bags. Right behind them, a teenage girl followed.

"You're not going to hold us back, I promise. We all move forward at our own pace. Last year, I taught a guy who walked with two canes. He's pretty lethal, now, if he needs to defend himself."

He wandered off to greet the newcomers.

I think I'm going to like this guy.

An hour later, Scott was tired and hurting, but happy.

After dismissing the class with a bow, Werbeloff said, "I'll be here again on Wednesday. I hope I'll see you here again." He laid a hand against Scott's shoulder. "Have you got a minute? I'll show you a couple of stretches you can start on at home."

Scott had all the time in the world.

While Werbeloff led him through the stretches, they talked.

"I expected you to be a lot older," Scott said.

"I think everyone did."

"It's cool that you know enough to lead a class when you're so young."

"I'm not quite as young as you think I am, I'll bet. I'm twenty-one."

Scott laughed. "No, you're right, but that's still not very old."

"I started studying when I was only nine. I was lucky to have found a good sensei. He gave me a lot of training."

"And now you are taking the time to pass it on to me. Thank you."

"I'll pass it on to anyone who is ready. The rest of the class is here just to check things out, which is fine. It felt like you have more of a purpose to coming, though. So, I'll help you."

"Do you get paid for doing these classes?"

"A little. That's not why I do them, though. To learn something you must do it. To master something, you must teach it."

"I think I heard Kwai Chang Caine say the same thing in this week's episode of *Kung Fu.*"

Chapter Twenty-Five

Scott figured out that even though he had gone to war and fought for his country, he hadn't learned much about hand-to-hand combat. There had been a few lessons with a tough instructor in basic training, but with so many soldiers and so little time, no one got more than a cursory lesson.

At the YMCA, Scott received much more individualized attention.

Isshin-Ryu consisted of learning a number of katas, or stylized movements, used to teach and reinforce specific techniques of punching and kicking. Because of the damage to Scott's lower body, he was never going to be as fully balanced as he had been, but Jerry taught him secrets and methods to overcome those limitations.

Many self-defense disciplines focused on outward achievements, like leveling up and claiming a new belt color. In Jerry Werbeloff's class, the aim was more on learning and self-improvement. That suited Scott just fine. When he inevitably found himself face-to-face with someone who wanted to do him serious harm, showing them his blue or brown belt wouldn't help. The ability to stay on his feet and fight definitely would.

In October, Earl Bell passed away again. Scott never got used to the pain of losing his grandfather. Each time it happened, it was a blow. It might have sent him spiraling into another dark hole of depression, but working out at the YMCA helped him maintain his equilibrium.

After Scott had been attending the self-defense classes three times a week for six months, Sensei Werbeloff brought a wooden stick to class with him. While the other students were working on their katas, he approached Scott.

"I think this is going to make a difference for you."

"A walking stick?"

"It's a jo. It looks like a walking stick, but it can be a lethal weapon when you need it." He handed it to Scott.

It was round, a little thicker in the middle and tapered on the ends. It was made of a lighter wood, so it felt almost alive in his hands.

"Did you make this?"

"Yes, I carved it for you. I make all my own weapons. I find it is better to be armed and not need a weapon, than to need a weapon and not have one."

"Can I buy this from you?"

"No."

Scott nodded and did his best to hide his disappointment. "It fits my hand so well. Can you tell me where I can buy one like this?"

"No, of course not. It's a gift. At first, I thought a bo might be right for you, but the more I thought about where you are in your training, the more I thought that might be too long and awkward for you. You can use this jo when you go on your walkabout."

Scott looked at Jerry. "Have I told you that I am going on a walkabout?"

Jerry shrugged. "Are you?"

"Yes, I am, and soon."

"There you are, then." He smiled and said, "Come on, let me show you a jo kata. It will take some practice."

It did take practice. Nothing about it felt natural at first, but the more Scott worked with it over the next six months, the more it became like a part of him.

The YMCA was three miles from the house he and Cheryl were once again sharing as she prepared to marry Mike for the two-dozenth time, from Scott's perspective. After he received the jo, he started walking to the "Y" and home each day and grew stronger and stronger.

Between the six miles of walking, the fifty laps in the pool, and three workouts each week overseen by sensei Werbeloff, Scott had worked his way back to some semblance of the condition he had been in before he was wounded.

In all the previous repetitions of this section of his life, Scott had kept to himself. Even when he spent huge amounts of time in the Rusty Bucket, he was something of a loner. In this life, he found himself more and more drawn to Jerry Werbeloff. Scott was a few years older than his young sensei, but that didn't matter. They were on the same wavelength.

Jerry was a newlywed, much to the disappointment of the many young women who flocked to the YMCA to take lessons from him. Over time, Jerry and his beautiful wife, Lynn, fell into the habit of having Scott over for dinner on Fridays.

They lived in a small apartment in a busy part of Evansville, not far outside of downtown. They shared food and laughs, and the three of them grew close.

Over a plate of hummus and chips one night, Scott posed a question.

"Let me give you a hypothetical scenario. You teach over and over that everything we are learning is for self-defense."

"Correct. I won't teach someone who just wants to make themself a tough guy to go out and pick a fight. That is against the way of the warrior."

Scott nodded. "Good enough. But, what if a situation arose where you knew with absolute certainty that a person was going to harm someone else, but they weren't threatening you directly?"

"That is an easy question. My code says that I must protect the innocent and those who are unable to defend themselves. If I know someone is going to harm someone else, it is incumbent on me to stop them."

Jerry stood up and wandered into a bookshelf in the living room. He flipped through the books stuffed into it, selected a volume, and brought it back to the table.

"Here. A gift for you. I can get another."

Scott turned the book over and read the title. *Hagakure: The Secret Wisdom of the Samurai.*

"That should answer your question and any others similar to it."

Scott nodded. "Thank you. It means a lot to have it from you." He hung his head for a moment. "I am leaving next week. I'll sure miss the two of you and our classes. When I get back to town, I'll come find you first thing."

"Why do I think that your hypothetical question and the fact that you are leaving have something to do with each other?"

Chapter Twenty-Six

Scott did his best to switch things up so that his entire life didn't feel like a rerun. To that end, instead of hitchhiking or riding a bus to Maine this time, he started his journey on a train. Aside from hitching a hobo's ride, he had never been on a train before. He soon found he loved the experience.

The rocking, swaying motion as the train rumbled down the tracks soothed him to sleep at night and he spent his waking hours reading or staring out the windows at the passing rivers, lakes, and mountains.

He caught a train to Chicago where he ended up spending a few hours before he boarded another train to Philadelphia. From there, he changed trains again and rode to Portland, Maine.

This time, he knew exactly where the Jenkins lived, and he had a plan. He didn't need to get there a month early to scope out Waterville. So, he had waited and hadn't left Evansville until June 30th.He arrived in Portland late on July 2nd. Train travel was soothing, but it wasn't fast.

That put him on a much tighter schedule, which was just what he wanted. He had found out last life what happened when he gave himself too much time to think. One of his grandfather's aphorisms came to mind: *those who think long, often think wrong.*

In Portland, he found an inexpensive motel within walking distance of the train station. After several days cooped up onboard the train, it felt good to stretch out his legs. He was once again traveling light—still just his single backpack, with his karambit and baton tucked safely into a zippered pocket. His only new addition to his travel kit was his jo stick, which was disguised as a walking stick.

He found a newspaper box outside his motel, put a dime into it, and fished out a copy of *The Portland Press Herald.* After grabbing a quick bite at the diner across the street, Scott shut himself in his room for the evening.

He had left all but the Classified section of the paper at the diner. Now back in his room, he searched through the classified section of the paper for cars for sale. He had waited until he was in Maine to look for a car because he wanted whatever he drove to have Maine license plates and be less conspicuous.

He made a few phone calls from the old rotary dial phone that sat on the stand next to his full-size bed. A few of the vehicles were already sold and several other numbers didn't answer, but he finally reached a man who had a 1964 Plymouth Valiant for sale. It met Scott's criteria—cheap, and a little dinged up, but not remarkably so.

Scott arranged to meet the man the next morning at 10 a.m. The man's home was more than five miles from his overnight accommodations, so he called a Yellow Cab to pick him up and deliver him to the address.

He tipped the cabbie a buck and let him go. He was either going to buy the Valiant or he would have a good long walk home. The car, looking a little sad and dilapidated, sat at the curb with a "For Sale" sign in the rear window.

Scott walked around it, taking in the faded paint, rust spots along the running boards, and the spring that stuck up through the back seat.

Perfect.

A man in a t-shirt and Bermuda shorts came out through the front door.

"She's a beaut, eh?"

Scott looked at the man but managed not to laugh.

"Does she run?"

"Does she—don't be crazy. Of course she runs!"

The For Sale sign said it had 169,000 miles on it and that he wanted $400.

"I'll tell you what. If she starts on the first go, I'll give you $350, cash. If not, but it starts eventually, I'll give you $300. Deal?"

"Well, she'll know it's a stranger trying to fire her up."

"Then you be the one to start her. Deal?"

The man squinted at Scott, but apparently gave a thought to how long he had been trying to get this car out of the front of his house. "Deal. Hang on."

Bermuda shorts in Maine. Now I've seen everything. Maybe he's going to take this money and run to Florida with it.

Two minutes later, the man reappeared holding two keys on a leather key ring.

He slid in behind the wheel, paused to say a little prayer, and turned the key.

The little Valiant lived up to its name and turned right over. It didn't exactly purr, but it ran steadily enough.

The man gave Scott a triumphant smile and said, "Hah! Just like I said. Every time."

Scott peeled three hundreds, two twenties and a ten off the roll in his pocket and gave it to the man. "Got the change of ownership paperwork with you?"

"Well, I wasn't really expecting to sell the old girl today. I'll make out a bill of sale for you and sign the title."

"Good enough." *And all the better for me.*

Ten minutes later, Scott had given the man a false name and accepted the bill of sale and title. He threw his backpack in the trunk, his jo stick across the backseat and headed out of town. His first stop was a gas station, because it's a universal law that people selling used cars will sell it with the least amount of gas in the tank as possible.

Scott filled the tank for five bucks and headed north. Waterville was only a seventy-mile drive from Portland, so he arrived there in time for lunch. He ate at the same little café he had taken many meals at in his previous life and got a room in the same little motel he had stayed in as well. The whole thing was familiar to him, but he was unknown to everyone in the town.

He didn't bother to look for a room to rent long term this trip. He knew he wasn't going to be in town for very long.

Chapter Twenty-Seven

The details of what had happened at the Jenkins' house in his last life was still clear in his memory. He had witnessed with his own eyes how it had played out that day, so he knew he didn't need to arrive early. He had a few preparations to make, but he had plenty of time.

He packed his bag and threw it in the trunk of the Valiant. He laid his jo stick, karambit, and baton across the passenger seat. In its sheath, even the karambit looked innocuous enough. The baton and jo looked absolutely ordinary. In all, his array of weapons was unlikely to attract unwanted attention.

He stopped at his favorite café in Waterville for what he hoped was the last time.

Either way, I swear this is my last time through this scenario. If I can't get it right this time, I'm going to have to admit I can't do this. Maybe I could get a job working as the world's greatest detective helping police apprehend people after they've already killed. That's fine for me, but not so hot for the victims.

It was just before noon when he sat down in the booth. He ordered a big breakfast—two eggs over easy, bacon, hash browns and a large OJ—because he wasn't sure when he would have a chance to eat again.

He stopped at a Shell station and topped off the tank of the Valiant, which ran him less than a buck.

Finally, he drove to Greenbrier Road. When he passed the Jenkins house, he saw that the 4th of July play day was in full force. The two girls were kicking a ball back and forth and the baby sat on Sylvia's lap.

Scott kept the needle pegged at an even 25 MPH and drove past without kicking up too much dust on the gravel road. He continued on past the house and woods. The last time around, when, he had to admit, he'd had no real, concrete plan, he hadn't found out what was at the end of Greenbrier. Did it dead-end, or funnel off toward the highway?

Two miles down the road, it veered off to the right. Scott followed the road until it T-intersected with the highway.

Perfect.

He had noticed the mileage on his odometer when he passed the Jenkins house and saw that was exactly 2.3 miles back. He drove back in that direction until he could see the trees that bordered the Jenkins property. He slowed until he saw what he was looking for—a small stone building that looked like it had been abandoned decades earlier. There was the hint of an old driveway that had once run alongside it. Scott turned the Valiant down what was now no more than a path. He circled behind the building, turned the car so that it faced back toward the road and parked.

He slipped the sheathed knife onto his belt, pushed the baton into his back pocket, and, using the jo as a walking stick, walked the short distance through the field toward the woods. He turned and looked back at the stone building, then out toward the road. The long grass he had disturbed when he drove in was already springing back up.

Unless someone looks awfully damn close, they're never gonna see the car back there.

He walked toward the Jenkins place at a comfortable pace, giving every indication he was just another traveler passing through. Before he even broke a sweat, he came to the stand of trees he had waited in during his last life.

Scott picked his way through the brambles until he was approximately across from the Jenkins house. He didn't have to worry about his pack this time—it was safely hidden in the trunk. He glanced at his watch. 4:30. He still had some time to wait. He sat on the cool earth and leaned his back against a tree.

No need to keep watch this time. I have a pretty good idea when he'll be here.

After a few minutes, he felt himself grow drowsy in the heat of the day, so he quickly stood back up.

No way. I am not living this whole damned life over again because I fell asleep on a hot summer day.

Moments later, Brock Jenkins' green Dodge pickup turned into the driveway.

Scott stretched out, touched his toes, and jogged a little in place.

Sylvia Jenkins walked around the yard scooping up toys and shoes, then ushered the kids inside.

There's my cue.

Scott walked out of the forest, making no attempt at being quiet.

Immediately, Brock Jenkins heard him approach and turned toward him with his head cocked at an angle.

"Can I help you?"

Scott shook his head and pointed to his left ear as if he couldn't make out what he was saying.

Louder, Brock Jenkins said, "Can I help you?"

Scott nodded, as if he finally understood what was being said. He did not answer though.

Brock Jenkins held his ground, but shifted so his weight was evenly distributed.

Not expecting it, but ready for a fight, just like last time.

Scott kept his pace steady and stopped a few feet away.

Brock Jenkins looked puzzled, as though Scott might be simple-minded and lost.

Scott didn't hesitate. He pulled his jo stick up into both hands and in one long-practiced, fluid motion, swung it in an arc that connected with Jenkins' head beside his left eye.

Jenkins crumbled to the ground, but reacted fast. He rolled away from Scott and sprang back to his feet.

Scott closed on him, still holding the jo in both hands and thrust it at Jenkins' throat. The other man was quick and tried to both turn away and grab the jo with both hands. Scott was expecting exactly that and twisted the stick as he thrusted. It scraped the right side of Jenkins throat, but didn't do serious damage.

The left side of Jenkins' face had been split open by the initial blow and blood flowed into his eye.

A shrill, ear-piercing scream tore through the air. Sylvia Jenkins stood on the front porch, her mouth open and ready to scream again. She dropped the beer bottle she had been carrying. It didn't shatter, but a geyser of beer shot up.

Scott had turned his head to see.

Jenkins hadn't. He bull-rushed Scott and hit him in the solar-plexus with his right shoulder. They both went to the ground, but Scott was on the bottom and all the air rushed out of his lungs with a loud "Ooof!"

Jenkins tried to wrap him up in a wrestler's hold, but Scott rolled away.

"Go call the police, and get the rifle!" Jenkins shouted at his wife.

Sylvia Jenkins fled inside, slamming the door behind her.

Brock Jenkins scrambled to his feet, quick as lightning.

The baton, still collapsed, had fallen out of Scott's pocket. He grabbed it off the ground in his left hand, opened it to its full length with a downward flick, and dropped into a fighting stance.

Jenkins wasn't interested in a fight, though. He had turned and run toward his pickup truck.

Scott was not fast, but he moved as quickly as he could and when Jenkins had to stop to open the door, Scott caught him.

He didn't hesitate. He raised the baton as he ran and whipped it down on Jenkins right arm as it opened the door.

Scott heard the bones break in Jenkins forearm. It was Jenkins turn to scream.

Gotta do this fast. Don't know how long it will take the cops to get here, but probably not too long.

While Brock Jenkins cradled his broken arm and cried out, Scott pulled the karambit out of its sheath with his right hand and slashed upward into the other man's exposed chest. The knife was so sharp, its curved edge went in almost without friction. Scott twisted it as he pulled it out and blood spurted onto his hand, his arm, his clothes, everywhere.

Brock Jenkins fell to his knees, but before he collapsed completely, Scott reversed his attack and slid the blade across his throat.

Jenkins' eyes glazed over and Scott let him fall.

Adrenaline rushed through Scott, but he knew he needed to focus.

Gotta get the hell out of here, right damn now.

He strode over to where his jo lay abandoned in the grass, grabbed it and turned for the road. He was almost there when the front door opened and Sylvia Jenkins pushed through. She held a rifle in both hands.

Chapter Twenty-Eight

Sylvia Jenkins wasn't screaming any more. She looked calm as she raised the rifle to her shoulder and sighted down the barrel at Scott.

Scott looked left and right. Cover was thin, but there were a few maple trees at the front of the Jenkins yard. He sprinted for one.

As he slid behind it, a shot rang out and the bark beside his head was vaporized.

If I stay right here, she can pin me down until the police arrive.

He ran for the next tree, then another and another.

Mrs. Jenkins' aim was fair, but she didn't seem to be familiar with the mechanism of the gun, as the shots did not come quickly. She took two more shots that were near misses, but then Scott disappeared behind the cedar fence that delineated the two property lines.

Far away, Scott heard the tinny wail of a police siren.

I'm stuck here, the cops are coming, and my car is the opposite direction down the road. If I run for the car, either she'll shoot me, or the cops will see me.

Scott made a split-second decision and ran along the fence line toward the neighboring house.

If anybody's home and sees me, I'm probably stuck. I won't hurt an innocent person. I guess if I get caught, I can just start over.

He ran, keeping his head low. As he did, he glanced at the neighbor's house. It looked dark and deserted.

Moments later, he reached the back of the fence, turned right, and ran directly behind the Jenkins house. As he ran along the fence line, the hairs on the back of his neck tingled.

She could be right there, on the back porch, aiming that rifle at me right now.

Scott didn't focus on being quiet, but instead tried for speed. A few seconds later, he was at the end of the fence, which also marked the end of the Jenkins property.

He peeked around the fence corner at the backyard. It was empty. He gauged the distance between the fence and the safety of the trees.

Maybe fifteen feet. Just a few steps. If she doesn't see me, of course.

Scott took a deep breath, tucked the jo under his arm and leaped for the woods.

His momentum carried him into the cooler shadows, but his foot landed on a half-buried rock and twisted. Pain shot up through his leg, but he managed not to cry out.

He peered through the bush and toward the front of the Jenkins house. Scott saw Mrs. Jenkins running out toward her husband's body as a Waterville Police Department cruiser skidded into the driveway. Scott didn't wait to see any more.

He worked his way along through the woods, limping badly on his twisted ankle—the same one that had been shot in Vietnam. He used his jo half as a walking stick and half as a crutch. He maneuvered his way through the tangle of underbrush and felled trees.

He couldn't see the Jenkins place anymore, but he heard the police car that had first arrived tear out of the driveway and turn in the direction he had initially run. Happily for Scott, that was the opposite direction from him at that moment.

Won't take him long to figure out he can't find me that way. I'm sure there will be a whole bunch more cop cars here any minute. A mur-

der surely doesn't happen every day in Waterville, although there would have been more today if I hadn't come.

He did his best to hurry across the field toward the Valiant. Scott was limping badly now. His ankle was swelling and his walking boot was much too tight.

He opened the Valiant and threw his stick, knife, and baton across the backseat. He twisted in the driver's seat and put both feet outside the car. With a grimace of pain, he unlaced the boot on his right foot and slipped it off.

Glad this is an automatic. Not sure I could drive a stick right now.

He said a silent prayer to a God he didn't believe in, then turned the key.

The engine turned over immediately. He pulled out from behind the stone building and eased toward the road. He leaned across the front seat and rolled down the passenger door window—no luxuries like power windows in this vehicle.

He listened.

Sirens again, but coming from his right, and once again sounding some distance away.

They're gonna stop any vehicle they see along here and question them, so I've just gotta hope they don't see me, right?

He stepped on the gas with his painful right leg and turned left, away from the Jenkins house.

His first instinct was to floor it, to do eighty down that gravel road and put some distance between himself and the trouble behind him.

That'll only kick up dust, though, and in this still air, it'll hang there forever, pointing them right toward me.

He kept his speed at twenty-five miles per hour or less and drove toward the highway. He watched the road behind him in the rearview mirror almost as much as he watched the road in front of him.

After a few minutes, which felt like forever to Scott McKenzie, he intersected with the highway.

He turned right onto Highway 137.

He looked down at his himself. Both his hands and clothes were covered in sticky, drying blood. He did his best to wipe his hands off on his shirt, but he would need soap and water to get it all off. He made sure to stick right at the speed limit and drove away from Waterville.

Behind him, he heard more and more sirens, but they were fading into the distance.

Twenty miles down the road, he felt safe enough to pull over onto a small side road and find a deserted place to park. He opened the door and tried to step out but immediately regretted it. His ankle wouldn't hold any weight and he pitched forward onto all fours. He turned around, grabbed his jo and again used it as a crutch to get back to the trunk.

Scott stripped off his jeans and shirt, rolled them into a ball and stuffed them into the corner of the trunk. He fished through his backpack and found a clean pair of jeans and t-shirt. He slammed the trunk, hopped back around to the driver's side and collapsed onto the seat. Slowly, painfully, he managed to get his jeans on, but knew that putting his boot back on his right foot was a pipe dream. He slipped the clean shirt on and felt a little better.

I've got to be better prepared for these situations. I need a gallon of water stored in the trunk, maybe some baby wipes for quick clean up. Always need to have a change of clothes ready to go.

He started the car, but didn't move. The horror of the memory of the scene washed over him.

Without warning, he felt onrushing nausea. He opened the driver's door, leaned his head out and threw up the remainder of his breakfast. He stayed in that position for a long minute, waiting to see if there would be a second spasm.

I killed a man. That was awful. I don't know if I can do this. I killed people in Vietnam, but that was so different. There, I saw a man a long ways away. Pulled the trigger. When I looked again, he was either still there, and I fired again, or he was gone. This is different. Looking into a man's eyes while he dies. I don't know if I can do this.

He put the car in gear and let it roll forward a few feet.

But if I don't? Then what? Live with the knowledge that I could have stopped these horrible things from happening, but didn't? I don't think there is a good answer here.

Scott turned right back onto the highway and drove on. Wanting to put as many miles between him and the Jenkins place as humanly possible, he drove west into the sun. As the miles disappeared under his wheels, more thoughts haunted him.

What else did I mess up there? Mrs. Jenkins saw my face, for sure. She'll be able to identify me if they ever arrest me. That was stupid. I don't think anyone saw the car, so it should be okay for right now.

Scott continued revisiting everything and drove until it was almost dark. He stopped at a gas station and used the rest room to wash the blood off his face and hands. A few miles later, he pulled into the parking lot of a roadside motel outside of Lancaster, New Hampshire. His hands were shaking as he turned the ignition key.

At least I made it to another state.

Using the jo, he limped into the office. The gray-haired lady sitting behind the desk raised her eyebrows in surprise when she saw him.

"Looks like you came out on the wrong end of whatever you ran into."

Scott gave her his best smile. "Just doing some hiking today and slipped off the path. I think I sprained it. Can I get a room for the night?"

"If you've got fourteen dollars, I've got a room."

"Sounds like a deal." He laid a ten and a five dollar bill on the counter. "I don't suppose you've got a couple of aspirin you'd sell me for the extra dollar?"

The bills disappeared into a cash drawer, then she went through a door at the back of the office. Scott could hear a television playing and guessed that was her home. A moment later, she returned with a mostly-empty bottle of Anacin.

"Here. You can keep these. Check out is at eleven."

"I might want to stay an extra day or two and let the swelling go down in my ankle. Will that be all right?"

The woman waved her hand at the barren parking lot. "We ain't even full on the 4th of July, so it'll be fine. As long as you've got money, I've got a room." She grabbed a key attached to a plastic fob. "Room number twelve. You can park right in front of it, so you won't have to walk far."

"Thank you, ma'am," Scott said with relief. He had been able to hold himself together to this point, but he knew he was almost to the end of his rope.

Two minutes later, he had moved the car, grabbed his backpack, and shuffled into his room. He turned the television on. The ten o'clock news was playing.

A well-coiffed local news anchor was reading the news. "...and there's the cutest footage you'll see all day, the puppy parade down main street. In more serious news, we've had reports of a strange murder in neighboring Maine. We don't have a live report, but word out of our sister station says that a homeowner was killed when a man attacked him with a knife. He might have killed the man's wife and children as well, but she had a rifle and scared him off. Brave woman. More details as they become available."

"That's the spin, huh? I guess that's the way it looks." Scott realized he was talking to himself, shut the television off and collapsed across the bed.

He slept twelve hours straight.

Chapter Twenty-Nine

Scott was serious about holing up in the little motel for a few days. When he woke up late the next morning, he was stiff and sore. He felt like he might have gone twelve rounds with Smokin' Joe Frazier the day before.

He took a long, hot shower to loosen his muscles up. His ankle was still swollen, and it had started to turn a deep purple color in places.

He wasn't even sure he wanted to move from his room to get something to eat. He hadn't put anything in his stomach since lunch the day before, and he had thrown most of that up. So he hobbled to the car and drove to a small café down the road.

As he limped into the café, he realized how handy his little jo was.

Great for hiking, even better in a fight, and it doubles as a cane, too. They oughta do late night commercials about these.

He took the notebook he had written all his memorized crimes into the café with him. He ordered a double cheeseburger, fries, and a chocolate shake, then opened it to the second page. In block letters across the top, he had written: *Ted Bundy, Lake Sammamish, July 14, 1974.* The rest of the page was filled with bits and pieces of things he remembered about one of the world's most notorious serial killers.

Suddenly, his eyes slammed back onto that date.

July 14. July 14? Goddamn it! That's clear on the other side of the country, and he's going to abduct and kill two girls in nine days. Why didn't I ever make the connection between one killing in Maine and another in Washington State being so close together on the calendar? Stupid.

Any thoughts of a relaxing few days, sitting around eating fast food and watching television fled from his mind. He could picture the faces of the two women Ted Bundy abducted and killed on that day. Scott remembered Bundy's confession when he was captured in Florida, saying he had taken them to the same place and made one watch while he killed the other.

No way I can let that happen.

He bolted his food, slurped his shake, and left three dollars on the table to handle the meal and the tip. He hurried back to the motel, threw his pack in the trunk and stopped at the front desk to tell them he was checking out after all.

He pulled his old, folded-up atlas from his pack and opened it to the two-page map of America. He looked at where he was, then looked at where Lake Sammamish was, just outside of Seattle. They couldn't have been much farther apart and still been in the continental United States.

Using his finger as a ruler, he estimated that it was close to a 3,000-mile drive.

I figure I'll need at least a couple of days to find things and get situated. So, that gives me seven days to drive three thousand miles. I can do that easily. Five hundred miles per day gets me there an extra day early.

He stopped at a gas station and filled up again, then headed west.

That day—starting late, a little beat up, and exhausted—Scott didn't make his five hundred miles. He took Highway 2 west, then caught I-91 south, until he hit I-90 at Springfield, Massachusetts. From there, he knew he was going to be on that coast-to-coast freeway all the way to Washington State. It would be a long, straight drive for the most part, and that suited him fine. The less thinking he had to do, the happier he was.

By the time he got to Springfield, Scott's ankle hurt him so much that he pulled off at a drug store along the interstate. He bought an Ace bandage and a new supply of aspirin. As swollen as it was, he knew that what he needed was some ice and to get it elevated.

He drove a few miles west, found a Motel 6, and pulled off the freeway. Motel 6s were originally called that because the rooms were actually six dollars per night. By the mid-seventies, the rates had gone up, but not all that much. He found a clean, comfortable room for twelve bucks that night.

Scott checked in, grabbed his dinner out of the snack machine in the lobby, got some ice, and hobbled to his room.

He had fallen asleep the night before in the same clothes he had worn since he had changed after the fight with Brock Jenkins, so he stripped those off and climbed onto the bed. He took the plastic bag out of the ice bucket and filled it with ice. He elevated his leg onto a couple of pillows, placed the jury-rigged ice bag on his ankle and lay down.

He awoke in the middle of the night to find that the plastic bag had leaked, but he was too tired to care. He rolled over and slept until morning.

SCOTT SPENT THE NEXT three days driving across the northern part of the United States on Interstate 90. That route took him through the northern part of Indiana, but he was on a tight schedule and didn't have time to swing by Evansville to see Cheryl. He pushed on.

On the fourth day, he hit the badlands of South Dakota. The small towns that dotted the route of I-90 soon became a blur. When he was a few miles away from Murdo, he noticed that his temperature gauge was climbing.

Steam escaped from under his hood and he pulled over immediately. When he lifted his hood, more steam boiled out. He opened the trunk and retrieved the bloody t-shirt he had balled up and used it to open the radiator. More steam, but not a lot of water left.

He grabbed the jug of water he had begun carrying with him and poured it into the radiator. When he looked inside, he still couldn't see the water level. He sat on the side of the road for fifteen minutes, watching cars and semis whiz by him at eighty miles per hour or more, rocking the little Valiant to and fro. When he turned the ignition, he saw that the temperature had dropped into the normal range.

Two miles down the road, though, the whole scenario played out again—rising temperature gauge, more steam. He didn't stop, but pushed on to the Murdo exit, hoping against hope he could make it there.

Immediately off the Murdo exit he saw a small motel, a car museum, a café, and a garage. Scott turned into the garage with a prayer of thanks, killed the engine, and coasted to a stop in front of one of the bays.

A mechanic dressed in blue overalls looked up from the Mustang he was working on and saw the steam. He nodded an acknowledgement at Scott.

"Sorry to block your bay door, I didn't want to run it any longer than I had to."

"No big deal," the mechanic said. "Leave the keys in it and go grab a bite in the café. I'll take a look and tell you how bad the damage is."

Scott's stomach tightened.

I'm already pushing my luck here, I know. Please don't let this be a total loss. The only time I know for sure where and when Bundy is going to be is at Lake Sammamish on the 14th. After that, I'll have to hunt him down, and there will be two dead women.

Scott reached into the car for his jo to use as a walking stick. His ankle was healing, but it was still swollen. He had finally managed to get his boot on, though. As he grabbed his jo, he saw the now damp, bloody t-shirt crumpled on the front seat. He grabbed it and stuffed it under the seat.

Let's face it. I am a terrible criminal. Sherlock Holmes would have me locked up before the end of the first chapter.

Scott limped over to the little café and ate lunch, although he spent most of his time worrying about his transportation situation.

I guess I've got enough with me to buy another old car, but I'll go broke pretty fast if I have to do that. If I can make it out to Seattle in time to catch up with Bundy, I'll have a break after that. Maybe I can get a job somewhere for a few months. That'll give me enough money to maybe buy a more reliable car.

He paid for his lunch and made his way back to the garage.

The mechanic saw him coming. "As these things go, it could be worse. You broke a belt, overheated, but it's not too bad. Your radiator's shot, but I can probably find one in the junkyard to replace it. I can do that and put a new belt on for around a hundred bucks."

Relief flooded through Scott. "Damn, that's good. I don't have much more than that to my name."

That wasn't true, but Scott didn't like everyone knowing he was carrying a few thousand dollars with him.

"Bad news is, I won't be able to get to it until the morning. I'm backed up this afternoon."

Scott did some time and distance calculations in his head.

Tight, but I can still make it. Just have to drive a little further every day.

Scott checked into the motel that was within walking distance, got out his atlas and planned the rest of his trip.

Chapter Thirty

The mechanic was as good as his word. He started work on the Valiant first thing in the morning and the total bill was a bit under a hundred dollars. By the time he finished and Scott turned back onto Interstate 90, it was early afternoon.

He focused on nothing but putting miles under his wheels. He made it through the rest of South Dakota, across the northeast corner of Wyoming and into Montana before he ran out of steam. He pulled off at a rest area a few miles past the site where the Battle of the Little Big Horn had been fought.

He didn't even bother to look for a motel. He knew he wasn't going to sleep that long. He laid the driver's seat back as far as it would go—which wasn't far—closed his eyes, and he was out.

Sleeping essentially sitting up in a Plymouth Valiant guarantees one thing—that you won't oversleep. Before the sun was up, Scott was awake, had splashed water on his face, and was once again tooling along Interstate 90.

He didn't break any more fan belts, and the little Valiant held together until he reached Washington State late that night. He spent one more night trying to sleep in a rest area, then crossed the Cascades at Snoqualmie pass and dropped down into western Washington midday on July 12th.

He stopped at a gas station and bought a map of the state. He found Issaquah, which was just ahead on I-90, and saw that Lake Sammamish State Park was very near that.

He pushed on to Issaquah, which still had a rural, small-town flavor in 1974. The biggest business in town seemed to be something called Skyport, where balloonists and parachutists launched themselves into the sky.

Scott decided to drive out to Lake Sammamish and do a reconnaissance mission. As he drove, he twisted through the radio dial, finally settling on 950 AM KJR. The afternoon drive announcer was full of energy. "Get down on your knees and pray for the hits, this is the mighty 95, KJR!" After a jingle played—*KJR, Seattle, Channel 95!*—a Tommy James song came on, then the disc jockey read the weather report. "Nothing but blue skies and sunshine everywhere within the sound of my voice all weekend long. Highs in the nineties both days. Boys and girls, this is what we dream of during those long, cold, lonely nights. Get out and enjoy it!"

That's why it was so crowded at the lake the day Bundy hit twice, then. Seattleites know they've got to enjoy the sunshine while they can.

The lake and park turned out to be smaller than he had seen it in his imagination. It was late Friday afternoon by the time he parked and walked out to the lake. It wasn't packed yet, but there was a good smattering of people laying out, soaking up the late afternoon rays. Once people were free of the shackles of their jobs, it would fill up quickly.

Scott scouted out the parking lot, the paths to the beach, and the way in and out of the park. He knew that Bundy had used some plaster he had taken from a medical supply house he had worked at and made himself a cast that day. All the better to appear vulnerable and less threatening to his victims. He had approached many women at the lake that day, asking them if they would help him get a small boat onto his car.

Most had just said no, they wouldn't. One woman said she would help, but fled when she saw the infamous Volkswagen Beetle with no boat on it. No one knew exactly how he managed to incapacitate the other two women and secret them out of the park unnoticed, but he had, one at a time. Bundy committed an amazing number of horrible crimes—and no one ever knew exactly how many he murdered— but this abduction of two healthy, strong women in broad daylight, surrounded by hundreds of other people, was his most famous.

Just a few months after the dual abductions from Lake Sammamish, Bundy moved to Utah to attend college there. The killings in Washington stopped, those in Utah and Colorado began.

Scott walked along the tree-lined parking lot, formulating a plan.

If I don't get him here, then what? Try and track him down somewhere? I know he lived somewhere in the University District, but I don't have the address. I remember he used to hang out at a bar called Dante's, but that would be hit or miss. This spot, two days from now, is the only time and place I know he will definitely be. This has got to be it.

Scott suddenly felt like he was at loose ends. He had no reason to believe that Bundy would show up at the park any time before Sunday morning.

He drove back to Issaquah, found an inexpensive place to stay on the edge of town and rested. He needed to recover from his mad dash across the United States.

After getting his recon out of the way on Friday afternoon, Scott barely left his motel room on Saturday. There was a little drive-in within easy walking distance, and an International House of Pancakes. That was more than good enough to keep him in calories.

He bought a copy of The Seattle Times and The Seattle Post-Intelligencer and combed through both of them, seeing if there was any news of the Jenkins murder in Waterville. The murder of a single man clear on the other side of the country wasn't big enough to be newsworthy in Seattle, and there was no mention at all.

If I settle down for a few months somewhere after this, I can subscribe to the local paper from Waterville, have them mail it to me, and see if they've got any information.

Beyond those minimal activities, Scott rested on Saturday, and thought through how he would attempt to take out Ted Bundy.

Chapter Thirty-One

Scott's eyes flew open at 7:30 Sunday morning. When he peeked out the window, the sun was already blazing.

Damnit! I never sleep this late. Today of all days...

The sign at Lake Sammamish State Park had said that the gates opened at 8:00 a.m. during the summer months. Scott had planned to be there shortly after that. He had no way of knowing what time Bundy arrived at his hunting ground—just that one woman had been kidnapped in the morning and another in the afternoon.

He had been sure he would wake up earlier and have time for a breakfast at IHOP, but he was still exhausted from the long drive, so he slept in and those pancakes would have to wait.

If I hurry, I can still get there a few minutes after the park opens and park close to the gate so I can watch for Beetles coming in.

He threw his few belongings into his pack, left the room key on the table and threw everything in the backseat of the Valiant.

I can still make it there on time.

He slipped behind the wheel, turned the key and heard nothing but the clicking of the solenoid.

Holy shit! Not now!

He twisted the key off, waited fifteen seconds, then pumped the gas once and turned the key again.

Click, click, click. Nothing more.

Scott slammed his fist into the steering wheel.

What the hell do I do now?

Scott was a decent mechanic, but not much more. He opened the hood and poked around under it.

Could be a dead battery. Could be the starter just conveniently went out all at once.

He glanced at his watch. 7:55.

The problem is, it's early on a Sunday morning. No one's going to be around that can give me a jump, or help me fix it, if it's something more than that. I have got *to get a more reliable car, pronto.*

He felt his stomach tighten and gurgle, not with hunger, but with fear and anxiety.

He pushed his way into the small office. A young girl, who couldn't be more than sixteen, was behind the counter.

"Hey, my car won't start. Is there anyone here who can maybe give me a jump?"

She looked at him blankly.

"You know, jumper cables?"

The steady stare, followed by a shrug.

Scott blew out a breath of frustration, then asked, "Can you at least tell me where the closest pay phone is? I left my keys to the room on the table and locked my door already."

She could have given him another key to get back into his room to use the phone, but she also could have answered his question about a jump. Instead, she pointed to her left. "Gas station next door."

Scott considered a few zingers about customer service, but he felt the pressure of a running clock in his head.

He hurried to the payphone and pulled the Eastside phone book up and spread it open. His first instinct was to call a garage, but common sense told him that no garage was open. Instead, he dialed a taxi and asked for a pickup at the motel.

He hurried back to the Valiant. He slammed his hand on the trunk in frustration, but that did nothing but hurt himself. The car remained unmoved.

He tried to start it again, but the result was the same.

Scott dumped his clothes and bathroom stuff out onto the seat, then placed the karambit and baton inside. He slung the pack over his arm, grabbed his jo and sat on the back bumper to wait.

Forty-five minutes later, he was still waiting. He was pacing back and forth on the sidewalk in front of his room, then walking out to the street, looking for an approaching Yellow Cab.

After an hour, he wished he had walked there.

It's only about five miles from here, right? I coulda almost been there by now.

Finally, at 9:15, the cab pulled into the parking lot. The driver rolled his window down. "You call for a cab?"

Scott didn't answer, but jumped inside. "Lake Sammamish State Park, please, as fast as you can get me there."

The cabbie flipped his flag up, which put a .75 charge on the meter. "Sure, no problem. Don't worry, the park, the sunshine, and the pretty girls in cutoffs will still be there when you get there."

Scott gave him an insincere smile and sat back, willing the driver to move faster. It's a well-known universal law that the greater the hurry you are in, the more your chances of missing every red light increases. Scott was almost in a panic, in a true race against life and death. That meant that they did indeed miss every light possible as they drove through Issaquah.

Finally, almost two hours after he had wanted to be there, the cab pulled up to the entrance to the park. The cabbie flipped the flag back down and said, "Five twenty-five."

Scott pulled a ten-dollar bill out of his pocket, said, "Keep it." He clambered out of the backseat with his pack slung over his shoulder and his jo in his right hand. He hurried through the park gate and cast his eye along the cars that were parked along the left side of the lot. Scott scanned where the cars butted right up against some trees and undergrowth.

It was early, but it was a beautiful day, and the park was filling up quickly.

Oh, shit. Unbelievable!

Sitting a few parking spots from each other were two tan Volkswagen Beetles.

I have no idea which one is his, but one of those has to be it. He's here. He's already here and hunting. Everything depended on catching him when he first got here and was getting out of the car.

Leaning on his jo, Scott stood on his tiptoes and craned his neck. Wavy lines of heat were already shimmering off the parking lot, which was momentarily empty of other people. He saw a couple walking up the path toward him. The man was wearing a tennis outfit—white shorts and shirt. The woman was pushing a yellow ten-speed bike. Scott took a few steps toward them, then stopped cold.

It was not just a couple. Walking toward him was a pretty young blonde woman and Theodore Robert Bundy.

Chapter Thirty-Two

Bundy had wavy dark hair that went over his ears and collar. His open, boyish face was split into a grin as he said something to the young woman beside him. A clean-looking cast and sling was on his left arm. He was pointing at the VW Beetle that was just ahead. The man who would come to be recognized as one of America's great boogey men today looked like nothing less than an all-American man.

Scott had an unexpected, visceral reaction at the sight of Bundy. His nostrils flared, his fingers curled and uncurled against his jo, and he unconsciously spread his feet, settling into a fighting stance.

Bundy and the woman approached close and were about to walk right by Scott, when he stepped in front of the woman. The two of them stopped in surprise.

"Listen," Scott said, and he could hear the anger and breathiness in his voice. "You need to get out of here. You don't know this man, but he is planning to rape and kill you today."

The woman's eyes flew wide and she took a step back from both Bundy and Scott, dragging her bicycle with her.

Bundy himself twisted his head to the side with a shocked, quizzical look.

"I know he asked you to help him get his sailboat, but look at what he's driving. It's a Beetle, with no roof rack on it. Think. How is he going get a sailboat on there?"

Bundy reached out a hand toward Scott. Anger flashed in his eyes and he raised his voice. "Wait a minute, what are you going on about?" Scott saw his cunning mind at work, already running scenarios.

The woman looked at Scott, then back at Ted. Any trace of her smile long gone. "I don't know if this is some kind of a joke you two cooked up, but it's not funny." She spit the words at them, then picked up her bike, turned it around and peddled back toward the lake.

Bundy's eyes narrowed as he tried to process this unusual set of circumstances. He was an intelligent man, but he had been convinced he was anonymous here.

"Who are you?"

"I am the last person on earth you wanted to meet today."

A car drove past them and parked further down toward the lake. Scott glanced at it.

How the hell did he manage to get these girls out of here without being seen? There's people everywhere.

An idea flashed through Scott's mind.

"Screw you, Ted Bundy. I know exactly who you are and what you've been doing. I know about every girl you've already killed. I know your every damn move before you make it. That's how I knew you were going to be here today. My next stop will be the cops. You may not know it, but you left a fingerprint on the bed of the girl you attacked in the U-District. Once I tip them off about you, they'll put you away for life."

The color drained from Bundy's face and he took one dangerous step toward Scott.

Scott turned and strode quickly toward the Beetle that he had seen Ted point at. He raised his jo and slammed it down on the driver's side mirror, snapping it off.

Bundy ran toward him, arms out, flailing, murder in his eyes. Scott turned to face him, waited until he was nearly on top of him, then turned sideways with his left leg stuck out. Bundy stumbled over it and splayed onto the ground between the two cars. He cursed and got on all fours to stand, but was hindered by the sling on his left arm, which had wrapped around itself.

Scott put his foot against the butt of Bundy's white shorts and shoved as hard as he could. Bundy pitched forward, landing face first out of the parking lot and in the surrounding greenbelt. His face dug up a channel of dirt and pine needles.

Immediately, Scott was on the attack. He continued to kick and jab at Bundy with his jo, forcing him deeper into the briars and brambles, herding him to where he wanted him. Finally, when they were far enough into the woods that he felt they had some privacy, he paused.

For one of America's greatest serial killers, Ted Bundy did not have a lot of fight in him. He was on his back, pushed up onto his elbows and held his right hand up as a shield. "Why are you doing this to me?"

Scott's anger and adrenaline pulsed through him. He unleashed a short kick at Bundy's head. Bundy attempted to ward it off, but only managed to deflect it as it connected with his nose, breaking it. Blood poured from his nostrils and ran down his face.

Scott fell on him, jo held out in front of him. Bundy grabbed the stick, but again the cast got in the way and it slipped from his grasp. Scott pushed the jo against his windpipe and leaned all his weight on it.

Bundy beat against Scott's arms and shoulders. He kicked and bucked, trying to knock Scott off of him. Scott tightened the grip his legs had around Bundy's midsection and continued to apply more and more pressure. He lifted his head and turned his face away from the increasingly feeble blows.

The struggle went on for long minutes, but eventually Bundy's face turned red, then became the color of old bricks, and finally took on a bluish tinge. The light of consciousness went out of his eyes and his arms flopped against the pine needle-covered ground.

Scott did not let up, but instead straddled him higher up, putting his knees on either side of the jo and letting his full weight press down. He stayed in that position for a full five minutes, wanting to make sure the job was done.

Finally, he rolled off and leaned against a tree.

That all happened so fast. Did anyone see us fight by his car?

Scott steadied his breathing and listened to the quiet. He could hear car doors slamming, happy voices carrying, and a radio playing far away.

He sat next to the corpse of Ted Bundy for quite some time.

Eventually, his breath and heart rate returned to normal and he stood. He found that he had a little shimmy in his legs and his hands were shaking as he picked up his jo. He couldn't tell if that was from fear, exhilaration, exhaustion, or a combination of the three.

He walked out toward the car and saw his backpack sitting on the ground next to the broken mirror from the Beetle. Turning, Scott looked into the woods.

We weren't as far in as I thought. Someone might see him.

Scott emerged from the cooler temperature of the woods into the glaring sunlight. He grabbed his backpack and kicked the broken mirror under the VW. He walked back into the woods, set his jo and pack down, and grabbed Bundy by the shoulders. He picked up the top half of his body and dragged it further into the cool darkness. After he had half-dragged, half-carried him another fifty feet, he dropped the corpse. He retraced his steps, kicking at the drag marks to erase them as best he could.

I wonder if that woman that was with him will report what happened. Probably not. I'd guess she thinks it might have been a joke be-

tween two friends. She will never know how close she came to being murdered.

Scott stood at the edge of the woods and watched the parking lot for a few minutes. All the normal activity of a summer day at the lake played out in front of him, but no one showed any sign of alarm.

He saw a payphone at the edge of the parking lot.

Don't think it's safe to hitchhike or call a cab here. That might leave more of a trail. Nothing for it, then, but to walk.

He forced his tired, leaden legs to start moving, away from the lake, the parking lot, and the body of the man who had once been destined to be one of America's most infamous killers.

Chapter Thirty-Three

Scott walked back to the same motel he had stayed in the night before.

Might as well, my car's already here.

By the time he made it back, his ankle was once again swollen from too much walking, the Valiant still wouldn't start, and he hadn't eaten anything in twenty-four hours.

He checked into another room and gathered up his belongings from inside the car. He stuffed them back in his backpack, and dropped it off inside his new room.

Beyond a poorly-stocked vending machine, there was no food at the motel, so he grabbed his jo, limped over to the IHOP and finally had the pancakes he had been hungering for since he had woken up that morning.

As he poured syrup over his blueberry pancakes and crunched on strips of bacon, he contemplated this adventure.

On the bad side, I had to kill someone. On the good, I don't know of any other way to have stopped him. He was caught and jailed twice, and he got out both times. I had to do it.

He chewed on a bite of pancakes, then washed it down with a drink of orange juice.

Just about everything that could have gone wrong today, did. But, I still got the job done. And, as far as I know, I got away without a hitch. I guess the woman who was with him could give police a description of me when they find his body, but I don't know if they'll ever put two and two together. They had a pretty good police sketch of Ted, and even people who knew him didn't recognize him from it. All in all, I guess it was a success. So, why do I feel so melancholy? Why do I feel like I lose a little of my own humanity every time I do this?

Scott finished his breakfast for dinner and made his way back to his room. He turned the television to KING 5 and watched the news, but there was nothing about a dead body being found at Lake Sammamish.

The next morning, he arranged for someone else who was checking out to give him a jump, and the Valiant started right up. His first stop was at a garage, where they installed a new battery for him.

The west coast of the United States was a hotbed of bad deeds in the sixties, seventies, and eighties, so Scott knew he would spend a lot of time here over the next few decades. He'd taken care of Ted Bundy, but there was still a Green River Killer, the Hillside Stranglers, and Michael Hollister, the West Coast Strangler in his future.

Before he could get to any of them, though, Scott had his sights set on a less famous but no less-heinous killer—Charles Rodman Campbell. The murders that put him on Scott's radar wouldn't happen until 1982, but the crime that started it all was just a few months away.

In December of 1974, Charles Campbell raped a woman by holding a knife to the throat of her infant daughter. It took two years, but eventually he was apprehended and the victim identified him in a police lineup. Both the victim and her neighbor testified against Campbell at his trial, and he was sentenced to forty years.

He ended up being released after serving only five years, due to his sentences running concurrently and because of his good behavior while in prison. Very soon, he returned to the scene of his original crime and killed his original victim, the neighbor, and the daughter when she came home from school.

Charles Campbell was vengeful, but he was not smart, nor a good criminal. He left many obvious clues behind at the scene and he was arrested for the triple murder within a week. He was put to death via hanging in 1994.

To Scott's way of thinking, the death penalty should have been carried out much earlier. What person, if given the opportunity to stop such a monster, wouldn't do so?

He wanted to find Campbell and stop him before he came near those victims the first time, if possible.

Those crimes were committed in Clearview, a small town north of Seattle in Snohomish County. That meant there was no reason for Scott to go too far, too fast, so he decided to stay a few more nights in the same hotel in Issaquah and use that as his base of operations.

He consulted his map and saw that he could get back on I-90, jump down to I-405, and not have to drive through downtown Seattle.

The weather was still beautiful, so he decided to take the Valiant and drive north through Bellevue, Kirkland, and up to Snohomish county. In his notes, he had written "Charles Rodman Campbell, Edmonds." He had also memorized the victim's address in case he wasn't able to find Campbell before the day he showed up at her door.

Scott rolled his windows down, turned the music up on 950 KJR, and rolled up I-405. With the sun beating down and the wind ruffling his hair, he felt better than he had in some time.

A mile later, he hit a traffic backup in Bellevue that lasted all the way up to where 405 merged with I-5.

Eventually, Scott did make it to Edmonds. He looked up "Campbell" in the phone book, but there were dozens of them listed. He tore the page out and decided to try and drive around to some of the addresses listed and see what he could see.

I don't want to ask a lot of people questions about him, because they might remember that when he goes missing, but I know what he looks like, so if I spot him coming out of a house, I'll recognize him. It's not much of a plan, but I've got plenty of time.

Campbell would be easy to spot. He was a big man, 6'5" and built like an offensive lineman.

He was a big, strong man. I'm going to have to be careful how I approach him. What I could really use is a Taser. This is the problem with living a lot of lives, though. I'm not even sure those have been invented yet.

Edmonds was a spread out city, so it wasn't easy to find many of the addresses on the phone book page. He did locate a few, and of course they looked like normal houses. He parked across the street from several of them, but after an hour or so of watching each one, he felt like he was wasting his time.

He abandoned his surveillance in Edmonds and headed inland toward the tiny town of Clearview. He had to stop at a gas station and ask for directions, but he did eventually find the house where the original crime would take place.

I hope I can find him and take him out earlier. But, if not, I'll be right here waiting for him.

Chapter Thirty-Four

It was ten days before anyone discovered Ted Bundy's body.

After the stretch of sunny, beautiful weather, temperatures had cooled and a rainy front set in, which held the number of visitors to Lake Sammamish State Park down.

Eventually, the sun returned and so did the visitors.

One Tuesday afternoon, a young woman from Federal Way drove to the park to walk her dogs around the lake. While she was getting her Chocolate Lab on its leash, her German Shephard slipped by her and made a beeline into the woods, where the partially decomposed body was discovered.

Scott had made a point of watching the 11:00 news every night, waiting for just that to happen. He was still staying in the motel in Issaquah when the newscaster announced that a body had been found at Lake Sammamish, but no further details were available.

I'm sure by now, someone has missed him and reported him missing. Eventually, they'll put two and two together and he'll be identified. His family will mourn him, but they were destined to do that eventually anyway. At least this way, they'll never know how he besmirched the Bundy name. And, there will be women in Utah, Colorado, and Florida, who will live their lives through, never knowing they would have been one of his victims. And that's just fine.

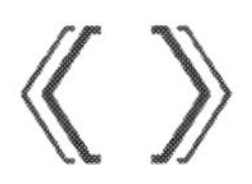

FOR A BIG MAN, CHARLES Campbell proved elusive to Scott.

Shortly after Bundy's body was found, Scott moved from Issaquah up to the University District, which was north of Seattle and closer to Edmonds. He could have gone all the way up to Snohomish County to stay, but he didn't want to show his face there for four or five months before Campbell was killed.

Instead, he used the same strategy he had in Waterville. He got to know the University District and found bulletin boards advertising for tenants for the upcoming semester at the University of Washington.

Classes didn't start until late September, so in early August, Scott had his choice of places to land. He found a room to rent in a house on Roosevelt Avenue, just north of the U-District. It was a small room, and he would eventually share a kitchen and bathroom with four other people. But, it was only seventy-five dollars a month, it came furnished with a bed and there was no lease.

Scott still spent time driving up to Edmonds a few times a week, but the longer he looked, the less hopeful he became. Eventually, it became easier to hang around home. He knew he had his date with destiny in a few months.

Overall, Scott didn't love large cities. Having lived his life first in Middle Falls, Oregon, and then Evansville, Indiana, he was used to the slower pace of non-metropolitan areas. The U-District felt different to him, though.

First, the UW campus was absolutely lovely, with open squares, majestic old buildings, and libraries that surpassed anything he had ever seen. Then, there was the community around the university. It was diverse, vibrant, and ever changing.

Over the weeks and months that Scott lived in the U-District, the summer sun became a forgotten memory and fog and misty rain became standard-issue weather. Still, he hated being cooped up inside all day with nothing to do, so Scott would walk the mile or so down Roosevelt onto the Ave. He found a tiny Russian restaurant that made incredible borscht for $1.50 a bowl and he took advantage of that several days a week. There were also half a dozen used record stores and even though he traveled too light to have a turntable, he still loved to browse through the albums and read the liner notes. He kept a small blue notebook in his pocket and jotted down album titles for a day when he was more settled.

Best of all, though, were the used bookstores. When he lived in Vermont, he had lived over such a store, but that had been the only one in town and, truth be told, it was on the smallish side. Here, he had seven bookstores within walking distance. The biggest was the University Bookstore itself, which took up most of a city block. From Scott's perspective, the other bookstores were better. One had a loft that you had to climb a ladder to get to. Once you were up there, though, you could settle in for a long afternoon's browse with no one to bother you.

Another specialized in lesser-known memoirs and biographies. Scott ended up hauling a lot of books out of that one.

One afternoon as he walked toward home, he saw a hulking figure ahead of him that set off alarm bells in the back of his mind. The man was with two other men, but he towered over both of them by at least half a head.

Have I been chasing him for months and he shows up right here in my back yard?

His knife and telescoping baton were tucked away back in his room—he never carried them with him unless he was expecting trouble. He had forgotten that sometimes trouble can come looking for you. He did have his jo, but he didn't want to think about getting into a brawl with a man who outweighed him by eighty pounds with only that.

The three men ducked into a coffee shop and stood in line at the counter. Scott hadn't seen the man's face clearly, but what he had seen matched the photos he had memorized of Campbell. Scott got in line behind the men and listened to their conversation.

He only caught snippets. "...we're gonna roll over them..." and "...of course, bro," and the like. Nothing that helped Scott at all.

The three men got their food and moved off to a corner table. The big man Scott was focused on sat with his back to him.

Scott ordered a cup of coffee to go. He walked to the door, then turned and loudly said, "Hey Charles!"

Everyone in the place, including the three men, ignored him.

Scott cupped a hand around his mouth. "Hey! Campbell!" As soon as he said it, he realized it was louder than he had intended.

This time everyone, including the men, turned and looked at him. As they did, Scott gave an embarrassed wave and said, "Oh, sorry, thought it was someone else."

When the man had turned around, Scott had noticed that he had a Husky football jersey on underneath his jacket. He looked as puzzled as everyone else in the café, but it wasn't Charles Campbell. Likely just another Husky lineman out with his friends.

I'm starting to jump at ghosts, I think.

Chapter Thirty-Five

After spending almost five months in the Pacific Northwest, the day Scott had been both dreading and anxiously waiting for finally arrived.

He knew that Campbell had attacked the woman and her baby while she was in her front yard, pushing his way into her house and assaulting her. Scott intended to be there to stop that, no matter what it took.

He had been planning and preparing for exactly how he would take Campbell out for weeks. It had taken another chunk out of his reserves, but he had bought another old beater off an ad in one of the small classified newspapers. He had given the woman he bought it from a fake name and she hadn't asked him for any ID. She was happy to get the old pickup off her front lawn. Scott was glad that it ran.

He had driven the pickup north to Clearview the day before. He had parked it in a deserted area down an old logging road and left a note in the window: *Not abandoned. Broke down. I will be back to get it.*

He had walked back to the highway and hitchhiked south until he was able to get a Metro bus to take him back to the U-District.

This morning, he had woken up and driven the Valiant over the same route. He parked it right next to where the pickup was, swapped out the note from the truck to the Valiant, and drove to the house he had been staking out in Clearview.

Just like the Jenkins murders, there was no record of exactly when the rape had taken place. Scott was sure it was in the afternoon, but he arrived at the house at 9:30 a.m.. He parked up the block and faced down the hill, the way he knew Charles Campbell would walk up sometime later that day. He had filled his Thermos with hot coffee before he left his room. He poured some into the plastic red cup that had come with the Thermos and leaned back to wait.

There was a Dodge parked in the driveway of the house, but he didn't see much activity. After he had sat watching for an hour, a woman emerged with a toddler in her arms, climbed into the Dodge and drove off away from him.

Scott relaxed, knowing that while she was gone, nothing was going to happen. He pulled the paperback he was reading out of his back pocket and read to pass the time.

The woman was gone until almost 1:00 that afternoon. As soon as Scott saw the Dodge approach, he put the book on the seat and sat at full attention. The woman pulled into the short driveway, bundled her baby into her arms and went inside.

Scott stared down the road for an approaching figure, knowing Campbell would approach on foot, but saw nothing.

It was a typical Western Washington December day. Forty-two degrees with off and on rain. Every twenty minutes or so, Scott turned the engine over and let it idle for a few minutes to warm up the cab and blow the moisture off the inside of the windshield.

At 3:00, the front door opened and the woman stepped outside again. She looked up into the gray, misting clouds with a squint, then pulled the hood up over the head of her little girl. She stepped off the porch and walked toward the driveway, then out to the mailbox.

Scott's fingers tingled and his heart beat fast.

He stared down the road and saw the shadowy figure of a man walking toward them at a good clip.

Scott turned the key and the engine turned and turned, then finally fired. Scott gave it gas and the engine sputtered, then caught and ran.

The woman stood at her mailbox, sorting through her mail, unaware of the danger approaching.

Scott pushed on the brake, revved the engine until the cab shook, then jammed the gearshift into Drive. The pickup jumped out of the parking spot, slipping a bit on the wet pavement, but quickly finding its footing.

Scott buried the accelerator and the truck surged forward. It roared by the woman and her baby, who jumped back with a startled "Hey!"

Scott drove as though he was going to hold his lane.

The huge man walking toward him moved slightly to the left to give him plenty of room to pass.

Scott glanced at the speedometer. He was already at fifty and accelerating.

At the last second, the man shouted and jumped to his right. If this had been a case of an inattentive driver, his good reactions would have saved his life.

Instead, Scott twisted the steering wheel left while still accelerating. He hit the man dead on doing better than sixty miles per hour.

Campbell flew up in the air ahead of the truck, but Scott was still accelerating. The man bounced off the hood of the truck, then smashed into the windshield, shattering it, and flipped again, landing momentarily in the bed of the truck, then tumbling out to lie in a heap on the pavement.

Scott slammed on the brakes, coming to a fishtailing stop. He reached up and pushed the smashed window out onto the hood. A hundred yards behind him, the crumpled form on the pavement might have been a man or a bear. It was impossible to tell.

Scott didn't bother to turn around. He jammed the transmission into reverse and gunned the truck again. He was watching the man on the ground for any sign of movement. As he closed, the man sat up, saw the pickup approaching again and screamed. He held his hand up to ward off the impact, but the truck ran right up over the top of him.

The truck died.

Behind him, Scott heard the woman with the baby screaming. All around him, people were coming out of their houses, staring.

Shit. Forgot.

He grabbed the blue ski mask he had brought with him and pulled it over his face, maneuvering it until he could see again.

He turned the key, but the truck wouldn't start.

An old man approached the truck with a puzzled look on his face. He looked at the masked figure behind the wheel and said, "Did you back up over that man? After you ran over him in the first place?"

Scott didn't answer, but stepped on the gas, let up, and turned the key again. He smelled the strong odor of gasoline, but miraculously, the truck started. He shifted into drive. The old man jumped back with an agility that surprised Scott.

He stomped on the gas one more time, aiming the front wheels for the mass of humanity that lay in front of him. Scott felt both passenger wheels raise and lower as he passed over the body. He accelerated and the windshield slid off the hood and onto the street.

Scott's adrenaline was too high to drive slowly. He whipped past the 25 MPH sign doing sixty and didn't slow. He raced to the edge of town, turned off the main drag, and dropped his speed. He followed a web of side streets he had planned out the week before until they led him to the Valiant parked in the woods.

He pulled the ski mask off and wiped the steering wheel, the door, the radio knob. Anywhere he could think of that he had touched. He grabbed his thermos and book, threw them into the Valiant and drove away.

Chapter Thirty-Six

Scott had enjoyed his time in the U-District, but after the stomach-churning reality of what he had done, he was ready to be gone from the Rainy City.

He gave his notice to his landlord on Roosevelt, sold the valiant little Valiant for half of what he had paid for it, and bought a ticket to fly back to Chicago. From there, he caught a train to Evansville. He hadn't called Cheryl in advance, although he couldn't have said why. He had gotten used to not answering to anyone but himself when it came to his comings and goings.

He did call her from the train station, though.

He picked up a pay phone, dropped a dime in, and dialed their home number. A few rings later, he heard Cheryl's voice say, "Hello?"

"Is there any room at the inn for a wandering stranger?"

"Scotty!" Cheryl cried. "Oh, it is so good to hear from you. There's always room for you. When are you coming to town?"

"About ten minutes ago. I'm at the train station."

"What? You're here? Foolish brother, you've got to let me know, and I'll be there to pick you up. Don't go anywhere, I'll be there in twenty minutes."

Eighteen minutes later, she pushed through the double doors, slightly out of breath.

She wrapped Scott in a hug. "You are so bad—not letting me know you are coming!"

"Guilty. Can I say I wanted to surprise you guys?"

"You certainly did that! I'm as bad as you are. I'm not even going to call Mike and tell him. I'll let him be surprised when he walks in tonight."

They walked together arm in arm to the car. Scott began to feel more human, less time-traveling assassin, almost immediately.

Unless my math is wrong, or something is different this life, she's pregnant with Andrea right now. I wonder if she knows yet.

Scott looked down on his baby sister. "You look like you're glowing a little today."

She smacked him in the arm. "Oh my God, you can tell, can't you? I can never sneak anything past you. We just found out a few days ago. How could you possibly know?"

Because I've lived this life a few times and things like that haven't changed. Every life I've made it this far, you've had Andrea on the same day.

When they got home, Mike was already there, but he was suitably surprised by his brother-in-law's sudden appearance.

He smiled a cat-who-ate-the-canary smile at Cheryl, but she shook her head. "Give it up. He guessed I was preggers the first minute he saw me."

Crestfallen, Mike said, "Are we never going to be able to surprise you?" He tipped Cheryl a wink. "We may have more than one surprise up our sleeve."

Cheryl gave Mike a look that warned him into quiet, but Scott was on the scent.

"What? You're having triplets? You've been elected the president of the local Rotary? What?"

Cheryl shook her head. "There will be no peace, now that you've brought it up." She turned to Scott. "It's getting late and I haven't started dinner because I was called away by a sudden errand this afternoon. Mike, what do you say we celebrate by going to Chen's for dinner?"

"I can always be talked into Chinese food," Mike said. "But you already knew that."

"And you, my bloodhound big brother, can wait until we get our chow mein before asking any more questions."

Half an hour later, they were seated in a comfortable booth in Chen's Chinese Restaurant. They had indeed ordered chow mein and half a dozen other dishes.

"Okay," Scott said, dipping a piece of BBQ Pork into hot mustard and sesame seeds, "what's the big secret?" He fixed Mike with an attempt at a menacing look. "Now that I already know what you've been doing to my sister while I'm away, what else is there?"

"Scotty!"

Scott had the good grace to look slightly abashed and smiled at Mike. "All right, kidding aside, what are you two crazy kids up to?"

Mike glanced at Cheryl with a "He's your brother, you go," sort of look.

"We want to sell the house."

Whoa, that's something new. They've never done this before. Maybe there will be more changes coming.

"Okay," Scott said, simply.

"Okay? That's it? No arguments at all?"

"Nope," Scott said. "I've run off and been gallivanting around the country, leaving all the upkeep to you guys. As far as I'm concerned, it's yours, not mine. If you want to sell it, that's absolutely A-OK with me."

Cheryl reached a hand out and laid it on Scott's. "Oh, Scotty, thank you for making this easy. We've been afraid to talk to you about it. We thought you might be mad."

"I can't even pretend to be mad. So, where are you guys going?"

Another glance shared between the young couple.

"You've already bought something, haven't you?"

Mike nodded. "We've got a sweet little two story being built out in Maple Glen Estates."

"Maple Glen?"

"Yeah, it's new. It's a little outside of town, but all the houses around us will be new, there will be lots of kids around for little Mike to play with—"

"Or little Andrea," Scott interjected and once again saw Cheryl's eyebrows shoot up in surprise. She fixed him with a narrow stare.

He smiled. "Sorry. Whatever you're having. Good for you guys. I completely understand. Gran and Gramps' house is in an old neighborhood. Most of the people around you are old. I really do get it."

"And, it will always be Gran and Gramps' house. We love them, of course, but we're ready to start our own story now, too."

Scott lifted his tiny cup of hot tea and offered it in a toast. "To starting your own story."

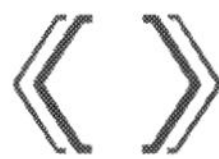

SCOTT STAYED WITH CHERYL and Mike through the holidays. Their new house in Maple Glenn wouldn't be completed until April, so they weren't planning on putting the old house on the market until after they made the move.

It didn't matter to Scott. Before he returned to the road, he said his good-byes to the house where his grandparents had taken him in. He wandered through Earl's basement shop, which was now Mike's. Earl's spirit was still everywhere there. A 1971 calendar with a picture of a duck in flight still hung above the workbench, not to mention that his array of hammers, chisels, wrenches and screwdrivers still hung in their proper spots.

I should pick out some souvenir of Gramps I can carry with me.

He walked along the bench, touching the hand tools one by one. Finally his fingers closed around an old 5/8" wrench. It may have been forty years old, but there wasn't a spot of rust on it anywhere.

You'll do.

Scott slipped it into the bottom of his pack, where he could carry it with him always.

By the time the first week of January arrived, Scott had experienced as much domesticity as he could stand, and his list awaited him.

Chapter Thirty-Seven

Scott was a busy traveler, not to mention, a busy vigilante, over the next five years. He traveled to all four corners of the country and crisscrossed the heartland any number of times.

When Cheryl and Mike closed on the house, they had insisted on putting half the proceeds into a bank account for Scott. Along with his check from the Army, as long as he kept his spending in check, he never needed to worry about money. In fact, each time he checked his balance, it was larger than it had been the month before.

Scott's arsenal had grown. In addition to his karambit, telescoping baton, and jo, he had added a canister of mace and one of the first consumer versions of a stun gun. More important than the new tools of the trade, was his sense of confidence. After resolving so many bad situations, he had grown sure of his own abilities and tendency to stay cool under pressure.

There were times when he felt that in saving the lives of so many others, he was losing his own soul. It was a dark night when he realized that he had killed more people than any of the other serial killers he had neutralized. There were still moments when he wondered how much of his own soul he was sacrificing in the service of others.

Not every target worked out perfectly. Sometimes situations had changed and there was no need for him to do anything.

In 1978, Scott had returned to Middle Falls, Oregon, to take out Michael Hollister, the West Coast Strangler. Hollister had begun his killing spree that year and even though he never revealed where or how he had taken his victims, Scott knew where he lived. He intended to take him out, quickly and quietly, before he had a chance to take his first victim.

Scott wasn't excited about returning to Middle Falls. It was the scene of his greatest nightmare, but he vowed to do his best to steer clear of the neighborhood where his father had killed his mother.

When he arrived to scout out the address, though, he found Michael Hollister didn't live there—it was an entirely different family. Scott looked in the phone book and found an address for Clayton Hollister, who Scott knew was his father.

He staked out his father's house—an impressive two story colonial on a large lot in Middle Falls' best neighborhood—for three days. An older man, who Scott surmised was Clayton Hollister, came and went, as did a housekeeper, but no other people.

Finally, Scott decided to risk direct contact. Scott had learned to change his appearance dramatically as he moved from town to town—the way he dressed, the way he wore his hair, whether he grew his beard and moustache out. At that moment, he had long hair and a moustache. After this, he would return to a barber and change his look.

He waited until the older man had left in the morning and the housekeeper had arrived. He parked on the street and walked up the walk to the front door. He rang the doorbell and listened to three deep, resonant notes play inside the house. He stood there for quite some time, waiting. Eventually the housekeeper, dressed in a gray uniform and a white apron, answered the door.

"Hi, is Michael here?"

A blank look sat on her face for several seconds. "Michael?"

"Hollister."

She looked as though that was a connection she should be making but wasn't. "Oh, Mr. Hollister's son. I've only met him once. He doesn't live here."

"You don't happen to know where he is, do you? I'm an old friend."

"No, I'm embarrassed to say, I don't. I never hear of Mr. Hollister speak of him."

Scott thanked her and retreated to his car.

Something's changed here. In all the research I did, Michael Hollister stayed with his parents until 1979. Then, his father died of a heart attack and Michael took over the company business. By then, he had also started murdering strangers up and down the I-5 corridor.

But now, everything seems to have changed.

Scott drove to the Middle Falls Public Library and asked where the copies of daily newspapers from previous years were kept. A librarian led him to a well-lit back room and showed him where both the paper and microfiche versions of *The Middle Falls Chronicle* and *The Oregonian* were kept.

Scott took out his increasingly dog-eared notebook and looked at his notes on Michael Hollister. It showed his first victim had been discovered in April, 1979.

Scott looked through every day's edition for both papers, but found no stories about a mysterious dead body being discovered at a rest stop, which is where he left all his early victims.

Scott looked up the dates around the second and third murders. Again, nothing.

Either you've chosen a better path this lifetime, or you've died before your time, Michael Hollister. Either way, I have no way to track you down. I'll have to let you go.

At least twice, Scott arrived too late to make a difference. Once, a multiple murder occurred earlier than it had been reported, and on another, yet another of his many cars had broken down on the way.

He mourned the loss of life that day and cursed himself for not being there to save the man who had been killed. At the same time, it reinforced the good he was doing and reminded him of the stakes he was playing for.

Most of the time, Scott accomplished exactly what he set out to do, taking the would-be murderers and rapists out before they had a chance to commit their crimes.

Next, Scott traveled north to Chicago, where he met the Killer Clown, John Wayne Gacy. Scott knew he was too late to save some of the victims, but he did what he could. He arranged to meet Gacy, who owned a construction company at the time, at a home under construction. He set the appointment for late in the evening and the site was deserted, but Gacy suspected nothing. It was the perfect site to kill the man who had already killed many young boys and was slated to kill many more.

Scott always disappeared from the community as soon as the murderer was neutralized, and he did the same with Gacy. As soon as he was three states away, though, he called the police, told them where they could find Gacy's body and explained exactly what they would find if they would look in the crawlspace of his house.

When the police went to Gacy's house to inform his mother of his passing, she invited them in. The smell from the crawl space sickened them. They got a search warrant and found exactly what their anonymous caller had promised.

The next day, *The Chicago Sun-Times* ran an article on the second page of the local news section headlined, *Avenging Angel?* The story posited that one of the parents of the dead boys had discovered the crime and taken justice into their own hands.

The murder of John Wayne Gacy remained an open file, but the police department did not assign many man-hours to solve it.

Scott worked on well-known criminals like Gacy, David Berkowitz, who never had a chance to be known as The Son of Sam,

Arthur Shawcross, and the serial killer Robert Yates. Yates lived and killed in Spokane, Washington, and Scott couldn't help but wonder if there was something in the water in Washington State that was breeding serial killers.

He didn't just stop serial killers and other mass murderers, though.

He also had crimes like the Jenkins murders on his list. Whenever he had a chance to stop a parent from killing their spouse or children, he would travel any distance to do so. He spent much of this life trying to make good a debt he felt for having failed his mother at age ten. It was something that would never be settled in full, but he slept better for having made the effort.

Chapter Thirty-Eight

In 1980, Scott traveled to northern California to stop a man named Jeff Pherigo from lighting his house on fire while his family slept inside. Pherigo had stayed inside long enough to get the smoke smell in his clothes and hair, then bolted outside, where he watched it burn. He was not a great arsonist, and was easily caught by the fire investigative team, charged with murder and insurance fraud, and sent to prison. None of that had brought his family back to life.

Scott had made a note that Pherigo had started the fire on the outside of the back porch, using an accelerant that was assumed to be gasoline. The fire had quickly spread to the second floor. The front door had a lock that required a key to unlock, even from the inside. Pherigo had pocketed the key to cut off that avenue of escape. The flames had made the back door impassable. The bodies of his wife, two children, and golden retriever had been found lying together on the kitchen floor.

The night Scott knew the fire would be set, he positioned himself among some pine trees in Pherigo's back yard. He had added a small crossbow to his arsenal, just for occasions like this. His plan was to hit Pherigo with a bolt while he was setting the fire, disabling him. Scott then planned to rush him and take him out. He intended to drag the body away so his family wouldn't discover it. They would no doubt be saddened by the loss of their husband and father, but they would be alive and able to move on with their lives.

Scott remembered that the first fire alarm had been called in by a neighbor at 2:35 a.m. The first responders had found Pherigo lying outside the back door, coughing and crying out for his family.

Scott checked his watch. 1:15.

Shouldn't be too long now.

Scott checked his small crossbow and made sure it was ready to fire. He peered around the trunk of the tree at the back porch.

Behind him, he heard the unmistakable sound of a shotgun ratcheting a shell into its chamber.

"Drop the bow, then turn around slowly."

Goddamn it! I've been doing this too long, and I got complacent. Now some neighbor thinks I'm stalking the place and wants to blow my head off.

Scott held the crossbow out to arm's length, lowered it toward the ground, then let it go. It landed softly in the fallen pine needles.

"Now, arms in the air. Turn around."

Scott did exactly that, and he couldn't help himself. He gaped at the man holding the shotgun. It was Jeff Pherigo.

"Not who you expected, huh? You thought you were gonna ambush me with that danged little bow of yours, then kill me, right?"

That was exactly Scott's plan, so he didn't say anything. He didn't want to be killed and transported back to his grandparents' couch. He didn't think he had the strength to do all this work again.

Pherigo took two steps toward Scott, but stayed out of easy lunging distance.

Scott took a mental inventory. His karambit was sheathed at his waist. The jo was leaning against a tree a few feet away. His Taser and mace were both in his backpack, which was a few feet away.

If I die here, I deserve it. I've lost my edge.

Pherigo kept the shotgun leveled at Scott's chest. The twin barrels looked huge and glinted softly in the moonlight that filtered through the trees.

An honestly puzzled look sat on Pherigo's face. "Why do you guys keep killing me?"

That set Scott back on his heels. "Wha—what are you talking about?"

"I keep living the same freaking day over and over. I wake up, go about my day, and every night somebody different shows up and kills me. Sometimes it's the same guy, but usually somebody different. You're different. I've never seen you before."

Scott's head was swimming so fast, he almost forgot he was pinned at the end of a shotgun.

"I have no idea what you're talking about. Seriously."

Pherigo waved the barrel at Scott. "Well, you're gonna danged well figure it out, or I'm gonna have to call the Sheriff and tell him I caught a man sneaking around my back yard, and I had to shoot and kill him."

"Hold on. Let's figure this out together. I'll tell you why I came here to kill you. Then maybe we can figure out how and why you keep getting started over. Fair?"

"It's hard for me to trust the motives of a man who starts a sentence with 'I'll tell you why I came here to kill you,' but go ahead. Shoot."

Bad choice of words, I hope.

"I came here because in my previous life, you chose this night to set a fire on your back porch that killed your wife and kids. This is what I do. I stop people from doing horrible, cowardly things like what you were about to do."

Pherigo shook his head. "So you keep living your life over and over, too? How many of us are there?"

"Until about two minutes ago, I thought I was the only one."

"Okay, I admit, I might have done something stupid, but I was punished for it. I got arrested, sent to prison, and things weren't pleasant for me. I found a way to kill myself, but I woke up right back here, and everything was fine. I thought I had a chance to make everything right. A chance to not kill my family. Right then, I knew I could figure everything out. I could find a way to put the money back I'd embezzled from the company. Or, even if I couldn't, what's the worst that would happen? Maybe I go to some country club prison for a couple of years and my wife divorces me? That's a lot better than the way things had worked out before."

"So what happened?"

"What keeps happening is, I wake up on the same darned day I set the fire in the life before. That's all fine and good, but that night, someone breaks into our house, slips into our bedroom, and cuts my throat. I bleed out, right there in my bed, with my wife screaming her head off."

"It's not me." Scott's head was spinning. It felt like everything he knew was shifting like loose sand.

"Yes, I know it wasn't you. I already told you, I've never seen you before. Are you slow or something?"

Scott very much wished their weapons situation was reversed.

"Anyway, it happened that way again and again. I wake up and it's the same day. Sometimes, it happens a different way. Once, someone showed up when I was out watering the yard and killed me. Sometimes they do it early in the day, sometimes they seem to be waiting for me to do something, but in the end, they kill me every damn time, and I'm tired of it."

Scott, hands still raised, weighed his options.

He's too far to rush. He'll blow a hole clean through me and I'll wake up back in 1972. If I make a move for my jo, same thing. I am well and truly screwed.

Pherigo went on. "After a few dozen times getting killed, I decided to do something about it. This time, I've taken this shotgun with me everywhere I've gone, but nobody showed up. Then, I am standing in my kitchen having a glass of milk with the lights off and I see you standing out here, thinking you're clever and hidden. So I take ole Bessie here and sneak around behind you. Now. We're all caught up. Your turn."

Scott opened his mouth to speak, but he caught a flash of movement behind Pherigo. Scott's eyes widened as he realized there was a man standing behind Pherigo with a gun pointed at the other man's head.

Scott instinctively ducked as a loud gunshot came from behind Pherigo. The man holding the shotgun pitched forward, dead before he hit the ground.

Chapter Thirty-Nine

F*rom the frying pan, into the fire. This isn't my night.*

A man who appeared to be in his late forties stood behind where Pherigo had been. He wore camo fatigues, had a rifle strapped over his shoulder, and held the pistol in front of him in a comfortable shooter's stance. It was aimed steadily at Scott's chest.

"I had to kill him. You'd told him too much already."

"A couple of things here. First, I was just talking, trying to not get my ass shot off, and second, who the hell are you?"

"I'm Joey Ramone."

In a night of weird happenings, that was just one more.

"You don't look like Joey Ramone. Joey was taller, and he looked like he'd never been outside in his entire life. You look more like some army dude."

"Joey Ramone is my team name. We all pick rock 'n roll names because the guy who founded the group liked the music." He lowered the pistol. "So what's your name? We've been seeing you off and on for years, but have no idea what your name is."

Scott hesitated. "Scott McKenzie."

"Come on now, you're having me on. Is that the best you can do?"

"Can't help it, that's my name.

"Couldn't you have picked a cooler cover name? You had to pick the '*be sure to wear some flowers in your hair*' guy? He only ever had that one song!"

"That's not a cover name. That's my real name."

Joey looked skeptical, but decided not to argue further. "Look, we've still got to deal with Pherigo here. Somebody heard my gunshot and will be along eventually to check it out. I'd just as soon not have his wife or kids find him like this in the morning. Give me a hand with him, will ya? I'm parked over yonder, right behind your rig."

Scott felt a little dizzy, as though he was standing on uncertain ground, but he picked up Pherigo's feet.

"Sure, sure. Leave the messy end for me, why dontcha?" Joey picked up the other end and they carried him to his pickup truck, which already had the tailgate down and a tarp waiting.

"Whoever you are, you're a lot more organized than I am, I'd say."

"It's not just me. It's the team. We're time traveling vigilantes, trying to fix things before they happen. We call ourselves the Time Operatives."

"I feel like I stepped into a Dean Koontz novel."

"Listen. It's late. Why don't you go get some sleep? I'll meet you tomorrow and tell you as much as I can. You know that little restaurant by the railroad tracks in town? Katie Bee's, I think it's called? I'll meet you there at noon tomorrow. If you don't show up, I'll figure you aren't interested in finding out what we're doing."

Scott nodded, a little numbly, and climbed into the little pickup he had bought a few weeks before. He drove to the inexpensive motel he had checked into that afternoon and soon fell into a deep, dreamless sleep.

SCOTT PULLED INTO KATIE Bee's at 11:45 the next morning. He found Joey Ramone waiting for him in the parking lot. Scott parked his pickup beside Joey's and hopped out.

"Hey, Joey."

"Scott," Joey said, and actually made the parentheses marks with his hands, as if he still didn't believe that was really Scott's name.

Did people even do that in 1979? I don't think so. He doesn't seem too worried about keeping the fact he is a time traveler a big secret.

"You want to talk out here, or you want to go in?"

"Are you kidding? They have an incredible French dip here. That's why I wanted to meet you here," Joey said. "Come on."

He seems friendly enough, even if he is a smart ass. He obviously doesn't want to kill me or I'd have been wrapped up in the tarp with Pherigo.

Joey pushed through the door, ringing a little bell above it. The attractive young waitress glanced at the door, then called back to the kitchen, "Hey, Hank, we still got French dips?"

A pause, then a man's voice answered, "Yep, just a couple more."

The waitress turned to Joey and Scott and fixed them with a look. "You're lucky. I thought we were out."

Scott slid into a booth across from Joey. "I take it you've been here for a while?"

"About a week. Which means a week's worth of their French dips. Wait'll you try one. Worth the trip all by themselves."

The waitress, who Scott noticed had a name tag on that read "Stacey," approached the table. She looked at Scott. "I already know what he's having. How 'bout you?"

"Who am I to say no to a French dip?"

Stacey nodded as though that was the answer she had expected. She took their drink orders and disappeared into the kitchen.

Joey leaned forward and lowered his voice somewhat. "So, you've never come across one of us before? As much as we've been tracking you, I figured you had made us a time or two."

"Nope. I must not be as aware of my surroundings as I thought I was, if both of you guys managed to sneak up behind me last night."

"Here's the thing. I called in to Peter, our group leader, last night. He told me it's time to invite you to join. I told him you already had your rock 'n roll name, but he'd never heard of Scott McKenzie, so I think you might want to make a better choice."

Scott started to correct him, but gave it up as a bad bit of business. Instead, he said, "Peter?"

"Yeah. Peter Frampton."

"Of course. I thought it might be Peter Cetera."

"I don't know if we can let you in. I think you like wimp rock too much."

"Are you guys ever serious?"

"The rest of the guys are more serious than me, but believe me, when the action goes down, the joking around stops in a hurry. Or, maybe you didn't notice when I spattered a bit of Pherigo's brains on you last night."

"I don't understand what you guys are all about."

"I'll try to explain. Peter started the group about ten years ago. He was a spook who did some wet work for the good old U S of A back in the sixties and seventies. I don't know when or how he met his demise—we never ask that question—but whenever he did, he woke up back in 1970. He started doing a little bit of revenge business, settling old scores and such, but he kept getting killed and starting over in 1970 again and again. He got tired of that."

"I can understand how that would lose its charm," Scott said.

"You, too, huh? Join the party. We're all members of a pretty small club, as far as I can tell. Anyway, it occurred to him that if he was in that situation, there must be others who are too."

Yep. Pretty logical, why didn't that ever occur to me?

"The man is a highly-trained observer of people and the human condition. When he focused his training on that, he was able to pick up on others who were started over. Slowly but surely, he built a micro-army of us. He trains us, he sets the rules, and we carry out the work." Joey shrugged. "I suppose I could decide to work on making myself rich and lay around by the pool all day, but that's not for me. I like the work." He formed his thumb and forefinger into a gun and sighted it at Scott. He pulled the pretend trigger and mouthed, "Boom."

He stared intently at Scott. "We've watched you for a while now. You're not the lay around the pool kind of guy either, are you? Peter wants me to bring you back to meet him and enlist you. Whaddya say?"

Chapter Forty

Just then, Stacey appeared with their French dips. Scott's eyes bulged a little and Joey enjoyed a little "I told ya so" moment. These were French dips in the same way Antarctica gets a little cold in the winter. They consisted of a big hunk of French bread sliced in half with rare roast beef thin-cut and piled at least three inches thick.

Stacey said, "Don't worry. The first time, everyone says, 'I can never eat all that.' We don't have to make up many doggy bags, though. Eat up, boys."

Scott still shook his head a little and poked at the mountain of beef and bread on his plate. The au jus sauce was served in a soup bowl, filled to the top. "That's more food than I eat in two days, usually."

"I know, ain't it great?" Joey said, speaking around his first mouthful.

While they ate, Scott lined up his questions.

Joey seemed happily lost in devouring his sandwich. By the time Scott was half done, Joey's plate was empty and he was dabbing at the corner of his mouth with his napkin.

"I'm afraid I'm going to be a disappointment to Stacey."

"I could polish it off for you."

"What, do you have a hollow leg? Where are you putting it all?"

Joey shrugged. "Suit yourself. Break Stacey's heart a little."

Scott pushed his plate away. "I've got questions."

"I would expect no less. I'm no recruiter, but I'll do what I can."

At the mention of a recruiter, Scott's mind returned to the sergeant who had recruited him into the army by promising him MP training.

"This just occurred to me. How do you guys communicate with each other? Ring each other up on the phone? Drop a letter in the mail?"

"Sometimes, sure. Those methods aren't as secure as Peter likes, though, so most often, we use classified ads."

That brought Scott up short. "You're kidding."

"Nope. You ever look at the classifieds?"

Scott thought of the endless hours he had spent poring over newspapers looking for info on killers and buying temporary automobiles. "Yeah, of course."

"You ever see an ad that didn't make any sense? Real mysterious like? Maybe a reference to an odd place, or time, or a phone number that didn't look like any phone number you've ever seen?"

Scott had to stop and think, but then he snapped his fingers. "Yeah. Yeah, I have. I just figured somebody was drunk when they typeset those."

"That's what we count on. We have a small team that spends their days placing those ads all over the country, wherever one of our agents is."

"And that's a signal to call in?"

"Nope. It's a code. A simple code, but you've got to know what book it's keyed on, or it doesn't do you any good. And guess what? I ain't telling you what it is. You're not part of the team."

"I don't blame you. This Peter seems to be pretty bright."

Joey nodded. "No doubt."

"So, has he figured out what we're all doing? Why we're repeating? Why we keep starting over at the same point? Because I haven't figured any of it out."

"That's not exactly his bailiwick. That falls more under Bob's auspices."

I'm afraid to ask, but I feel compelled.

"Bob?"

"Bob Dylan."

"I should have guessed. What does Bob Dylan have to say, then?"

"Bob's not an operative, like the rest of us. He's a deep thinker. He has come to the conclusion that the world's religions have got it wrong—all of them. He says the only conclusion you can draw is that this is what he calls a multiverse, or multiple-dimension universe."

"I'm a high school graduate. Definitely not a deep thinker. What's that mean in single syllable words?"

"Bob says that he thinks each time one of us dies, another reality is created, an exact copy of this reality, but starting back in time at whatever point we have reset to."

Scott considered that. "That's a lot of worlds. Or, dimensions, or whatever you want to call them."

"Bob also says that the universe, and time itself, are infinite, but that the human mind can't understand the concept of infinity or eternity in a real way." Joey took a drink of his Coke. "Me? I'm a foot soldier, parroting what he says. I'm no deep thinker, either. If you join us, you can likely sit down with him and ask him these questions yourself. I say 'likely' because Peter values Bob over everyone else, so he doesn't let anyone close to him until they've been vetted."

"That's a whole bunch to absorb. I can't argue with it because that's more than I've managed to figure out in twenty-four lives."

Joey closed his eyes and nodded. At that moment, he looked twenty years older than he had. "It gets old, doesn't it—not getting old, I mean."

"I'd like to figure a way out of the loop, that's for sure. Weird to think that I've managed to start twenty-four separate worlds all on my own. It doesn't make any sense, you know? Here's a question I'd ask your resident genius. If the world starts when I wake up, what happened to all those worlds when I die? Do they wink out of existence because I'm not there?"

"I don't think so."

"Why not?"

"Because I've known a lot of travelers. This is a dangerous business, so I know a lot of travelers who have died. But," he spread his hands out in front of him, showing there was nothing up his sleeves, "here I still am. And, there you still are."

"But, it would only matter if the prime person died, right? Like, if this world started when I woke up here, but if Pherigo had killed me, would you still be here?"

Joey chewed on his cheek. "Hmmph. You're right. Those others who have died might have been part of the copy. Which is a short way of saying, I am easily stumped by all this stuff, and it's why I don't dwell on it. I do the best I can with the situation in front of me."

"Every good soldier's philosophy, right?"

"Did you serve? I only ask because most of us did. That's the most common element among us."

"I did. Vietnam. My birthday was the first date pulled for the draft, so I signed up."

"You are one unlucky son of a bitch, aren't you?" Joey shrugged. "I volunteered because that's what you did in my family. My dad fought in World War II. My Grandfather in World War I. My uncle in Korea. Which brings us back full-circle."

"How so?"

"Signing up. I've done my best to fill you in on the operation. At least, as much as I am allowed. So, are you interested?"

Am I? What would it be like to be part of a team? To have that camaraderie again? To have brothers who are willing to lay down their life for you, and you know you'll do the same for them? Yes, that would be good. This is a long, lonely road I've been walking.

Scott stalled by taking a long drink of Dr. Pepper.

But, when I got out of Vietnam, I swore I'd never enlist in any man's army again. What would it be like to take orders from someone else? To kill for someone else again?

"You're a pretty cool dude, Joey Ramone. But, I don't think I can do it."

"The whole 'lone wolf' thing, huh?"

Scott smiled. "I guess so."

Joey smiled as well, but it faded from his face. "That's too bad. I'm going to have to kill you then."

Chapter Forty-One

Scott's hand drifted to his side, where his karambit was sheathed. He eased it halfway out.

Joey's face split into a huge grin. "Settle down, cowboy. I'm just joking. I mean, who are you gonna tell about us? Anybody that's not one of us will think you're loony. Tell enough people, the men in the white suits with the butterfly nets will be after you."

Scott relaxed and let the knife slide back into the sheath.

Well," Joey said, "I've gotta split. More disasters to avert, ya know? It's a never ending stream." He tossed his napkin onto his plate and stood up. He offered Scott his hand, which Scott shook. "Be careful out there, lone wolf, and don't let anyone sneak up behind you like that again. They might not be on your side. I'll let you buy me lunch in exchange for saving your life last night."

He strode to the door, but handed Stacy a five dollar bill. "He's taking care of the tab, but this is for you." Then, he was gone.

Stacy came to the table, laid the check there, and said, "Your friend's pretty cute. He from around here?"

"Definitely not," Scott said as he fished a few bills out of his wallet.

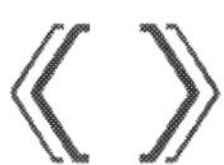

SCOTT HUNG AROUND NORTHERN California for a few more days. He wasn't in a real time crunch to get to the next job he had chosen. He sold the pickup truck he had purchased the week before. He had bought and sold so many vehicles since that first Valiant that he had lost count years before.

Sometimes he would keep something he liked for a few weeks or maybe a month, but he was still careful about covering his tracks. He always gave a fake name when he bought a vehicle and still changed his appearance regularly.

At the moment, he looked like a typical ex-Vietnam vet, hair a little shaggy and grown over his ears and collar, and a droopy moustache, which seemed to be the only kind he could grow.

Since the next place he had to be was on the east coast, he decided to give himself the luxury of an airline flight, although he was still careful to pick an airport one state over. That meant he would have to ditch his crossbow, but it had been an inexpensive model that he had never fired – despite his plans to the contrary.

He caught a Greyhound to San Francisco, then hopped a city bus to the airport. He wasn't even tempted to visit the VA hospital where he had spent more than a year of his life. One of his goals was to never step foot in that building again.

He flew into Philadelphia, then caught the Amtrak up to New York City. Even when he had dispatched David Berkowitz a few years before, Scott had managed to avoid the most crowded part of Manhattan. He didn't like being around so many people, loud noises, and hustle and bustle.

He stepped out of Penn Station and a cruel wind bit into him while a freezing rain slapped his face. He turned up the collar of his green army jacket.

First trip to Manhattan and it's gotta be in December.

He tried hailing a cab, but that proved difficult. It was as though the cabbies sensed Scott was a fish out of water and enjoyed passing him by. After half an hour of observing others, he realized he was being too polite and timid. He put his fingers in his mouth and whistled shrilly at the next passing cab. That caught the driver's attention and he pulled over.

"Westside YMCA."

"The one by the Park?"

"Yeah." Scott wasn't actually sure, but he knew that Central Park was near to where he wanted to go.

The driver turned the meter on and merged into the late afternoon traffic. The cabbie was Middle Eastern and wore a turban. After the first exchange, he seemed to forget Scott was in the cab at all. Although he seemed outwardly calm, the guy drove like a maniac and used his horn like a proctologic exam tool. At one point, they sat behind another cab, which was stopped at a crosswalk full of crossing pedestrians. Nonetheless, the cabbie leaned on his horn.

Finally, Scott asked, "Where do you expect him to go? He'd have to run over a dozen people to go anywhere."

The cabbie looked at him in the rearview mirror and shrugged. The concept of not leaning on his horn wasn't part of his thought process.

Scott was tremendously glad when the taxi pulled to the curb. He handed some bills across the seat and was glad to escape with his life.

I think I'll stick to shoe leather from now on.

Scott didn't have a reservation at the YMCA. He didn't even know if it was possible to make a reservation there. The man at the front desk was happy to rent him a room, though, and it was only sixteen bucks a night. Comparing that to what everywhere else charged, that was an unbelievable deal.

When Scott saw the room, he understood why. It was, technically, a room. It had four walls, a floor and a ceiling. However, it could have been called a closet as well, and no one would have argued with you. It was a narrow room with no window, no bathroom, a single cot and rickety table with a lamp. There was a bathroom, but it was down the hall and Scott got to share it with all his best friends he hadn't met yet.

Scott had been in the army, though. Spartan conditions were not going to put him off his feed. He dropped his pack on the bed and grabbed his jo, which he'd managed to use as his carry-on luggage on the plane.

By the time he walked out into the spitting rain, it was full dark. He popped his collar up again and started to walk.

He didn't have a real destination in mind, he just wanted to get a feel for the layout of the city. He turned left, right, and left again completely at random. The temperature continued to drop, but walking kept him warm.

Without knowing where it was, or where he was going, Scott walked directly toward his ultimate destination for this trip. Towering above him, like a holdover from another century, was The Dakota Apartments, home to many of New York's rich and famous. Most importantly to Scott, it was home to John Lennon and Yoko Ono.

Scott had been walking in a daze with no real destination in mind, but now that he was here, he stopped and mentally retraced his steps.

Not too bad a walk. Good. Now, one day to scout the place out, then I've just got to stop the nutjob from Hawaii who's here to kill John Lennon, and I can be on my way.

Scott turned and walked away. He had to decide whether to cut across Central Park, which would have been quicker, or walk back the way he had come.

It was late, it had been a long flight, and he was tired. He decided to cut through the park.

Much of the park is well-lit at night, but some of the paths had dark and twisty sections. Scott was walking through one of these when two men stepped out of the shadows in front of him.

One was a few inches taller than Scott and bulky. The other was smaller, but wiry.

The shorter man said, "Can you help a brother out?"

Scott pulled up short and said, "What do you need, brother?"

"Whatever you've got," the big man said in an incongruously high-pitched voice. Scott heard the soft *snick* of a switchblade knife.

Scott didn't bother answering. He took a single step forward and half-kneeled, while whipping his jo up. He used it as a stabbing stick and blasted the end of it into the big man's forehead. He stumbled backwards, then collapsed onto the wet grass.

Before the other man had a chance to react, Scott whirled and cut a smooth arc with his jo. It slammed into the smaller man's throat. A wordless cry that sounded like *Gaaagh!* issued from his throat before it cut off in mid-yell. He crumpled to his knees.

Scott took one step toward him and executed a perfect front kick into the side of his head.

An action hero would have made a quip.

Scott shook the tension out of his body and walked back to the YMCA.

Chapter Forty-Two

The next morning, Scott was up, showered, and out the front door of the YMCA before anyone else on his floor stirred. The spitting rain from the night before had intensified, but it didn't bother him. His Oregon-born resistance to rain kept him in good stead. He stopped at a café and had two cups of strong coffee and a full breakfast. By the time he exited the café, the dim pre-dawn glow had just started to light the eastern sky.

He had left his jo in the room. He didn't want to do anything to attract too much attention, and people tend to notice a man with a walking stick. He stuck his hands deep in his pockets and walked back to The Dakota.

When he arrived, a doorman was on duty, standing under an overhang so he didn't get soaked. There was a deep vestibule that led back into the entrance to the building. In the early morning hour, businessmen and women were streaming through, carrying umbrellas and briefcases. None of them paid attention to the small group of people who had already gathered around the entrance.

Scott approached a young couple standing inside the vestibule. "Hey, how are you guys?"

"Guess we could be better if the sun was shining, but other than that, all is good in our world," the young man said. He had the look of a young ad man or record executive, although it was possible he was just trying to look the part. That's always possible in the city.

"So, how come there's so many people here so early?"

The man looked around and laughed a little. "This? This isn't much at all. By this afternoon, there will be five times this many people here. We're here because we heard through the grapevine that John and Yoko were at the recording studio last night. When they are recording, they usually roll in about now. We're hoping to see them and say hi."

"And maybe give them a cassette of our music," the woman said. She was a pretty brunette with her long hair pulled back. She produced a cassette and shook it like a tambourine.

"Well, good luck. I hope he signs you right up."

The woman shrugged. "Probably not, but standing here is free and where else am I going to have a chance to meet a Beatle today?"

"Nowhere I know of, that's for sure. I mean it, good luck."

Scott faded away from them and moved back onto the sidewalk so he had a better view of his surroundings. Over the years of being a hunter, he had developed a keen sense of patience and waiting for the prey to come to him. He went into his waiting posture and when he looked up, two hours had passed. People had come, people had gone, but nothing of import had happened.

Then, Scott noticed him. A pudgy man with large dark glasses. He had a long dark coat on and a watch cap on his head. Scott hadn't seen him approach, but he was standing alone in the vestibule. He held a copy of an album.

Tricky bastard. How'd he get past me? Must have been daydreaming.

Scott walked across the sidewalk until he was standing on the same side of the vestibule as the would-be assassin, just a few feet away.

If this was a regular situation, I'd take him out right here. But this is anything but regular. Whatever happens here is likely to be big news.

"You here to see John Lennon?"

The question yanked Scott out of his reverie and he realized it was the man he had come to stop.

Scott shrugged and didn't answer. He looked pointedly away.

"I'm going to stand right here until I meet him." If he noticed that Scott was ignoring him, he didn't show it. He smiled ingratiatingly and held up the album he was holding. "I'm going to ask him to sign my album."

How long will he keep talking, if I never respond to him?

Scott would never find the definitive answer to that question because the man talked and talked without an end in sight. He talked about John Lennon, the Beatles, a trip he had made from Hawaii to meet him before, and how he had failed in his mission to meet John that trip, but wouldn't this time.

Scott tried turning his back on the chattering man and staring out toward the street. It didn't matter. He continued to talk to his back.

If he doesn't shut up, I might kill him right now in front of all these people.

Scott walked out to the street, where he saw more people were gathering. As he walked, he heard the man behind him say, "Hey, where you going? Who's your favorite Beatle? Is it John? He's mine..."

Scott took up his original spot, where he could keep an eye on the man, but not have to hear him. The rain had slowed and it was warming up. Scott took inventory of the people. Most of the crowd was younger, under twenty-five. The couple with the cassette they wanted to give to John had split, but their place had been taken by many others. His eye settled on one man who was alone, which was unusual in and of itself. It seemed more normal for people to treat it as a social occasion.

The man was young—Scott guessed maybe twenty—and was talking to the doorman, who seemed to be doing his best to ignore him. He walked away from the doorman and momentarily looked out at the street. When he did, Scott saw a large birthmark covered the left half of his face from his forehead clear down to his chin.

Tough break, kid. We've all got our crosses to bear, but I feel for you.

Scott was watching the kid with the birthmark instead of his intended target. Meanwhile, the kid saw the man holding the album. His eyes swept across him, then his head snapped back and he locked on him. He took a couple of automatic steps toward him, then caught himself.

Interesting. Why would this kid be so interested in my guy? He's not one of Joey Ramone's team, is he?

Scott looked him over more intently. Jeans, tennis shoes, a flannel shirt and a jacket that probably wasn't warm enough. He held a black umbrella that still had the price tag dangling from the handle, but nothing else.

He could have a small gun strapped somewhere, but he doesn't have the vibe of a guy who kills people regularly. Looks more like a kid on a senior trip to New York City than an assassin.

The kid moved into the vestibule and stood directly opposite the would-be killer who wouldn't shut up.

You're gonna regret that, I'll wager.

The kid did his best to not stare directly at the man in the pea coat, but it was obvious that he was keeping him under sly observation. Soon, the man noticed and started talking to the kid. Scott couldn't hear what was being said, and he was pleased about that. He hoped to never hear the soft-voiced man with the undeniable trace of a Southern accent again.

Scott watched the two of them converse across the vestibule. After a minute, he saw the kid start to edge away, one step at a time.

I coulda told you, kid.

Finally, just as Scott had done before him, he turned and walked away, toward the sidewalk. The man called after him, "Hey, where you going?"

The young man stood street side, waiting for the traffic to clear, then jogged across Central Park West to the park. It was the same route Scott had followed back to the YMCA the night before. Scott glanced at the man in the entryway, who seemed to have forgotten about being abandoned again.

There's something about that kid. If I hadn't just run into Joey Ramone, I might not have noticed it, but there's something going on with him. I've gotta have a little chat with him.

Chapter Forty-Three

Scott crossed the street after the kid with the birthmark and jogged to catch up. He gave a little whistle, but the kid didn't hear him.

Finally, he got close enough that he could say, "That guy's a bit much, isn't he?"

The younger man had been lost in his own thoughts and wasn't expecting someone to speak to him. He glanced around with a slightly worried expression on his face.

Ah. He thinks I might be the other guy, chasing after him to either kill him or chatter endlessly about the Beatles.

"Sorry?" the young man said, obviously puzzled.

"That dude back there that wanted to be your new best buddy. He's a little too intense. He did the same thing to me a couple of hours ago. He makes me nervous."

Scott watched him carefully to see how he reacted to this.

The kid gave him a nod of agreement, but still seemed unsure of who Scott was or why he was accosting him. Scott thought back to his small adventure the night before and realized that not all people have good intentions for you in the big city.

"Anyway, didn't mean to disturb you. Just wanted to let you know I noticed it too. There's something off about that guy."

Scott thought that one hit home. *He already knows there's something off with him. He's here to do something, too. He's another person like me.*

"I appreciate it." The other man reached his hand out to Scott. "Joe. Joe Hart."

Scott gave him a quick grin. "Scott McKenzie."

"Wait a minute. Scott ... *McKenzie?*"

"Yep. Just like the guy that sang the 'put flowers in your hair' song in the sixties. You can bet your ass my buddies gave me some shit about that."

"I'll bet," Joe said. "Probably doesn't happen so much anymore, does it? He hasn't had a hit in a long time."

"That's one of those songs that seems to stick in people's minds, though, for some reason. Woulda been a lot cooler if my name was Jim Morrison or something."

"Good point."

Scott examined Joe Hart up close. He decided his first impression was right.

Young. Innocent. Out of his element. What's his game? He doesn't look like he's on the same mission to me. Is he some time traveling tourist, showing up to watch John Lennon get killed?

"Well, nice talking with ya. See ya around," Joe said, and set off across the park.

"See ya around, buddy," Scott said and headed off in a different direction.

It almost feels like I should double back and make sure he gets wherever he's going. It's the middle of the day, though. He'll be all right. He's a big enough kid. He can take care of himself. I think I'll head back and make sure the weirdo doesn't get up to anything. He's not supposed to start anything until tomorrow night, but maybe an opportunity will present itself to take him out before then and I can get out of the city and be on my way.

Scott jogged his way back to the Dakota and took up a post he thought was far enough away to not be the target of a conversational diatribe, but close enough to keep an eye on him. The pudgy man in the pea coat and blue watch cap was deep in conversation with two young women, though, and paid Scott no attention whatsoever.

They all held their positions until an hour or two after darkness fell. Finally, the man and the two women seemed to give up on seeing a Beatle today and left the entryway. They turned left and walked along the sidewalk past Scott. He let them go until they were half a block ahead of him.

He followed a safe distance behind for a few blocks, but they stepped into a diner.

I can either wait here in the rain and cold and follow them all over the city, or I can pick up the trail tomorrow and stop him in the act.

Scott's eyes traveled down the block and he saw a warm pool of light emanating from a place that had a yellow neon sign that read "Steinman's Delicatessen." His stomach reminded him that he hadn't eaten since before sun up, which was a long time ago.

He took one last look at the pudgy man with the gun no doubt in his pocket. The two women he was with were laughing, and he was looking through the plate glass window, directly at Scott.

Definitely time to be moving along.

Scott walked to Steinman's, ordered a corned beef sandwich and a coffee to go. He took the same route through the park he had the day before, but today it was clear sailing all the way back to the YMCA.

He shut himself in his small closet of a room, ate as much of the huge sandwich as he could manage, and dropped off to sleep. Tomorrow was a big day, complicated by the arrival of Joe Hart, since he didn't know what role he intended to play in the drama.

Chapter Forty-Four

Scott's notes on the John Lennon assassination were more complete than virtually any of the other crimes he was trying to stop. Killing one of the world's most famous people in the middle of one of the biggest cities in the world brings a lot of attention.

Oddly enough, he didn't have an exact time for the killings. Only that the killing took place late in the evening on this day, December 8, 1980. Since Scott knew he was going to be at the Dakota until the whole thing was over, he wasn't in much of a hurry to get there early. Even so, it was still dark outside when he woke up. He spent a few hours walking around New York. When it got late enough for businesses to open, Scott stopped at a used bookstore and was pleasantly surprised to find that those are essentially the same no matter where you are. As soon as he opened the door, the familiar aroma filled his nostrils and he relaxed.

He spent the next few hours happily browsing the stacks. In the end, he limited himself to two books—*The Wanderers* by James Michener, and a collection of the year's best short stories. He had made a big loop around midtown, and so was only a few blocks away from his home base. He stopped back at the YMCA, put the books in his room and locked it up tight.

If everything went to plan, he wouldn't be sleeping there tonight, but he didn't want to haul his bag and jo around with him all day. Specifically, he didn't want to have the karambit on him, in case he had to explain himself to a police officer. He could probably explain away the collapsible baton as sensible self-defense, but the wicked-looking knife was another matter. So, he paid for another night at the "Y," but had everything packed and ready for a quick getaway should one be needed.

He put the baton in the back pocket of his jeans, then put on his old army jacket, the one that still had "McKenzie" etched above the pocket. It was long enough that it easily covered that weapon.

By the time Scott got to the Dakota, it was almost 2:30 in the afternoon. He immediately found the man he was looking for. No watch cap today, but the same chilling expression on his face—a jack-o'-lantern grin that masked violent thoughts. He also saw Joe Hart, standing not far away, but just out of the conversational arc of the gunman and a couple of other men.

The interesting thing is, this guy seems undeniably creepy to me. And, to Joe Hart. But, to everyone else, they seem to accept him as normal. Normal, that is, if there is such a standard for those who wait outside the Dakota for a glimpse at fame.

Scott was slightly surprised to see Joe Hart give up his post. He walked down the sidewalk in the same direction the man and the two women had walked the night before.

Scott stood where he was and focused on the man who he knew had a .38 pistol tucked into the front pocket of his coat, along with a copy of JD Salinger's *Catcher in the Rye.*

Before long, Scott saw that Joe had returned, this time with food. A few minutes later, Joe walked up to Scott.

"Hey, man. I got a sandwich at the deli and could only eat half of it. You want the other half?"

I can relate.

"What's the matter, you don't want it?"

"I did my best, but I could only get through half of it. I don't have anywhere to store it, so I'm either gonna have to give it away or throw it away. I hate to throw a good sandwich away."

"I'm not turning down a free sandwich, and not to look a gift horse in the mouth, but what kind?"

"Corned beef."

"Oh, man, brother. I had one of their corned beefs last night. I had the same problem—couldn't eat the whole thing."

But that was last night and this is now. I could use something to get me through the night.

Joe gave Scott the sandwich. Scott said, "Thank you very much," in a terrible Elvis imitation. He was able to make short work of it. Scott smoothed out both the waxed paper and the paper bag, folded them, and stuck them in the deep pocket of his jacket.

Scott noticed that Joe was looking at him with sudden interest. He raised his eyebrows as if to say, "Yes?"

"Hey, if it's rude to ask, just tell me to shut up, but what's your story, Scott? What are you doing hanging out here in front of the Dakota for two days in December?"

"That's not rude at all. Stories are a good way to pass the time. What's mine? A full telling of that requires more time than we have here, even if we stand here several more days. The truncated version is that I grew up in Evansville, Indiana, and got unlucky when my birthday was the first number pulled for the draft. I took a tour of exotic Asian locations on Uncle Sam's dollar. After I got my ass shot off in Kompong Speu, they shipped what was left of me home and put Humpty Dumpty back together again. If you look close, you can still see the cracks."

Joe nodded, but didn't speak.

"Since I've been back, I've been wandering. I get disability checks sent to my sister back in Indiana, and she deposits them for me. I live pretty simply. When I want to go somewhere, I stick out my thumb and off I go."

"And you decided to come to New York City in December."

"I never told you I was smart. I could have enrolled in college and maybe found a deferment, too, but I never did. I think I might get on a bus and head south for the winter after today. And so, Joe Hart, turnabout is fair play. What's your story?"

And I'd be willing to bet, you're going to have to leave as much out of your story as I did mine.

"Not nearly as exciting as yours. My parents are both dead, I live by myself, and I decided to take a trip to the Big Apple."

"Also, I might point out," Scott said, "in December."

"As you say, I've never claimed to be smart."

Just then, they heard a ripple of excitement in the crowd behind them. Scott looked over his shoulder and saw that a white limo had pulled to the curb behind them. It wasn't quite dark yet, but dusk was settling in. Scott saw a small Asian woman approaching, wearing a full-length fur coat. He smiled and nodded at her, and stepped out of her way.

Strolling along behind her, as if he didn't have a care in the world, was John Lennon.

Scott nudged Joe, whose mouth was slightly agape at the sight of Lennon. "We may have chosen a crappy time of year to visit New York, but where else are you gonna be standing around and see a Beatle?"

The man with the gun hidden in his pocket approached John Lennon. Joe tensed and took a step further, which further confirmed what Scott had come to believe—that he was on a journey similar to Scott's own. Scott didn't tense. He had now seen many people right before they committed acts of violence, and he had learned the clues. This man was showing none of them. In fact, he appeared so nervous and tongue-tied being near to Lennon that Scott thought he was likely incapable of doing anything at that moment.

Scott stood far enough back that he couldn't hear what John Lennon was saying, but the other man held out his copy of Double Fantasy, which Lennon signed.

A man with a camera—the same man whom the pudgy man had been talking to all afternoon, took picture after picture in the fading light.

Lennon looked around, saw that no one else was waiting to see him and stepped to the limousine. As he approached, he gave a little wave at Scott.

Man, there really is something about that guy. I make eye contact with him for a few seconds and I feel butterflies. What's it like to live your whole life like that?

Chapter Forty-Five

The crowd in front of the Dakota moved to the edge of the sidewalk and watched the limousine disappear down Central Park West.

"That's it, folks," the doorman on duty said. "They won't be coming back tonight. Might as well go somewhere warm."

Most of the crowd broke up into groups of three or four and drifted away.

Scott turned around and found himself face to face with a lanky black man who was dressed remarkably similar to Scott, right down to the green army jacket.

"Hey, brother," Scott said. "What's up?"

"Hello, Scott," the man said, making the same quotation mark gesture with his fingers that Joey Ramone had.

"Ah, you must be with Joey Ramone."

The black man laughed. "Oh, man, don't tell me he tried all that BS with you?"

Scott flushed a little. "It's all BS, then?"

The other man shrugged. "Not for me to say. You're not gonna catch me calling him Joey Ramone, though, that's for sure." He held his hand out to Scott. "I'm Freddy. And if you say, 'Freddy Mercury?' I might have to punch you. It's just Freddy, okay?"

Scott smiled and laughed a little. "I admit, that all sounded a little fishy to me."

"So," Freddy said, "you're here on the case?"

"Yep," Scott said, nodding toward the gunman-to-be. "I'm on the case."

"I'm supposed to be here for this, too, but I've got a girl waiting for me, if you know what I mean. If you've got a handle on this, I'm going to let you take care of it."

Scott lifted his chin toward Joe Hart. "He's here for it, too."

"Man, tourists are getting thicker every day." He looked Scott up and down. "I'm gonna leave you to it, then. Have a good night, man."

"See ya, Freddy."

Scott watched as the man hustled away. Wherever he was going, he seemed to be in a hurry.

. Scott walked back to where Joe was standing. "Well, is that it for you, then? You came, you saw a Beatle, and now you can head back to Oregon?"

Joe shook his head. He stared at Scott for a long moment. It was obvious he was debating with himself about something. Finally, he decided. "You see the guy over there?" He gave a slight nod toward the man Scott had come to take out.

"The guy reading the book that wanted to be your best friend yesterday?"

Joe nodded. "I've got a bad feeling about him. I think he's up to something bad. I heard him muttering some weird stuff to himself a while ago. I also think the doorman said they'd be gone all night so everyone would leave. I know it sounds crazy, but I want to be here in case something happens."

"What are you going to do, if he does try to do something bad? How are you going to stop him?"

"Honestly? I have no real idea, but I want to stay close."

"Well, I was going to head back to my room at the 'Y', but I guess I'll hang around for a while and see what's up."

Scott had never intended to head back. Nothing short of being arrested and thrown into the back of a cop car could have dragged him away at that moment. But, he didn't want to let Joe know what his real story was. At least, not yet.

"Nah, you don't have to. I'm sure I'm just being crazy. The wind's starting to blow, and it's gonna get cold soon."

"Have you ever stayed at the 'Y'?"

Joe shook his head.

"Well, if I say, 'spartan conditions,' a certain image might come into your head. Whatever image that is, the reality is worse. It's only sixteen bucks a night, but it's not much more than a cot in a closet."

Joe smiled and nodded.

"So what I'm saying is, given a choice between hanging out with you in the cold for a few hours, or lying on that uncomfortable cot, this doesn't seem so bad. Even so, what sounds good to me, is a cup of hot coffee. How 'bout you? You drink the stuff?"

"Sure, of course."

"The deli makes great coffee. I'll run and get us some to go. Black okay?"

"Yes, that's great."

Joe dug some bills out of his pocket and tried to give them to Scott.

"Nah, I got it. I'm not gonna let you buy lunch and coffee both. I'll be back in a flash."

Scott enjoyed being on the move again. Even after all these years, and all the stretching exercises he did every day, he still stiffened up when he stood in one place too long. He grabbed two large coffees at Steinman's and hurried back to the Dakota with the coffee still hot.

Joe accepted the coffee, lifted it toward Scott in a small salute. "Salud, and thanks."

They killed time over the next few hours by telling more stories of their lives.

Joe told Scott an almost-unbelievable story of escaping death the day Mt. St. Helens blew.

Scott decided to tease Joe a little. "It's almost like you knew exactly when the mountain was going to blow, the way you timed it."

Joe shrugged that off. "Yeah," he said with a chuckle. "Almost."

At 10:00, Joe looked at his watch. He said, "The problem with coffee is, you don't buy it, you only borrow it. I gotta run to the deli and use the can. You want another cup?"

Scott shook his head. "No, same problem with me. I'm going to have to go after you get back. In the meantime, I'll keep an eye on Mr. Catcher in the Rye while you're gone."

Joe looked relieved. "Thanks, man, that's great."

And, I'm going to hope this all goes down while you're gone, so you don't have to be at risk. You're a good kid, Joe, but you're over your head.

It didn't happen that way, though. Ten minutes later, Joe ran back, huffing and puffing, but all was quiet at the Dakota.

Damnit. I wasn't kidding about having to go myself. It's gotta be getting close to the time when John and Yoko are going to get back. But, if I stand here too much longer, I'm going to bust a kidney. The best thing I can do is hustle there and back and get it over with.

Scott leaned into Joe and said, "I've got the same problem you did. I'll be back in a few."

Scott did hustle. He took the two blocks at a steady jog, bordering on a sprint. He burst into Steinman's, saw the sign that read, "Restrooms are for customers only," and had to stand in line to grab a pack of gum. Every second that passed, Scott's gut twisted a little tighter. He ran into the bathroom, did his business, and ran back toward the Dakota.

His heart sank as he saw the same white limousine that he had seen earlier in the day. It had already dropped off its occupants and was pulling away from the curb.

Scott sprinted forward and grabbed his baton out of his pocket as he ran. He flipped it open in one smooth, downward motion and ran like a sprinter at the first leg of a relay race.

When he was closing in on the Dakota, he heard two loud gun blasts.

Too late! I'm too late!

Scott was forced to slow as he approached the opening or he would have skidded right past it. When he turned, he saw a scene he never would have expected. John Lennon was picking himself up off the ground and still had his back turned to the action. Joe Hart was lying on the ground in a rapidly spreading pool of blood. The killer was scrambling to his feet. He had the .38 in his hands and had settled into a shooter's stance—legs wide, arms extended in front of him. The gun was pointed at John Lennon.

Chapter Forty-Six

Scott leaped forward, whipping his right arm in a complete circle. The steel baton slammed down on the shooter's right arm. In the eerie quiet of the moment, he actually heard the bones in the man's arm break.

The gun hit the pavement with a metallic retort and Scott pounced on it. He grabbed and held onto it.

The man with the gun was now simply the man with the shattered arm and he fell pitifully to the ground crying. In another situation, Scott would have had his karambit or his jo, and he would have dispatched the man on to whatever was next for him. This was the Dakota in New York City, though, and there were witnesses everywhere, including John Winston Ono Lennon, who was staring at Scott open-mouthed.

Lennon rushed to Joe's side. He'd been shot through, but he was still conscious. Scott put a boot in the back of the shooter and pushed him forward onto his broken arm. The man cried out, but no one paid attention to him. Scott kneeled with Lennon beside Joe.

"Lay still, lay still, bloke. You're going to be all right." He turned his head away and raised his voice. "Jose! Jose, are you there? Call the police!"

Lennon took off his jacket—leather, with a black fur collar—and laid it under Joe's head.

"Thank you," Joe said, weakly.

"Lad, I owe you me life. I think he was here to kill me."

Joe turned his face to Scott. "And thank you. I blew it. You did it."

"Be still now," Scott said. "You're losing a lot of blood."

Scott looked at the wound in Joe's left arm and realized the man had loaded the gun with hollow point bullets. There was a hole all the way through Joe's bicep and he was losing blood at an alarming rate.

Sirens filled the air and moments later, both red and blue lights lit the vestibule.

An ambulance was first on the scene and Scott stood and waved them over to Joe. He hurried toward them as they approached. "Left bicep. Shot all the way through. He'll need blood."

The ambulance crew went to work and Scott, John Lennon, and Yoko Ono, stood back out of the way, concern etched on their faces.

"I don't know what both of you were doing here tonight, but it's my lucky day you were," Lennon said. Yoko nodded, eyes wide.

Half a dozen police cars screamed onto Central Park West.

The first officer on the scene was going to put Scott in handcuffs until he got things sorted out, but Lennon stopped him. He pointed to the man cradling his broken right arm and said, "There's your culprit, officer. He wanted to kill me. These two"—he pointed to Joe and Scott—"stopped him. I think they saved my bloody life."

The officer put the handcuffs on the injured man and whisked him away.

As the gurney was wheeled into the ambulance, Scott called to the EMT's, "Which hospital?"

The EMTs didn't hear, but John laid a hand on his shoulder and said, "It'll be St. Luke's. I expect he'll be in surgery tonight, but Yoko and I will go see him tomorrow."

A man who appeared to be in charge of the scene—not in uniform, directing others to keep everyone away until the scene could be secured—stepped forward. "Mr. Lennon, we're going to need a full statement from you. We can send someone here in the morning, if you'd like."

"Mother and I are going to the hospital to see the young man who risked his life for me in the morning. Can we give you our statement there?"

The man nodded, jotted a note in a small notebook. "That's fine, Mr. Lennon. I can be there myself."

He turned to Scott. "We'll need the same from you."

"I'm planning on leaving town tomorrow. Can I give you my statement now?"

The investigator paused, but John Lennon stepped forward. "I'll tell you this—I wouldn't be here to give you a statement tomorrow, if it wasn't for this man. He saved my life."

"That's fine, then. Can I ask what you were doing here at the Dakota so late?"

Scott smiled his thanks to John. He had rehearsed a story, and he told it well.

By midnight, he had given the police Cheryl's address in Evansville as his own permanent address, and they had given him a ride to the YMCA. On the way there, the cop had taken in his disheveled appearance, considered where he was taking him, and offered to buy him dinner—a small thank you for his night's work.

Scott demurred, and asked to be dropped off at the "Y."

The next morning, Scott reversed his trip from Penn Station, but this time did it on foot, taking in the sights and sounds of New York. He was in no hurry. Every newspaper box he walked by, every television he saw on, and every radio he heard was focused on the attempted murder of John Lennon and the two strangers who intervened. Scott walked among it all, happily anonymous.

And now, I hope, I can disappear from the scene. I hope the press doesn't hound Joe too much. He's a great kid with a big heart, but I don't think he's much interested in being famous.

Scott got to Penn Station by late morning and was on a train heading south by mid-afternoon. He rode right past Philadelphia this time, and went on to Washington, DC. Through all his travels, he had never had reason to step foot in the capitol. He didn't have another event scheduled for months and he wanted to lie low for a time after being involved in such a high-profile happening. So, he found another inexpensive room in DC and spent a few weeks exploring.

Washington D.C. is a great place to visit on a limited budget. There's so much to see for free that you rarely have to take your wallet out of your pocket except to eat.

Living in Middle Falls, Oregon, then Evansville, Indiana, Scott had never had a chance to explore a lot of history. In Washington, though, he couldn't turn around without finding a historic spot of some sort. Best of all were the Smithsonian Museums. He found that if he arrived right at opening and stayed all day, he could get through one each day.

Two weeks later, he judged that he had seen what he wanted to see and it was time to move on. Scott estimated that he hadn't spent more than two weeks in one place in the last six years. Moving on had become a habit.

The weather in DC was no better than it had been in New York, so he stuck his thumb out again and rode it all the way to Pensacola, Florida. He found a roadside motel, hung his green army jacket up and traded it for t-shirts and shorts.

It was nearly Christmas so it wasn't too hot, as it had been his last trip through Florida. But after the chill of an east coast cold snap, it was good to get some warmth back into his bones. For the first time in this lifetime, he actually got a little bit of a tan.

Also, for the first time in years, he felt relaxed and less driven.

Seeing Joe Hart's guileless innocence had reminded Scott of himself as a young man. Laying on a white sand beach and soaking up the sun, he felt far away from the violence he carried with him wherever he went.

Scott thought back to the moment he had first realized he could dedicate his life to fixing so many of the world's wrongs. For the first time since that day, he asked himself if he had the strength to continue along the path he had chosen.

Scott McKenzie was growing tired.

Chapter Forty-Seven

As he always did, Scott called his sister on Christmas day.

"Scotty!" Cheryl exclaimed when she heard his voice on the other end of the line. "What have you gotten yourself into?"

Scott's stomach tightened. "What do you mean?"

"A police detective from New York called me, wanting to know if this was where you lived."

"What did you tell him?"

"I told him the truth, of course—that you didn't really live anywhere, but this was as close to home as anywhere for you."

"Good enough."

"I asked him why he wanted to know, and he wouldn't tell me. I've been so worried about you. What's going on?"

"Nothing bad, little sister. You can stop worrying." In as few words as possible, Scott told her about his role in saving John Lennon's life.

"That was *you?* That was all over the news a few weeks ago."

"And now, the world is already forgetting about it, right? There are a lot more pressing issues in the world than that. The hostages are still being held in Iran and there's a new president about to be inaugurated."

"But, did you just happen to be there when it happened? The news said that the man who tried to kill John Lennon ended up with an arm broken in two places."

"Let's talk about happier things. I think I'm going to come home for a while."

"Wonderful! It's been forever since we've seen you. The kids barely remember their Uncle Scott. We'll make room for you."

"No, I don't want you to do that. You've got a houseful now. You have a three-bedroom house with the two of you and three kids. I'm not going to put one of the kids out of their own room. I've already got a reservation at a place there in town."

"Liar. You've never made a reservation in your life. You're forgetting who you're talking to."

Scott laughed. "Okay, you caught me. I just want to see you guys and the kids. I'll be around plenty, but I'm gonna lay my head down somewhere else. Deal?"

"Deal. Just come home, Scotty. We miss you and I'm worried about you."

Scott absorbed the Florida sunshine for a few more days, then hopped a bus heading north. He knew from experience it wasn't fun hitchhiking through the Midwest in the middle of winter.

Two days later, he stepped out into the blowing wind and rain of an Indiana New Year's Eve. He didn't want to interrupt any celebrations Cheryl and Mike had planned, so he caught a cab to a motel on the edge of town. He managed to make it to midnight before he fell asleep. He watched the ball drop in New York before he dropped off himself.

SCOTT SPENT A FEW WEEKS with Cheryl, Mike, and the three kids. The kids, especially, enjoyed having Uncle Scott around as their own personal amusement ride. Seeing a normal family living a normal life, including kiddie squabbles, burnt dinners, and relaxing with a glass of wine when the house was quiet helped Scott center himself.

While he was in Evansville, he got in touch with Jerry and Lynn Werbeloff and they insisted he come over for dinner.

Their family was growing, too, with two kiddos running around underfoot. They had moved from their small apartment to a house in one of the new developments near the city limits. Jerry had moved his dojo from the YMCA to a building of his own long ago.

It was a mile and a half from his motel to the Werbeloff's new home, but Scott was glad to walk it. He didn't want to get too out of shape while he was taking a hiatus.

Scott found the address without any difficulty. It was a two-story house with Christmas lights still glowing from the eves.

Feels like everyone else is moving on with their life. Finding a life partner, having children, building a life together. And what am I doing? Crisscrossing the country trying to kill bad people before they kill good people. It's my chosen path, but if I could go back and whisper in my ear, I might tell myself to think more carefully.

Scott rang the doorbell and Lynn answered. Having two children had only made her more beautiful. She hugged Scott and said, "We thought you'd disappeared forever."

He saw Jerry over her shoulder and pointed up. "Christmas was a while ago now, you know."

Jerry shrugged and said, "We're not all that bound up by convention. We might leave them up all year. The Homeowner's Association will likely pass a new bylaw just for me. Come on in, dinner's almost ready."

"...he says, as though he was the one who had cooked it," Lynn added.

There are people in your life that it doesn't matter how long it's been since you've seen them, you can pick up a conversation like you had just stepped out of the room for a moment. So it was for Scott, Jerry, and Lynn.

When Scott walked into the warmth of their living room, Jerry held out his hand for Scott's jo.

He tested its strength, twirled it easily with a swoosh, and said, "Holding up pretty well."

"It's gotten me a lot of miles."

"Weathered now, that's good," Jerry said. He held it up against a lamp. "Looks like a few blood stains. Yours?"

Scott shrugged, but then shook his head.

"We can talk about it after dinner. Oooooof," Jerry said as a small bundle of energy jumped into his arms, followed by another who looked exactly like the first. "Meet the twins, Brittany and Connor." He held them up, one in each arm, then said quietly, "Attack time is later. This is dinner time, and we have company."

The twins hopped down, bowed slightly to Scott and then stood quietly.

"I didn't know kids came with off switches."

"Just have to talk to them like adults, right? Besides, they both know they've got some growing to do before they can take on their old man."

"My parenting skills stand at zero. I'm a decent uncle, though."

The six of them sat at a rectangular table and ate the beef stew and salad Lynn had made. The meal was delicious, but there was something Scott wanted to talk with his sensei about.

Chapter Forty-Eight

Dinner done, Jerry and Scott sat on the low couch in the living room, drinking hot tea with honey.

Jerry leaned forward. "You almost look like a different man than when I saw you last, and I can tell something's on your mind."

"I don't know if I am the same man. But, before I tell you what's going on, I need to know what your capacity for believing things that can't be seen and can't be proven is."

Jerry mulled that over. "It's hard for anyone to truly believe those things, but I think my capacity for holding the possibility of them in my head is greater than average."

"All right. Here's that thing, then. To a certain extent, I know what's coming in this world. It's not a hundred percent, because things change over time, but for major events, it's pretty damn accurate."

"You know the next question. How?"

Scott gazed levelly at Jerry for a few long seconds, considering. As he did, Lynn came in and joined the conversation.

Jerry laid a hand on her knee and said, "He's about to tell us his deepest, darkest secret." He was joking, in a way, but Lynn looked at Scott expectantly.

"Oh, good," was all she said.

"I can't tell you everything, but I do need to talk to someone about all this, or I might go a little crazy."

Lynn leaned forward. "Tell us what you can, what you need, and don't worry about Jerry. He's constantly curious."

"Do you remember a conversation we had before I left, six years ago? About whether it's acceptable to aggressively harm someone if they were going to harm an innocent?"

"Of course. I told you that in the way of the warrior, you have no choice. You must protect the innocent. Why?"

Scott discovered the teacup in his hand and took a sip.

"I can't explain why, but I know bad things that are going to happen. Very specific bad things. I've been spending my life doing my best to stop them. So far, I've been mostly successful."

Jerry and Lynn sat quietly, knowing more was coming.

"I've been traveling the country, killing people who were going to do those bad things."

"That either makes you a very good vigilante, or a deranged murderer. Without more information, it's hard for me tell which," Jerry said.

"Yeah, that's fair. Even knowing everything I do, I still wonder about that. I haven't wanted to tell you what this actually is, because I've valued our friendship, and I have a feeling that after I tell you my story, you're going to never trust me near your kids again."

Jerry's eyes turned steel-hard. "Then you better tell me."

Rushing through it, Scott told them the truth of his life, from the death of his parents, to being wounded in the war and all the lives he had lived through since. He ended by saying, "The Iranians are going to do everything they can to spite Carter. They're not going to release the hostages until the moment Reagan becomes President. They'll have the hostages in a plane, idling on a runway, but won't allow them to take off until Reagan puts his hand on the bible to say the oath. At least, that's how it played out the last time I made it this far. Things change from life to life, but not usually world events like that."

Jerry sat back on the couch, lost in thought. "That would make this a multiverse, then, which is certainly possible. Like Billy Pilgrim, you've come unstuck in time, except not quite, right? You travel linearly, but reset to the same spot each time you die."

"Right. Which is what allows me to know the bad things that are coming."

"What kind of things?" Lynn asked.

"When I left here, I went straight to Maine. A man there was going to kill his wife and children. I stopped him the only way I knew how. I hesitated once before, and he ended up killing me."

"So this is the life after that for you, then. Did we meet in that previous life?"

"No. I started studying with you in this life because I knew I needed to know more than the army taught me. I needed to know how to kill people before they killed me."

Lynn glanced at Jerry, but he kept his gaze steady on Scott.

"It would be pretty easy to find the man you killed in Maine after you left here."

"Yes. I've just given you enough to put me away for life, if you want. It's a risk I'm willing to take, because I've begun to feel like I've lost my way. I've got to have someone to talk to about this."

"For the moment, then, let's say we accept this story. I'll be honest. I don't, but for the sake of further conversation, let's say I do. What did you want to talk about?"

"Using violence to stop violence. It feels like every time I do it, I lose a little more of my self. Did you know that I've killed more people than anyone I set out to stop? But, if I stop, I don't know if I could live with myself. What if I knew that someone was going to come and harm your family while you were away, but didn't do anything about it? How could I live with myself?"

"Philosophers have been asking themselves whether the ends justify the means for thousands of years, and no one's come up with a satisfactory answer. I'm no smarter than any of the people who have gone before me, that's for sure. John Brown's raid on the armory at Harper's Ferry is a classic example of that. His ultimate end—ridding the country of slavery—was undeniably good, but kidnapping and murdering people to accomplish that? Was that okay? I can't say it was. Here's what I do know. When your core values are clear, your decisions are easy."

Scott let that settle into him.

"What are your core values?"

"That's a good question. Honesty. Empathy. Dedication to others, I guess."

Jerry nodded sympathetically. "The first thing that occurred to you was honesty. But, you haven't been able to be honest with anyone, have you? You've essentially had to hide who and what you are from everyone. That's a conflict that will grate on your spirit. Then the second core value—empathy. That's a beautiful trait, but can you be empathic with everyone? If you feel empathy for those you have dedicated your life to stopping, that's another conflict. If your life is in conflict with two of your core values, how can you be happy? The answer is, you won't. You'll constantly feel like you're at war with yourself."

"That's pretty close to the way I've been feeling. For those reasons and others, I suppose. I was trained to kill, but killing in the army is different from what I've had to do. In the army, you're a hundred yards away and pull a trigger. With what I do, I'm often looking into their eyes when the light goes out of them."

Lynn stood and held her hand out for Scott's teacup. "I'll get you a refill." She stepped into the kitchen and turned the water on to boil. When she came back, Jerry and Scott were each absorbed in their own silence.

She said, "Let me ask you something. When you kill these people, what do you feel?"

"A little tormented, I guess. Sadness that I've put myself in this position. But, satisfied that I'm helping someone else."

"And what would you feel if you didn't kill them? If you just let them go?"

"Overwhelming guilt about the people they would kill. Completely innocent people."

"I have a suggestion, if you're open to it," Jerry said.

"That's why I'm here."

"Two suggestions. For one, you've got to weigh this whole situation out. Weigh out the cost of what you're doing versus the cost of the guilt you'll feel if you don't do it. Those aren't likely to be equal. One will be heavier. My best advice would be to give yourself permission to follow the path that is heavier."

Scott nodded. "And the other suggestion?"

"You're racking up negativity on your spirit each time you do this, but you're not refilling the positive. You said the first man you killed was going to kill his family. How old was the oldest child?"

"He had a daughter that was twelve."

"And that was 1974. So, she would be eighteen now. Have you ever looked her up? Or the man's wife? Seen what her life turned out like?"

"Honestly, I was hoping to never return to that little town."

Almost said, and there's no internet for me to look things up on yet, but let's not complicate things any more than we need to.

"Maybe you should."

"You're right. Maybe I should. It would help me if I could see some of the good that has come out of my life."

"Right now, I think you need to decompress. Why don't you grab your gear and come stay with us? I've converted the garage to a workout area. I can set up a cot for you out there. You can come and help me at the dojo if you want. I can always use the help. Have you been doing your katas?"

Scott looked away. "No."

"They will help center you too."

"Do you really want a man who just confessed to multiple murders staying in the same house with your kids?"

"I know you. Plus, anyone who tried to attack those two holy terrors would find themselves with blood spurting out of several orifices. They are warriors already."

Chapter Forty-Nine

Scott did stay with the Werbeloffs for a few months. He was close enough to be able to drop in on Cheryl, Mike and the kids every other day or so, and he was able to help Jerry out at his dojo.

Werbeloff Karate was located in an older building in downtown Evansville. It was a little drafty, and the plumbing made odd sounds, but it had plenty of open space for the growing number of students.

Scott went there to work with Jerry every day. He swept up, unclogged the toilet, caulked around old windows and did other equally glamorous tasks. It was the closest he had come to having an actual job since he had been a gofer at the car dealership in his first life.

In exchange for his hard work, Jerry let him have free lessons. Working out six days a week went a long way toward healing what was wrong inside him.

On January 20th, Jerry and Scott stayed home from the dojo and watched the news. Scott held his breath, wondering if any of the changes he had made would change the way Inauguration Day played out.

It didn't.

Immediately following the inauguration ceremony, the news anchor announced that the plane holding the hostages had cleared Iranian airspace.

Jerry and Lynn looked at Scott, then at the television, then back at Scott.

"I guess I always believed you on some level, because I could tell how sincerely you believed it yourself. What you were saying was so impossible, I thought you might be delusional, though."

Not much I can say to that, is there? 'No, my friend, I am not crazy?'

The full realization of what this meant seemed to soak into both Jerry and Lynn's brains. Scott could see the wheels turning.

"So you've already lived through this day, this week, this year, before?"

"Yep. For the most part, I was out of society, so aside from the things I read in the newspapers, I didn't know too much."

"Out of society?"

"I lived most of my life in a cabin in the Vermont woods."

Jerry got a faraway look in his eyes. "If you're going to hide from the world, a cabin in the Vermont woods is a pretty damn good way to do it."

"Regretting your life choices?" Lynn asked, pointedly.

Jerry snapped out of it. He smiled at her and hugged her. "Of course not. I wouldn't trade this life for any other. But what thinking man doesn't dream of a life of solitude, alone with his thoughts, from time to time?"

Jerry gave Lynn the side-eye to see if she was buying it. Based on the expression on her face, she was not.

"But still, you know big things, right? Natural disasters, scandals, new inventions, things like that. So, what about—"

Scott held his hand up. "Nope. Doesn't matter what you're going to ask. I'm not going to tell you. Believe me, you don't want to know what's coming. It kind of sucks the air out of the moment."

"You're right. Life is for living in the moment. Thinking too much about the future steals the happiness away from the now."

"I lived like a hermit in that life, because I just wanted to study where crimes had happened, and decide if I could stop them or not.

I ignored things like robberies and what not. People can always get more stuff, more money. I wanted to be there when something horribly undeserved and unfair happened. Like happened to me when I was a kid."

Jerry and Lynn exchanged a puzzled glance.

"When I was ten, my father shot my mother with my little sister and me in the house, then shot himself. That's how we came to live in Evansville. Our grandparents came and got us and brought us home."

"Wow, okay," Jerry said. "And if someone had been waiting in the bushes outside your house when you were ten years old and killed your dad, things would have been better."

"I sure think so. No way to know for sure, of course, but my mom would probably still be alive. It would have been terrible in the moment, losing my dad, but our house was always filled with so much anger and violence, I think it would have been a relief just to get away from that."

"You've been carrying a heavy load by yourself for a long time. No wonder your spirit is flagging. Working out with me at the dojo is helping though, right?"

"It is."

"Let's keep it up for a while. We love having you here with us. The kids love beating up on you every day." Jerry drummed his fingers on his knee. "I think this is something you shouldn't be tackling by yourself."

Lynn dropped her chin and looked at Jerry. "No." It wasn't loud, but that one word carried weight.

Jerry nodded. "You're right. Of course, you're right. I can't take off and leave everything we've built behind. But, we could get a little camper trailer and make a few trips a year to help out with the bad ones." He turned to Scott. "I'll bet you've had some tough ones, haven't you?"

Scott thought back to Charles Rodman Campbell and a few others. "Yeah, but so far it's been fine. There's a reason I am not married and don't have any kids. If I screw up and get killed, or arrested and sent to jail for the rest of my life, so what? It's all on me. Fair enough."

"How far ahead do you know these events?"

"2001."

Werbeloff whistled. "And you've got things you want to change all the way up until then? How in the world do you remember all that?"

"I've got a system, and a damn good memory. Thank you for the offer to keep letting me stay here and work out with you at the dojo. I'd like to take you up on it for a few months. That would feel good, if I'm not imposing too much."

"We'd love to have you here," Lynn reiterated.

"Good enough. I'll stick around for a while, then. In a few months, I think I'll take a trip back up to Maine."

Chapter Fifty

Scott fell into a routine, which was something he had been missing in his life for a long time. If the dojo was open, he went in with Jerry and helped with whatever he could. He worked his body hard, which freed his mind to see things from different perspectives.

Three nights a week, he spent the evening with Cheryl, Mike, and the kids. He got to know his niece and nephews better. Well enough that he knew he would miss them when he was gone. It was the same with the Werbeloff kids, not to mention Jerry and Lynn themselves.

Scott was tempted to find a little place, maybe use his VA loan to buy a house, and settle down. One night, as he was lying on the cot in the Werbeloff's garage, he got his notebook out and reviewed the crimes of the late 20th century. There had been a gap of seven months between the John Lennon assassination and the next event on his calendar. Soon enough, though, he knew he would be needed somewhere else. If he didn't go, someone would die, and he would feel responsible.

In mid-April, he was having dinner at Cheryl and Mike's house when the evening news announced from the other room that John Lennon had died.

The adults all moved to the living room to hear the details, which were sketchy at best. Essentially, Lennon had suffered a heart attack that morning in his apartment at the Dakota and he couldn't be revived. As the newscaster read the story, they showed footage of the night someone had attempted to kill him. In the background of that shot, talking to a police officer, was Scott McKenzie.

Cheryl hugged Scott close and said, "I'm sorry, Scotty."

"Better this than him being gunned down a few months ago, right?"

The revelation hit Scott hard, though he didn't want to admit it in front of his sister.

I keep swimming, constantly swimming, like a shark. I never stop to look back and see if what I am doing is actually helping anyone. I think it's time to do that, if I can.

The next day, he begged off of going to the dojo with Jerry and instead went to the Evansville library.

Once there, he had a difficult time deciding where to begin. There was no Internet to search, of course, and the microfiche was of only limited help. The Evansville Library System was good, but it wasn't world-class. They had the Indianapolis Star on microfiche and a subscription to the New York Times and Washington Post, not to mention Time and Newsweek, but Scott needed to drill down further.

After a frustrating few hours chasing information that wasn't there, he changed tactics. He began searching the way he had in his previous life, when he was trying to decide on what crimes to stop before they occurred. As he looked back over the previous months and years, he naturally discovered that the people who would have been famous—Ted Bundy, John Wayne Gacy, the BTK Killer—were nowhere to be found. What disturbed him, though, was that there were a number of people that would have crossed his radar, but hadn't.

There was a serial killer in Florida who had killed at least seventeen victims. He had been caught in 1979 and was currently on trial for his life.

I know I would have put him on my list. So what does that mean? Is there so much evil in the world that when one serial killer is disposed of, another will pop up to take his place?

The more he looked, the more he saw the same. Killers that would have easily made his list, but who he knew nothing about.

Is that the way it is, then? No matter what I do, the world, the universe, balances itself out? If I take out one, another pops up somewhere to take his place? Or, would these killers have come about anyway in this existence? I know I am changing things in this world by what I am doing, but I hope it is for the better. There's no way to be sure, is there?

IN MID-MAY, SCOTT DID something he had never done before. He purposefully returned to the scene of his crime. His very first crime, in fact—Waterville, Maine.

He had one last dinner with Cheryl and Mike, then hugged and said good-bye to the Werbeloffs. He packed his few belongings into his backpack, including the karambit and telescoping baton, grabbed his jo and walked through town to the train station.

Just as he had long ago, he caught a train to Chicago, then on to Philadelphia and up to Portland, Maine. Again, he perused the classified ads and bought a used car—this time a 1976 Chevy Nova—and drove to Waterville.

As he made the short drive, he remembered how he had felt when he had last made this same drive—uncertain, nervous, wondering if he could go through with the life he had planned. Now, almost seven years later, he knew the answer to that question. He could, and he had. Now he wanted to see the results of what he had done.

He wasn't certain how he would do that, but he knew he could accomplish it better on the scene than he could from far away. If nothing else, he would have access to the local newspaper again.

Scott knew he was running something of a risk by showing his face in Waterville again. To lower the risks, he had let his hair grow long and shaggy. He had let his beard grow out. In addition, he knew that the previous seven years had been hard on him. He guessed he might look fifteen years older than he had in 1974.

He also stayed in a different motel, on the other side of town from where he had stayed his last trip through.

First thing the next morning, Scott went back to the Waterville Library. Same building, same smell of books, different librarian.

Scott went to the area where they kept the last few months of the Waterville Morning Sentinel. He intended to start with the most recent issue and page through, again not sure of what he was looking for, but believing he would know it when he saw it.

On the front page of the Local section of that day's paper, there was an announcement about the graduation ceremony for Waterville High School, Class of 1981. The ceremony was to be held in the high school gym and the public was invited. There would be speeches from the pastor of the local community church, an address from the mayor, and the valedictorian, Brenda M. Jenkins.

Jenkins? That's gotta be more than a coincidence. And valedictorian? Pretty damn good. That's one speech I'd like to see. But do I dare? Her mother will surely be there. Would she recognize me after all this time? The last time she saw me, I was dodging her gunshots.

Scott flipped idly through the rest of that day's paper and opened another, but his heart wasn't in it. He realized that he had found what he had been looking for on the very first try. He returned the newspapers back to their proper location.

I'm gonna risk it.

Chapter Fifty-One

Walking into the gym the next night, Scott felt a little out of place. He had worn the best clothes he had with him, or that he owned, for that matter, but he still felt underdressed. His blue jeans, boots, and chambray work shirt stood out a little in the crowd of people dressed like they might be going to church.

Still, no one paid him a second glance. All sorts of people attend high school graduations—parents, relatives, friends, community leaders, and people that just want to be a part of a happening in their town. Scott did his best to look like one of those.

He accepted a program from a young volunteer when he walked in, then found a seat three-quarters of the way back and settled in.

The seats filled up quickly, and the ceremony started on time. The principal made a few opening remarks that stretched into a few-too-many opening remarks. The pastor of the local community church was much briefer in his blessing of the occasion. Scott approved and believed that brevity in these events was a positive.

The principal returned to the podium. He talked about what a special class this was for a few minutes, while the parents in the crowd glowed a little and silently agreed. After pumping up the crowd, he introduced Waterville High's Class of 1981 valedictorian, Brenda Jenkins.

A tall girl with long, straight, dark hair approached the podium. To Scott's eye, she looked nervous, but determined. The whole gym applauded for her, but two rows in front of Scott, and just to his right, a small group whooped, and a man whistled loudly.

Holy cow, that's got to be her family. He stared at the back of the head of the woman.

Scott's eyes flitted to the two other Jenkins children that sat with her.

Seeing them there, hair combed, dressed in their Sunday best to celebrate their sister's accomplishment, brought a tightness to Scott's throat.

Brenda Jenkins was not the most naturally gifted speaker, but she was sincere. Her speech was titled "The Gifts We Are Given," and it focused on finding blessings everywhere. It was a standard-issue graduation speech, with homely homilies and lessons well-earned.

Scott sat on the edge of his seat anyway, absorbing every word.

At the end of her speech, she paused, and looked up from her notes.

"I think most people know that my father was killed the summer before I went into sixth grade. It was the hardest thing I've ever lived through."

Scott leaned back slightly, glancing slightly to his left and right, wanting to see if anyone was looking at him. They weren't.

"Out of our greatest pain," Brenda continued, "can come new gifts. A few years after my father was killed, a new man came into our family and helped to heal us all. He has been a gift to all of us. I love you, Dad."

The man who sat next to the woman Scott guessed was Sylvia Jenkins took out a handkerchief and blew his nose loudly. People around him chuckled.

Brenda paused for a moment, then added, "You too, Mom."

A ripple of laughter spread through the gym.

The ceremony went on.

Scott would have liked to get up and make an escape before it was complete, but he didn't want to draw attention to himself, so he sat quietly.

Finally, it came time to hand out the diplomas. When each student's name was called, their own personal rooting section would stand for a few seconds and shout encouragement for them.

When Brenda Jenkins was once again called to the stage, the people two rows in front of Scott stood, applauded, and shouted her name.

Immediately, the next name was called and the two children and the man sat back down. The woman who had once been Sylvia Jenkins did not. She remained standing and slowly turned around until she was looking directly at Scott.

She held eye contact with him for several seconds.

Scott wanted to look away, but could not break her gaze.

She didn't look alarmed, or angry, or surprised he was there. It was as though she had simply sensed him.

Finally, she gave him the slightest of nods, then turned back around and sat with her family.

Scott's heart took a few seconds to start beating again. Again, no one around him seemed to notice anything.

That's impossible. How would she know I was here? She hadn't so much as looked this way all night, but she turned and looked directly at me.

Scott wiped a sudden burst of perspiration off his forehead.

But then, it didn't seem like she cared.

When the graduation ended with one last prayer, the families all drew together into tight bunches for photos taken with Kodak Instamatics or Polaroids.

Scott did an end around into the least-crowded area he could find, smiling and saying, "Excuse me," time and again.

He saw an opening and stepped toward it when he saw that the younger Jenkins children were surrounding Brenda right in front of him. They were smiling with excitement and happiness. Scott veered to the right and escaped into the cool night air.

Chapter Fifty-Two

Emerging from that high school gym in Waterville, Scott felt a bit like a new man. Seeing the reality of what he had made happen buoyed him.

I can't always assume that the ends justify the means, no matter what. But, seeing that family in there, alive and flourishing, at least this time, it feels like it did.

Scott never came to enjoy the mission he had set for himself in this lifetime. The work was too grim for a fundamentally gentle soul to find happiness in it. He did find satisfaction, though. In his travels through the country from that point forward, he did his best to look up people who would have been victims of horrible crimes. They lived normal lives, never knowing the fate they narrowly missed.

For the next four years, he crisscrossed the United States, eliminating those who would have killed innocent people whenever possible.

Right after meeting Joe Hart in New York, Scott had intended to pay him a visit in Middle Falls, Oregon. Four years later, he decided it was time.

He was in Arizona, having just dispatched a man who had been about to break into a family's home in Flagstaff and kill everyone inside. His plan, not to mention his life, was ended by Scott in an efficient fashion. The family slept inside, unaware they had been minutes away from death.

There was a gap in Scott's schedule, although he was feeling guilty that he hadn't managed to get to the Pacific Northwest to deal with the Green River Killer yet. He planned to stop and say hello to Joe, then travel north to stop Gary Ridgway from killing again.

He was in no terrible hurry, though, so he walked, hitchhiked, and caught rides on freight trains north. Oregon had the most liberal hitchhiking laws in the USA. It was the only state that allowed pedestrians and hitchers to walk on freeways, instead of having to congregate at entrance ramps.

If there was a long line of hitchers in one spot, Scott could simply walk on the side of the freeway, thumb out, until he got to a more agreeable spot.

It was odd for Scott to return to Middle Falls again. The infrastructure of the city hadn't changed that much since he had last seen it. A few new businesses and a new bridge, but it still matched the memories he carried with him.

He contemplated looking for the house where his father had shot his mother in 1958, but after so long, he couldn't even remember the name of the street. Instead, he found a phone booth, looked up Joe Hart's address and asked at a service station how to find it.

An hour later, he stood on the sidewalk in front of an impeccably well-maintained cottage in a quiet neighborhood.

I should have known you would live somewhere like this, Joe Hart. Surprised it's not made out of gingerbread.

Scott walked up the walk and knocked on the door. Immediately, barks and growls came from inside the house. A few seconds later, Joe Hart stood uncertainly in the doorway, a question on his face.

"Yo, Middle Falls boy."

Joe recognized Scott and his expression changed to surprise and delight. Joe stepped onto the steps and wrapped Scott up in a brother's hug.

A medium-sized dog with reddish fur and an infectious smile jumped up and down, wanting in on the action.

"Oh my God! The mysterious Scott McKenzie! The invisible man! I thought you were in the wind forever!"

In the wind. Well said, Joe. That's exactly what I have been.

"Hey, it takes a while to hitchhike to Oregon."

Joe tilted his head, which only served to highlight the terrible birthmark on the left side of his face.

"Four years?"

"Well, I may have had a couple of detours."

Joe nodded, opened the door wide and swept his hand into the house. "Come in, man, set your bedroll over there in the corner." Joe shook his head in disbelief. "I swear, I thought I'd never see you again."

"Ah, I thought I would make it here sooner, but as always, things pop up. I stopped in Indiana and saw my sister, and I had some business to attend to."

Joe looked interested, but didn't ask what that business was, exactly.

"The years slip away, that's for sure. I was so bummed when I woke up in the hospital, and you weren't there. I never got a chance to thank you for saving my life. And John's."

I think it's time to let him know I'm onto him. It'll be good to have another person to talk with about these things.

"I couldn't believe I almost missed it, when I got back. I am such a dummy."

"Yeah, you were definitely there in the nick of—wait, what? What do you mean 'missed it?' Did you know that was going to happen?"

You're quick, Joe. Don't miss a thing.

"Of course. And so did you. I could tell that right away. I've met a few others of us, though. I'm guessing maybe you haven't?"

Joe opened his mouth to speak, thought better of it and shut it. A moment later, he repeated that process.

"From the expression on your face," Scott said, "I'm guessing you haven't run into many, or maybe even *any* other people like us."

"I met one lady. In a library. Her name was Veronica. I was searching for anyone else who was going through this. She was about to *reset* her life, though, and she wouldn't stay and talk to me. That's been more than five years, so I thought I was never going to meet anyone else going through the same thing. So, you were in New York just to save John's life then?"

You and I weren't the only ones there to do that, but no need to complicate things any more.

"Just like you, brother. It's what I do. Or, at least, what I've done."

Scott took off the cap he was wearing and showed Joe his hair, which had already begun to turn gray.

"I'm getting old. I've decided to do my best to ride this life though to the end. There's only so many things I can change, but I'm getting to as many as I can."

Joe looked thoughtful and Scott recognized a familiar sadness in him.

"I wanted to do the same—do things that changed the world and made it better. I have a hard time remembering what events happened when, though. I can never be sure when and where I need to show up. Do you have some kind of super memory or something?"

"No, not at all. I spent quite a few lives indulging myself. When you find out there's no real consequence to your actions, it can make you into a bit of a prick. It certainly did me."

Scott smiled ruefully at the memory of so many wasted lives.

"Eventually, I got all that out of my system and figured out that maybe the best way to help myself was to help others. I spent an entire life reading through newspapers and magazines, looking for things I wanted to change. A mother drowning her children in Tennessee. A father murdering his whole family in Maine. Serial killers. That sort of thing. Then, I memorized the list and started over."

Chapter Fifty-Three

"By 'started over,' you mean..." Joe mimicked cutting his own throat.

"Yep. Exactly. I've done that so often, it didn't bother me. It's not suicide, it's just starting over. Or, resetting, as the woman you met in the library called it." He paused, thoughtfully, staring at his shoes. "I was pretty messed up when I got back from the war. I challenge anyone to live in a VA hospital, in the conditions we did, and not end up a little crazy. If the war didn't do it to you, that place sure did. Also, living a couple of dozen lifetimes helps a lot. It took me a long time to get some distance from all that, but I've got my feet under me now."

Joe sat down suddenly on the sofa. "Holy buckets, Scott. You are rocking my world. Two dozen lives? I'm on my third, and I lose track of things. I have so many questions! How old are you when you start over each time? Don't you ever get confused about what's happened before, and what's happening in this life?"

Scott held his hand up, looking for a pause in the rapid-fire questions.

"I wake up not long after I got my honorable discharge and I was out of that hell hole of a hospital. If I woke up further back, and I had to spend that year there again, I don't think I would have ever done it a second time. Of course, if I went a little further back, I could have chosen to head for Canada and saved myself the trauma of the war. The hell of it is, I wake up on the day after my grandmother dies. For my sister and my Gramps, it's like she's just died, but for me, she's been gone for lifetimes."

Joe found his feet again and wandered out into the kitchen. "Want something to drink?"

Scott waved him off and said, "No, I'm good."

Joe came back into the living room with a glass of iced tea tinkling in his hand.

"So do you interfere in these bad things happening, then just disappear like you did in New York?"

"That's the plan, but it doesn't always work out that way. Sometimes, people get suspicious about how I happened to be in a particular place at a particular time. That scene at the Dakota was a little different. Most of the things I do aren't high profile like that. I had intended to jump into action that night, when I realized you were there to do the same job. But, I was prepared just in case."

Joe dropped his eyes to the floor. "After I blew it."

"Don't be so hard on yourself. The first time I tried to do something like that, I blew it. The guy killed me and I had to start over again. But you? You didn't hesitate. You jumped right into the line of fire. I should have been there, then you wouldn't have been shot."

"But, do your changes stick? I mean, if you save someone, they get to live out their normal lives?"

"That's the way it's been every time I've been able to check, anyway—with the possible exception of John Lennon, that is. Why?"

"Because I changed two events. I saved John Lennon and two friends. Then, they all three died on the same day, less than a year later. I can't figure out why the people that I saved died again right away, but the people you save don't."

That's interesting. He's right. He makes changes and the universe seems to push back. I make changes and people get to go on living. Why would that be? Unless...

"Maybe I've found my calling, and yours is to be something else. I think if God, or the universe, or whatever machine is out there, running things, didn't want me doing this, the same thing would have happened to the people I saved."

Scott watched Joe turn that over in his mind, find some truth in it. He abandoned that line of questioning. "So, what are you planning on doing next?"

"I'm not sure where I'm going next. I know who the Green River Killer is, and if I don't do something about it, he's going to keep going for a long time."

"How you going to do that?"

How much do you want to know about what I do, Joe? You're pretty innocent, and it's best that you stay that way.

"Haven't decided yet. I could hang out on his hunting grounds and hope to get lucky, or I could put together a few reasons why I know it's him and take it to the King County Sheriff up there. He's a tricky one though. He lived in the shadows, so it's harder for me to catch him in the act. Ted Bundy was easier."

"Ted Bundy? He's one of the big ones."

"You've heard of him, right?"

"Of course. Everyone's heard of him. Mark Harmon played him in that made for TV movie, he's famous."

"Not anymore."

"What do you mean?"

"I mean we are well after the time he stopped killing in our other lives, right? He should be famous. But, ask anyone you know if they've ever heard of him. I guarantee you they haven't."

Scott saw understanding come over Joe. "I get it. No one has heard of him, because you stopped him before he became well-known, right?"

Scott nodded and smiled.

"What did you do?"

"Do you remember when he abducted and killed two women at Lake Sammamish?"

"Of course. Anyone who lives in the Pacific Northwest would remember that. He had his arm in a cast, asked women to help him, then killed them."

"Right. Except this time, he didn't. Before I reset, I memorized the date he did that. Young Mr. Bundy didn't take anyone that day, but he got taken himself."

"You killed him?"

"Do you think anyone would miss him?"

"Maybe his family, but the world at large? No. Certainly not me. I know what he was capable of. How did you do it?"

"Certain stories are better left unsaid. I don't want to spoil your appetite."

"Speaking of which, it's getting close to dinner time." Joe walked into the kitchen again, pulled two steaks out of the freezer and set them to thaw. "Got time enough to hang around here for at least a couple of days? I've got a pretty nice little house in the backyard that you can stay in for as long as you want. It's not the New York YMCA, but it's not bad."

Scott leaned back in the chair and said, "Yeah, I think I could take a little time off the road. I've got some laundry that needs doing."

"Washer and dryer are right in the house. Come on, I'll show you. You can get unpacked while I get the barbecue fired up."

Chapter Fifty-Four

Joe let Scott into a fully-furnished little house that was completely contained in his backyard. Joe had said it had once been for the mother of the couple who he bought the house from. He had lived in it before he bought the cottage in front.

However he had come to it, the little house was nice. It was newer, but somehow it reminded Scott of his little cabin on the woods in Vermont. Except here, every right angle was straight. Maybe it was the feeling of solitude it gave him, like he was tucked away from the rest of the world.

It was just one bedroom, a living room, a small kitchen and bathroom, but the bath had a stackable washer and dryer. What else did a single man need?

It never took Scott long to unpack. How could it, when his entire wardrobe consisted of three pairs of jeans, a few shirts, half a dozen pairs of socks and underwear and not much more? In fact, he rarely unpacked. He preferred to live out of the backpack, which made for quick getaways when needed. He did appreciate the fact that he could get his laundry clean, though.

Scott had been on the road for a few consecutive days, so he grabbed a hot shower and felt like a new man.

Eventually, Scott wandered out into his front yard, which also happened to be Joe's backyard. Joe was already there, with a nice barbecue set up. He had something wrapped up in foil resting directly on the coals and two huge steaks sizzling.

"I knew this would get you out here."

"Smells good, brother."

"Want a beer?"

Scott shook his head. "Nah, I don't do so well with that stuff. That was my downfall quite a few times, along with some worse things. No more of that for me."

"Smart man. Problems with it ran in my family, so I avoid it too. I keep some for company, though. How about the more gentle beer, then? I've got root beer, and a few other pops in the house. Pick your poison."

"You know, a root beer sounds pretty damn good. Perfect with whatever you've got cooking there."

Joe stepped back inside for a moment then emerged with two bottles of root beer. He popped them open and offered one to Scott.

Joe tipped his as a toast. "To friends."

"I agree. To friends. I don't have a lot of them. Being a vagabond crime fighter, moving from state to state, doesn't allow you a lot of time to develop friendships."

Joe opened the lid of the barbecue and turned the steaks.

He pointed to a couple of lawn chairs with a TV tray between them. "Here, take a load off. I never did get a chance to thank you for saving my life. The guy was drawing down on John, and I have no doubt I would have been next. There would have been two dead bodies at the Dakota that night instead of just one."

"It was nothing. Seriously. If the roles were reversed, tell me you wouldn't have done exactly the same thing."

"Oh, sure, if I could have, but I think you were better prepared. No one ever told me—what did you use to break his arm? Some kind of Special Ops Jiu-Jitsu or something?"

Scott smiled. "I am no kind of special operative. I was regular army. It was my trusty twenty-four inch collapsible baton. It packs a wallop. Perfect for the vigilante on the go. My adrenaline was pretty high that night, so I might have used a little more force than was absolutely necessary. I heard his radius break on the first swing. Whatever happened to him, do you know?"

"He's locked up in some mental hospital. I've got a connection with a few of the police officers who responded that night. They told me they'd let me know if he ever got out." Joe looked wistful. "That doesn't matter as much, now that John's gone. That was my worry—that he'd try to get to John again."

"No way for us to know what happens now. Everything with him will be different."

"John recorded one of my dad's songs, you know."

"I know. I was eating lunch in a diner and heard Kasey Kasem talking about it on *American Top 40.* That's a pretty cool story."

"I'd like to split the proceeds of the royalties from the song."

Would that be good? To profit from this? It would make life easier. I could maybe buy a new pickup or Jeep instead of the beaters I usually drive. It wouldn't feel right, though. That's not why I'm doing this.

"Nope, no need. You keep all the money and the worry. I'll take my freedom and happiness."

"You're a wise man. Just know that the money's not going anywhere. If you need it, let me know. One thing's for sure—it woulda meant the world to my dad. It does leave me with a little problem, though. I am the sole heir of my dad's estate, and all those royalties are still coming in. There's money in the bank that I have no idea what to do with. I wanted to give half of it to you, but now you say you don't want it either. Are you sure I can't change your mind?"

"No, I won't change my mind. Hey, you burnin' those steaks, or just cooking them?"

Joe opened the barbecue to a rush of smoke. He grabbed the steaks and smacked them onto a plate. "Soup's on."

"I am ready. In fact, I was ready when I first smelled the steaks. I might be a little past ready now."

"Would you like some steak sauce?"

Scott made a face. "I feel no need to insult the cook with that."

"Medium-rare okay?"

"Quit kidding around and give me the damned steak before I have to go get my baton."

Joe raised his hands in surrender. "Okay, just kidding around. Let's eat!"

For the next fifteen minutes, they ate in silence while they watched the sun set.

While he ate, Scott let Joe's problem roll around in his mind.

What would I do, if I had more money than I knew what to do with? It's a lot of money, but not enough to change the whole world. It won't end hunger or cure cancer or any Miss America speech like that. But, it could make a difference. And I know who deserves to get a better shake.

"If you're still looking for a way to unload some of that money, I think I've got an idea."

"If you're serious, I would love that. I do my best to ignore the pile of cash accumulating in my bank account. If I could, I'd rather do something useful with it."

Scott McKenzie suddenly looked very pleased with himself.

I don't have a lot of great ideas, but I think this is one.

Scott leaned forward in his lawn chair, excitement suffusing his face. "There are a lot of vets who haven't had the benefit of a few dozen lives to get their heads screwed on straight."

Joe nodded. "I can't imagine what you and everyone who fought over there went through."

"Right. I could tell you horror stories all day. Wiping out villages, killing kids when we thought we were only hitting the enemy, things worse than that. But, none of those stories will capture what it was like to actually be in the shit there. Vietnam was the last time the U.S. forced young men to join. We ruined a big chunk of a generation by doing so. A lot never came back, but those who did were never themselves again. The rates of mental illness, suicide, and homelessness for veterans is astronomical."

Joe was leaning forward now, too, so close to Scott their knees were almost touching. "So, that's an area of need. I know the government has programs for vets. Education, home loans, medical care, disability checks. What's missing?"

"Government programs are fine for broad brush areas like that. But, the truth is, a lot of vets slip through the cracks. I've been wandering around America for quite a while now, and I see them in every city. I hate to say it, but some are so lost, I don't know if they can ever find their way back. But there's a whole group that's wandered off the path a little. I think the right kind of helping hand could make all the difference."

As the impact of the idea hit Joe, he leaned back to take it all in. "I like it. What kind of specific thing are you thinking about?"

"Maybe some kind of housing, where a vet could come and spend a week, or a month, or whatever's necessary. It would need to have things to keep them busy. It would be good if there was a therapist or two that would be available if and when they were ready to talk."

Joe looked up at the darkening sky. The clouds had parted and there was a patch of clear sky where bright stars were twinkling.

"You done with your dinner?" Joe asked.

"Unless you want me to eat the plate."

"Let's go inside and sit down and hash things out. I already have a million questions."

Chapter Fifty-Five

Scott and Joe sat at the kitchen table for hours, trying to get a handle on what this project actually looked like.

Eventually, the little red dog, who Scott learned was named Jenny, quietly laid her head on Joe's knee.

Joe laughed a little. "She's reminding me that it's past time for her walk around the neighborhood so she can smell whatever secret messages the other dogs have left for her. Wanna come on the walk with us?"

"Of course. I need to do about ten miles to work off that steak you fed me. Let's go."

Spring evenings can be chilly in western Oregon, but this night remained warm. Scott didn't walk Jenny on a leash, but just opened the door and let her out. She knew their route and Scott and Joe followed along behind.

As they walked, the two men quietly batted ideas back and forth about the upcoming project to help out veterans. The whole plan began to take shape in their minds.

They had walked half a mile from Joe's house when Scott looked up and stopped cold.

They were in front of a one-story house with a small porch off the front door and decorative shutters on the windows. It was a cute house and looked like most of the other homes in the neighborhood.

"When were the houses in this neighborhood built?"

Joe had to focus on the question, as his mind had been on what they had been talking about a moment before. "Ummm, I think most of this neighborhood was built for families of men returning from World War II. So, maybe late forties? Why?"

Scott stared at the little house. If he had been asked if he might recognize his old home, he would have said no. That was a long time ago. Many lifetimes, literally.

He would have been wrong. "Is there still a little park up ahead on this street? Swings, and teeter totters and things like that?"

Joe reconnoitered where they were and said, "Yeah. How in the world would you know that? Did you walk through here on the way to the house today?"

Scott shook his head. "No. It doesn't matter."

They started to walk again, but twice Scott looked at the little house, with its porchlight on, looking absolutely non-threatening in every way.

That house was the stuff of my nightmares for so many years. Seeing it from this perspective, I can see it for what it is—an ordinary house where something extraordinarily bad happened. Nothing more.

Joe, who had been chattering a mile a minute about their new project, stayed quiet and let Scott have his thoughts.

I was a child. Ten years old. The two of them picked their own path to that moment and there was nothing I could have done about it. I think I can let that go, now.

Scott flashed a little smile at Joe—a thank you for the break in their conversation while he kept his own counsel. "So, do you have a place here in Middle Falls where we can put this whole thing?"

THE NEXT MORNING, SCOTT woke up a few minutes before 6:00 a.m. He had never learned to sleep late, no matter where he was.

He found a bookshelf in the living room and riffled through the books until he found one by Kurt Vonnegut that he hadn't read—*Breakfast of Champions*—and sat down to read. At a more civilized hour, he poked his head in through Joe's backdoor and smelled coffee brewing.

"Come in, no need to knock!

They looked through the notes they had scrawled the night before and came to a conclusion. This project was too big for both of them. It required skills and expertise neither of them possessed.

Scott leaned back in his chair. "I love that we're doing this. I can't imagine all the good we are going to do for the people who deserve it. But, there's a reason I'm not a middle manager in corporate America somewhere. As much as I love this project, overseeing a lot of details just isn't me."

Joe chewed on his pen. "It's not really me, either. I've got a high school education. We need to bring in people to help us. A project manager. A lawyer to help us with all the legal stuff. Luckily, this is one place where having a big bank account will help."

Joe walked over to the wall phone and dialed a number he had written on his pad. He waited a few seconds, then said, "Hello, this is Joe Hart. I'm in need of some legal advice on a project I'm preparing to launch, and I wonder if your firm handles that type of project?"

Two minutes later, they had an appointment with a local attorney named Ben Jenkins for that afternoon.

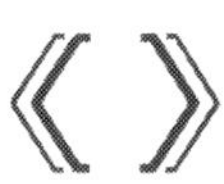

BY THE TIME THEY HAD finished with that appointment, they had retained Jenkins—who, it turned out, had gone to high school with Joe—and they had a recommendation for a project manager.

They met with the potential project manager—a young woman with a penchant for organization named Samantha Straley—for dinner the following night and both knew she was a perfect fit.

That left Joe as the man with the vision of the project and Sam Straley as the woman in charge of everything else. It also left Scott at loose ends.

He stayed in the comfortable little mother-in-law in Joe's backyard for six weeks. He enjoyed the time there. It was nice to have someone who knew who and what he was. They had coffee together every morning and dinner together most every night, but Joe instinctively left Scott alone for long stretches of every day.

Still, Scott wasn't used to staying around in one place for long, and he did feel the pull of the road.

One morning in early July, as they sat drinking their morning coffee, Scott said, "I've gotta head out, brother. I haven't been in one place this long in years, and my feet are itching for the open road."

Joe glanced at the back door and saw Scott's backpack was there.

"You're not gonna leave me to do this all alone, are you?"

"Absolutely not."

"Good," Joe said. "I thought you were serious, hauling your bug out bag around with you like that."

"Oh, I'm serious about leaving. But, you won't be alone, and you know it. You are the money and idea man. Sam is the person that actually does all the work. Happily, that means you don't need this old soldier."

"Damn. I was hoping you were going to hang around through the duration of the project."

"This project is bigger than both of us. It's going to take years. No insult intended to the tiny hamlet of Middle Falls, Oregon, but if I had to stay here until then, I'd be crazier than I am now. It's not my nature to stay in one place this long."

"Tell me that you'll at least check in, so I can tell you all the ways I'm messing up."

"Deal."

Scott set his empty cup in the sink and headed toward the front door. He was never one for long good-byes.

"Hold on, brother," Joe said as he grabbed Scott in a bear hug. "Don't stay gone too long, all right?"

Scott gripped Joe on the shoulder. "I won't. I'm going to be out there, scouting for our first customers, remember?"

Joe nodded. "You're right. That was our plan."

"For now, though, I've got a few people on my list I want to get to before I get too old to wield this baton. Right now, a certain Green River Killer should be looking over his shoulder, because I'm coming for him."

Chapter Fifty-Six

In the life Scott used as a baseline for all his missions, Gary Ridgway, also known as the Green River Killer, had been actively killing women throughout the eighties and nineties. However, he hadn't been arrested for his crimes until 2001. Scott had died before Ridgway had pled guilty to forty-eight murders in exchange for not receiving the death penalty, so he had limited details.

He knew his name and what he looked like, though, and the approximate area in Puget Sound where Ridgway lived. Scott had been to the area so often, he had become comfortable with navigating the area.

Ridgway had a familiar *modus operandi.* He had lured prostitutes along Highway 99 south of Seattle into his vehicle, then strangled them. He counted on the fact that when sex workers disappeared, they were less likely to be noticed and reported. It wasn't unusual for days or weeks to pass before someone reported the murdered women as missing.

Scott thought it would be good to have a vehicle, so he stopped in Olympia, Washington's state capital, and bought a 1977 Chevy Luv pickup. It was small, dinged-up, and somewhat underpowered, but it would serve his needs nicely.

He drove north from Olympia, through Lacey, then Tacoma. He pulled off Interstate 5 at Auburn, a sleepy little town that would eventually become one of many bedroom communities of Seattle. He stopped at a gas station and filled up. While he was there, Scott tore the page out of the South King County phonebook that had the listing for Gary Ridgway.

Scott wasn't familiar with the address, or the area around Auburn, but he wasn't in an incredible hurry. He had been bedded down in one spot for a month and a half. He was enjoying the freedom of being in the wind, as Joe Hart had said.

It got dark before Scott found the address, so he retreated to a busy street he had passed a mile back that had a lot of fast food franchises and a few inexpensive motels. He checked in and noted for the thousandth time that all crappy motel rooms looked the same. Cheap television on an equally cheap dresser, a bed covered in a glossy bedspread that repelled stains and with sheets and pillowcases that smelled strongly of bleach. Although they were thousands of miles apart, the myriad motels he stayed in had taken on the feeling of home in this lifetime, and he was glad to have it.

The next morning, he had breakfast at the Denny's down the street from his motel and read the newspaper. An article buried in the local news section mentioned that another body had been found in a remote area. It was attributed to the unknown person known as The Green River Killer.

Unknown to everyone else, but not to me.

After breakfast, he drove the Luv to the quaint downtown area of Auburn. There was a used bookstore there. Although Scott loved to while away the hours at bookstores, this time he was looking for something specific.

An older lady that might have been the spiritual twin of Greta back in Waitsfield, Vermont, sat behind the counter, sorting books out of a brown paper bag. She peered at Scott over her half-spectacles and said, "Can I help you?"

"I'm new to the area and I find myself getting lost. I've got a state map, but that's not helping me. Have you got something that's got the local streets on it?"

"Of course," she said with a slight groan as she pushed herself off her stool. "You need a Thomas Brothers Guide." She glanced at Scott. "Never heard of Thomas Brothers? Huh. They've been around forever. Or, sixty years or more, I guess, which counts as forever in these times."

She walked to a spinning rack of oversized books and plucked one from the top row. She handed it to Scott. "9.99, and it's got both King and Pierce counties in it. Can't go wrong."

"Well, I seem to keep coming back to the area for business, so it's worth the investment," Scott said as he laid the map book on the counter next to the cash register.

The older lady punched some keys on an old-fashioned cash register and said, "Ten seventy-nine." She glanced at the ten-dollar bill Scott was offering, then back at him. "Got to pay the Governor, you know."

"Right, right, of course! Scott pulled an extra dollar from his wallet and handed it to her. He walked out of the bookstore into typical western Washington weather—cool, misty drizzle. He hurried to the cab of the pickup and flipped open his new purchase. It didn't take him long to figure out how it worked. A listing of all streets were in the back, along with what map pages they appeared on.

Within thirty minutes, he was parked across the street from the house listed for Gary Ridgway in the phone book. It was a smallish house, one story, one-car garage. There were no cars in the driveway and no lights on inside.

Scott sat watch on the house all morning and afternoon with no luck. The house was located in a rural part of town, so there weren't a lot of inquisitive neighbors out walking their dogs and wondering who he was and why he was there.

Scott's patience was rewarded at 5:45, when an old pickup pulled into the driveway. Scott slipped low in his seat so he could barely see over the steering wheel. Gary Ridgway emerged from the truck, glanced around, unlocked his front door, and disappeared inside.

I've got the right place. I know he was married to three different women, but I don't know when. I don't want to go charging in and find him enjoying a cozy domestic scene with his wife and scare her half to death.

Scott sat and watched the house for another hour, but nothing changed. Finally, he started the Luv and eased away from his parking spot. He drove to a little café for dinner, then returned. Still no change.

For the next three days, Scott drove by the house at odd hours. He never saw another vehicle besides Ridgway's pickup, and he never saw another person.

Over the weekend, Ridgway's schedule became more unpredictable, coming and going at odd hours, which concerned Scott. No one knew exactly where the Green River Killer had taken his victims, but one popular theory was that he had brought many of them to his home and killed them there.

Scott decided to stakeout the house and follow him if he left. He parked a block-and-a-half up from Ridgway's house and kept an eye on his truck through binoculars. Time dragged and eventually Scott nodded off. When he woke with a start, the pickup was gone.

He glanced at his watch. Just past midnight.

Where does your friendly neighborhood serial killer go in the middle of a Saturday night? Cruising for victims, probably.

Kicking himself, Scott threw the Luv into gear and drove down the hill in search of Ridgway. After a few miles, he realized it was a lost cause. He pulled into a 7-11, got a large coffee, and returned to his same parking spot.

Hours passed, but Scott didn't nod off again. At a quarter past four, Ridgway's pickup rolled up the road and into his driveway. The truck sat idling for two, three, four minutes. Finally, Ridgway and a woman dressed in high heels, a tube top and a neon green miniskirt emerged and went in the front door.

Chapter Fifty-Seven

Adrenaline spiked through Scott McKenzie. He sat bolt upright.

Shit! This wasn't the way I wanted this to go down.

He fumbled around in the cab of the truck, grabbed his pack, then ran for the house.

He slowed as he approached the front door. The porch light was on, but the bulb was weak and barely illuminated anything. Scott melted into the shadows along the side of the house. He tried to look in the windows, but the blinds were pulled snug.

He reached the front door and gently tried the knob. Locked tight.

Scott glanced around, saw all was quiet in the neighborhood. He slunk along the deep shadows that ringed the house and ran into a tall cedar fence that marked the back yard. The gate had a piece of string hanging through a hole. He tugged on it and the gate latch clicked open. He hurried through and found the back door.

It was locked as tight as the front door. Scott put his ear against it and listened, but heard nothing but silence.

Nothing for it. He might be killing her right now. Gonna have to break it down.

Scott unslung his backpack and set it beside the door. He backed up four paces, then ran forward and slammed his shoulder into the center of the door.

The frame split slightly, the blow reverberated through the entire house, but the door held. Scott bounced off and fell onto the muddy ground.

Before he could pick himself up, the door flung open and an enraged Gary Ridgway screamed, "What the hell is going on out here?"

Scott launched himself from his kneeling position. His shoulder hit Ridgway dead center, driving him backward into the house. Scott's momentum carried him right along and they both landed in a heap in what turned out to be the laundry room.

They scuffled in the darkness of the room for a few seconds, then Scott was able to disentangle himself. He retreated to the back door and reached inside his pack. His fingers closed around his baton. He flicked it open and jumped back inside.

Ridgway was gone.

Scott charged after him, but the house was dark and he stumbled against a piece of furniture in the living room and went down in a heap.

A woman screamed, but Scott had no idea if it was because Ridgway was killing her or if she was afraid of Scott, the sudden intruder. Scott picked himself up, limping slightly and followed the sound of the scream.

He ran down a narrow hallway, seeking Ridgway. As he moved past an open door, Ridgway stabbed at him with a hunting knife, slashing at his side.

Scott cried out, but instinctively swung his baton, catching Ridgway flush in the face, shattering his glasses and smashing his nose.

Scott didn't wait to see how badly he'd been stabbed, but pressed his advantage. He delivered a vicious front kick that caught Ridgway in the groin. He fell to the ground and Scott was on him.

Ridgway was blinded by the blood spraying from his ruined nose, but he thrashed around under Scott's strong hold, desperately trying to break free.

Scott swung the baton, slamming it against Ridgway's head again and again.

Ridgway lapsed toward unconsciousness. That was the opening Scott needed. He unsheathed his karambit and slid it up under Ridgway's chin and into his brain. Warm blood sprayed over Scott's face. He jammed the knife up with all his strength, then rolled off him.

From the other room, he heard the woman's voice—loud and near-hysterical.

"I don't know what address I'm at. I'm at someone else's house." Her voice rose again, becoming almost unintelligible. "He's killing him, I can hear it!"

Scott walked out of the room, wiping his knife against his jeans and slipping it back into the sheath. He remembered his baton and turned around to retrieve it. It had rolled under a desk and he had to flip the overhead light on to locate it. He avoided looking at the corpse of Gary Ridgway and flipped the light back off.

He staggered back out of the room and waves of pain from the wound in his side washed over him.

He moved down the hall, leaving a long, bloody streak on the wall. The woman stared at him, covered in blood and panting. She opened her mouth to scream, but nothing came out. She ran for the front door, fumbled with the lock, then fled, high heels tapping a staccato rhythm against the sidewalk.

Through the open door, Scott heard the faraway wail of sirens. Someone in the neighborhood had heard the ruckus and called the police.

Scott wanted to go through the house and wipe down anything he might have touched, but he knew he was running out of time. He stumbled to the back door, grabbed his pack and hurried around to the open gate.

Scott moved as fast as he could to his pickup and jumped in the cab. He closed the door behind him and slunk down low in the seat.

The blue lights of a police car lit up the darkness as it flew up the hill and parked sideways across Ridgway's driveway. An officer sat inside his prowler for a minute, then emerged with a flashlight in one hand and the other resting on his gun.

Scott watched him approach the wide-open front door cautiously. He stood to the side of the light coming from inside, then called out, "Police!"

A moment later, he disappeared inside.

Scott turned the key and the Luv started on the first try. He shifted into first gear and coasted past the house as quietly as possible.

He checked his rear view mirror anxiously until he was out of sight of the blue flashing lights behind him. Before he got to the bottom of the hill, he saw more sets of flashing lights—a combination of red and blue this time—approaching him.

Before they reached him, he switched off his lights and turned into the driveway of a darkened house. He waited until the two squad cars and an ambulance had passed him, then got back on the road and drove to the motel.

Inside his room, he checked the knife wound, which was throbbing now. It was a stab wound, not a slash, so it was deep but only an inch or so wide.

During his vigilante years, he had been injured enough times that he always carried medical supplies with him. The lips of the cut were clean and needed stitches, but there was no way Scott was going to go to a hospital with a knife wound—especially when he had left the hunting knife at the scene. Knife wounds were reported, and there was every chance that someone would eventually put two and two together.

He gritted his teeth and dabbed an antibiotic ointment all around the wound. The bleeding had slowed to an ooze. He applied a double-folded bandage, then added several layers of medical tape.

Finally, he took an ace bandage and wrapped it all the way around him three times.

That should keep my insides on the inside and hopeful absorb any blood that makes it through the bandage.

He rolled up the bloody flannel shirt he had been wearing and stuck it inside a plastic laundry bag.

What he wanted more than anything was to lie down on the bed and sleep for twelve hours.

Self-preservation told him that what he needed to do was put as many miles as possible between him and the crime scene.

He popped three aspirin to help with the pain, checked out of his room and got back on I-5 heading south. He drove straight to PDX, the Portland, Oregon airport. Parking the pickup at a convenience store, Scott left the keys in the ignition and walked away.

No time to sell it, but this will be just as good. Someone will steal it within a few hours and it will be gone.

He grabbed a taxi to the terminal, bought a ticket to Chicago and collapsed into an uncomfortable chair until it was time for his flight.

Chapter Fifty-Eight

The next three years played out much like the previous ten. Scott spent most of his life on the road, doing his best to right the wrongs that he knew were coming. Spiritually and emotionally, he was more centered. He had made peace with his life's work, and he now had two home bases to work from—Evansville and Middle Falls.

When he got banged up from a confrontation, he made his way as quickly as he could to one of them. Both the Werbeloffs and Joe Hart became adept at sewing and bandaging him up.

Physically, he was starting to wear down. He had never fully recovered from the wounds he had suffered lifetimes earlier in Vietnam. Add in more than a dozen years of brawls with bad men who knew they were fighting for their lives and the picture becomes clear. Even when he wasn't recently injured, Scott walked with a limp and he woke up to an entire menagerie of pains every morning.

He looked over the remainder of his list and knew he would likely never get to all of them. In the end, the body could only do what it could before it broke down completely.

Each time he went to Middle Falls, he and Joe traveled to the edge of town where their dream project had taken physical form. When Scott had made the initial suggestion, he hadn't had a specific form in his mind, but long conversations with Joe had solidified the idea.

They had created a small village of its own, with tiny houses modeled on the guest house Joe had in his backyard. Those were for vets who needed solitude, peace, and quiet to get their heads straight. There were bunkhouses for those that desired company and socializing.

There was a huge community center with pool tables, card tables, an industrial kitchen, and a massive great room where everyone could gather to hear a speaker or watch a movie. There was also a counseling center, manned during the day five days a week, for those who wanted or needed someone to talk to.

Joe's favorite part was the no-kill animal center he had built right in the middle of the complex. It served a number of purposes. It saved animals and helped them find their forever homes, of course, but it did much more. It gave the vets who were staying there a place to work and bond with the animals. It also gave the townspeople of Middle Falls a reason to come onto the property and learn that it was a positive thing for their community.

It all sat on twenty wooded acres with walking paths, a duck pond, and benches to sit and contemplate the world.

The one thing Joe couldn't figure out was what to call the whole enterprise.

A few months before the place was ready to open, Scott took Sam aside for a meeting. They walked through the grounds, inspecting the finishing touches on the buildings and landscaping.

"Come up with a name, yet?" Scott asked her.

"Yeah, but nothing great. Nothing that quite fits." Sam shot a sideways glance at Scott. "You've got an idea, don't you? I know you."

"Joe's dad Rodrigo was a vet, you know. Korea."

"Right. He did mention that one night."

"So then, what about 'The Rodrigo Hart Oasis for Veterans.'"

Sam stopped. She stared up into the tops of the trees that ringed the project. "The Rodrigo Hart Oasis for Veterans. Scott, you are a certified genius."

"Nope. I have a lot of time to think when I'm traveling."

'I've been meaning to ask you. What do you do when you're traveling? What are you looking for?"

"Peace, love and understanding?"

"Okay, fine. Don't tell me. I still think you're a genius. And now *I've* got an idea. I'm going to put a little side project together and get a sign made up for the Oasis. We'll surprise Joe with it."

"*You'll* surprise Joe with it. Me? I'm hitting the road again. I think this place is about ready for some occupants, don't you? I'm gonna go look for them."

And that's exactly what he did.

As he had so often, he traveled to the four corners of the country, crisscrossing the middle states over and over. This time, instead of dealing out vigilante justice, he looked for veterans living on the fringes of society.

Unfortunately, they weren't hard to find. The difficult part was picking the right person. The truth was, some of the homeless vets were homeless by choice. They never felt like they fit in when they returned home, or they didn't fit in with their families, or a thousand other reasons. They chose to live without a roof over their heads every night and found a certain amount of freedom and contentment from the lack of commitment. On the other end of the spectrum were those who were almost beyond help—so mentally ill or drug-addicted that Scott knew a few weeks or a month at the Oasis wouldn't be much help.

He looked for people more in the middle. Vets who hadn't ever gotten a break, who had been abandoned by the system, but were still fighting to get back on their feet.

The only way to identify who was who was for Scott to live as they did. And so he did. He stopped flying, riding the bus, or staying in even the most inexpensive motels. Instead, he hopped freight trains, rode his thumb, and slept under the stars or tucked into a cramped space somewhere. The men and women who lived on the fringes of society looked out for each other and communicated through what they called the hobo network. Someone always knew something, or someone. Where to find a safe place to sleep, where the best place to hop trains was, or who might have an extra can or two of food.

When Scott found someone that he knew would benefit from a stay at the Oasis, he bought them a bus ticket to Middle Falls and gave them enough money to eat on the journey. He knew that some cashed the ticket in and smoked or drank the proceeds, and he was okay with that. He wanted to extend the hand of possibility to those who needed it. It was up to them whether they accepted the opportunity or not.

Enough did that a steady stream of "Scott's people" found their way to the Oasis. Word of Scott's largesse and scouting trips spread along the hobo network. No one knew his full name. They just called him the Angel.

Chapter Fifty-Nine

Scott enjoyed his scouting trips more than he ever had his other life's work, but he still did his best to combine the two.

By the spring of 1990, though, he was forty-one-years-old with the body of a seventy-year-old man. Sleeping in doorways or around a fire outside the city limits was fine, but he found he was having a harder time standing up straight after he did.

A reputation is a wonderful thing, though, and eventually word spread when he was in town and he found that he didn't need to actually bed down beside them every night. He knew he wasn't the only one who was hurting from that lifestyle, though, so that only increased his urgency in getting more people back to Joe, Sam, and the Oasis.

Eventually, Scott sent so many on that Joe and Sam had to apply for new permits and build more bunkhouses to accommodate the stream of veterans. They encouraged Scott's evangelical work, though, and told him they would keep building more buildings until they either ran out of space or money.

Whenever he needed a break, he headed back to Middle Falls and stayed at the Oasis. When Joe saw that Scott was returning regularly, he built him his own cabin, placing it inside the trees that ringed the buildings for a little privacy. Scott only asked for one thing—a front porch he could sit on like he'd had a lifetime before in Vermont. Joe was more than happy to accommodate the request.

The porch opened out onto a small meadow, then the tranquil duck pond. It finally felt to Scott like he was living his own Walden dream.

For the most part, Scott skipped the vigilante duties he had once embraced. His body was too broken to be able to do what he had once done.

Still, he kept his notebooks. Whenever something came up that he thought he could still handle, he left his little cabin in the Oasis and hit the road once more.

One of those happened in October, 1994. Joe and Sam gave Scott a ride to Portland, where he caught a flight to Charlotte, North Carolina. He left his weapons at home. He knew he wouldn't need them this time.

In Charlotte, he rented a car and drove a little over an hour to John D. Long Lake, a man-made lake in South Carolina. He drove around the lake, found the boat launch, and parked. He got out of his car and surveyed the surroundings. He hiked around until he found a spot where he could be essentially hidden from view, but could still see the boat launch.

He paced off the distance between his hiding spot and the launch. Seventy-five feet. He certainly didn't have sprinter's speed these days, but Scott judged he could run that far when called upon.

He drove to the nearby town of Union, and found a small motel.

Scott had hoped to combine this one last job with finding a few more lost souls for the Oasis, but as he drove around Union, he knew that was unlikely to happen. It was the kind of small town that took care of its own. It was far enough off the beaten path that it didn't attract a lot of itinerant vagrants.

He grabbed a burger at Dairy Queen and vowed to start eating better when he was off the road to stay. He knew he had a full day the next day, so he gratefully crashed in his little room next to the highway.

The next morning Scott was up early, as usual. He knew that what he was there for wouldn't happen until later, but not unlike his very first job, he felt nervous about this one. He stopped at a convenience store, bought two bottles of water, a sandwich and chips, and a cup of coffee to jump start his brain.

He drove back to the lake and looked around. He didn't want his car to be seen from the boat launch, so he drove it half a mile away and parked it in a spot that would look like someone had taken off for a hike.

He grabbed the equipment he had brought with him, along with his food and drinks, and hiked to the spot he had scouted out the day before.

By 11:00 a.m., everything was set up and in place. It was a Monday, exactly one week before Halloween, and the lake was deserted. Scott sat for hours, watching for vehicles, but aside from one pickup that cruised in then turned right around, there were none.

Finally, at 3:45, a maroon Mazda four door rolled in and came to a stop.

Scott took a deep, calming breath.

He moved to the edge of his cover and waited.

The car idled for several minutes, smoke curling up from its tailpipe. Finally, a young brunette woman opened the door. She leaned inside and fidgeted with something. Scott didn't hesitate. He began to run.

The woman stepped back from the car and stood mute while it rolled toward the lake, slowly picking up speed.

Scott sprinted. Through the back window, he saw the tops of two car seats.

The driver's door was still open, swaying as the car bumped over the approach.

Scott planned to get there before the car hit the water. He didn't make it.

The car slowed a bit as it hit the resistance of the lake and Scott managed to catch up. He dove for open door, leaped inside and slammed on the brake. Cold water rushed in and filled the front of the Mazda up over the seat. Scott jammed the car into Park, pulled the emergency brake, and turned to look in the back seat. Two boys, one almost a baby, the other only a toddler, were looking at him with wide frightened eyes. The youngest was crying.

Scott clambered out of the driver's side, making sure to unlock the back doors as he did. He threw the back door open and got the smallest of the boys loosened from his car seat. The older boy had somehow managed to get out on his own.

Scott did his best to smile reassuringly at them. He reached out his arms to the older boy. "Come on, champ. Let's get you out of there."

Scott's world turned upside down as the woman threw herself at him, beating at his face.

"What are you doing to my children! Help! Leave them alone! Police!"

Scott righted himself, picked the woman up, and threw her into the water. He knew she was desperate and didn't know what she would do next.

The oldest boy screamed "Mommy!" and tried to clamber across the seat. Water continued to rush in.

Scott grabbed both boys and hurried them up the launch to dry land.

The woman had picked herself up and chased after them.

She plucked the two boys up and screamed, "I'm going straight to the police!"

"No need," Scott said. He pulled the cell phone he had bought for the trip from the pocket of his coat. He had stored it inside a plastic zipper bag in case he had needed to go into the water. He opened the bag, dialed 9-1-1 and said, "Hello. I just watched a woman try to drown her two children in John D. Long Lake."

In the background, the woman was screaming hysterically.

"We're at the boat launch. Can you please send someone here immediately? I'm afraid she's still trying to hurt her children."

The woman had vented her hysteria and spoke more quietly. "They'll never believe you. Why would I do that? I'm going to sleep at home in my bed with my little boys, and you'll be spending the night in a jail cell."

"Anything's possible, but I doubt it." Scott reached up and touched his cheek. His fingers came away bloody.

One last war wound, I guess.

Almost immediately, the wail of sirens approached. Two local police cars came skidding toward them, tossing up a gravel rooster-tail.

The woman became hysterical again, pointing at Scott and screaming, "He hijacked us and drove my car into the lake. He tried to murder my children."

Scott stood quietly.

The first officer on the scene escorted the woman to his prowler with her two boys.

The second officer approached Scott. "Turn around and put your hands behind your back."

Chapter Sixty

Scott did as the officer asked.

The cop clicked the cuffs on him and in a low, reasonable voice, said, "Why don't you tell me what's happening here?"

"Sure. I've been here for a few hours. I was over there," Scott indicated his spot in the woods with a nod of his head, "taking some videos of the lake."

The officer looked at the spot Scott had indicated, then turned and looked at the lake.

"Not much going on here this time of the year. Why were you here, taking shots of the lake?"

Scott shrugged. "It's a hobby. Back at home, I like to put videotapes of peaceful scenes on my television and just let them play."

The cop squinted at him. He was used to be lied to.

"Uh huh. I don't suppose you happened to be running this camera when this all happened?"

"As far as I know, it's still running. You want to walk over and check it out?"

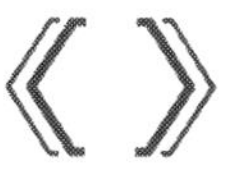

TEN MINUTES LATER, another half dozen vehicles had arrived at the scene. Two more local cops, two county sheriff's deputies, a South Carolina State Patrolman, and, for some reason, the local fire chief.

All of them gathered in a circle around the cop who had put the cuffs on Scott. That officer held Scott's camera out, with the small screen extended. He showed everyone else what Scott had shown him.

"I'll be goddamned," the cop who seemed to be in charge of the scene said. "Damndest thing I've ever seen." He looked at Scott, who was standing a few feet away from the circle of men, still wearing the handcuffs. The cop in charge, whose black name tag read "Rose," turned to the cop who had put the cuffs on Scott. "Bill, get those cuffs off of him."

Scott turned around and let the officer free him, then rubbed some circulation back into his wrists. "Thanks."

Officer Rose said, "I can't imagine what would have happened if you hadn't been here. Looks like she was fixin' to drown her kids. Damndest thing I've ever seen," he repeated.

Rose turned to look at the woman in the back of his car. She was holding the two children protectively against her.

"Bill, find out the name of her husband and how to get ahold of him. Then get him down here to get his kids."

Rose turned to Scott. "Are you passing through, or..."

"I'm staying at the Barkley Motel out at the highway."

"I'd appreciate it if you wouldn't mind staying around town for a few more days."

"I've got a ticket to fly home on Saturday. Do you think that will be a problem?"

"No, sir. What's on that tape of yours is pretty clear. I'm going to need that as evidence, of course. I'd just like you to stick around for a few days in case we have some more questions for you."

As it turned out, the officer named Bill knocked on the door to Scott's room the next morning.

"Officer," Scott said when he opened the door.

"Morning. Want a cup of coffee?"

"Always."

"C'mon, the department's buying. You can ride over to Margie's Café with me."

Once they were seated in a booth and each had a steaming cup of coffee in front of them, Bill spoke up. "You wanna tell me what you were doing out there yesterday?"

"I told you—just taking shots of the lake."

"Mmm-hmm. I watched that whole tape myself last night. It was the most boring hour of my life."

"Different strokes for different folks," Scott said with a shrug.

"I noticed something funny, though. It looked like you started running toward the car before it was obvious what was happening. It was almost like you knew exactly what was going to happen, and set that camera up right there to capture it all."

"How would I know that, do you think?"

Bill leaned back in the booth, studying Scott.

"No idea, and that's the worst part of it for me."

"Take a minute and think about what would have likely happened if I hadn't happened to have been standing right there. You saw the tape. She stepped out of the car and not only didn't help those kids, she was backing away from them."

"I'm glad you were there. You did the right thing, and you did it fast. But you know how sometimes you look at something, and it just doesn't all add up? That's the way this is." The cop poured some creamer into his coffee and stirred. "But, that's that. Just thought I'd ask." He looked at Scott with a keen eye.

Scott took a sip of his own coffee.

"In any case, the Chief wanted me to let you know that you're free to leave town. We might ask you to come back and testify at trial, but I've got a hunch once her attorney sees that tape, it'll never see the inside of a courtroom."

"Good enough. Tell the Chief thanks, and thanks for the coffee."

Bill offered to give Scott a ride back to his room, but Scott declined.

"It's not a bad day, and when am I ever going to be back in Union, South Carolina? I think I'll walk."

Scott checked out of his room and drove back to Charlottesville. He got another, somewhat nicer, room by the airport and waited for his flight to leave town.

He lay on his bed that night, thinking.

Wish more of these could have been like this, but most didn't present a bloodless solution like I saw here. I think this is it for me. A good way to go out.

Chapter Sixty-One

Back at the Oasis in Middle Falls, Scott fell into the rhythm of the next phase of his life. He still went out on the road, looking for veterans to offer a helping hand to, but those trips became less frequent with the passing years.

Something wonderful happened—the Oasis and its mission to help veterans took on a life of its own. Other wealthy people around the country saw the successes that they were having in Middle Falls and pledged money to build a similar village in their own community. Scott, Joe, and Sam took turns traveling to those towns and helping them get their own village for vets off the ground.

Meanwhile, word spread on the grapevine about these places where all vets could get a hand up. Whatever they needed—medical or dental care, counseling, or just a place to commune with other people who understood them—they found it at the Oasis. New people showed up every day, but new beds were constantly opened by those who felt like they were ready to face the world again. Somehow, it struck a balance and it worked.

Scott, meanwhile, spent a lot of time on his front porch, whittling, reading, and watching the raindrops fall. He spent some time each day in the community center, playing pool or just having coffee with people who got him.

The counseling center at the Oasis handled mental health needs for those who needed it most, but Scott found himself as a de facto counselor as well. There were a lot of men who wouldn't dream of walking into the counseling building and signing up for a session. But, they had no qualms about sitting down and talking things over with Scott.

In 1998, Joe and Sam invited Scott over for dinner at their house. They'd gotten married a few years before, to the surprise of absolutely no one. They had a daughter, Chandra, named after Joe's mother. Even as much as Joe gave away to fund the Oasis every year, they were still the wealthiest couple in Middle Falls.

They continued to live in the same little cottage that Joe had bought fifteen years earlier and showed no sign of moving anywhere else.

It was a gorgeous summer evening, and Joe had emphasized that they would be grilling steaks that night. Sam was good at almost everything, but the one exception was her cooking. Joe said that was how he managed to never gain any weight.

The three of them sat in the same backyard where Scott had first suggested the idea of the Oasis, ate steaks and once again had root beer to drink. Chandra lay on her stomach in the grass and watched the fish in the pond endlessly swimming.

"Things are going pretty good, don't you think?" Joe asked.

"Which makes me think there's another shoe to drop."

"No, not really," Joe said with a laugh. "A lot of the veterans we're seeing are getting older and older. Vietnam is fading further in our rear view mirror. Just want to let you know we've managed to buy the twenty acre plot next to the Oasis, and Sam and I have been planning."

"When you guys put your heads together, good things happen."

Joe reached his hand out to Sam sitting next to him. She held it with a smile.

"We're thinking we're going to need more medical facilities than the Oasis can handle. So, we're going to build a fair-sized hospital and staff it with doctors and nurses. We're going to have a wing that can help dementia and Alzheimer's patients, because there are so many vets living and suffering on the streets."

"Then, we're going to build our first section for women vets. They're out there, too, and there will be more coming," Sam added.

"Of course, of course. That's all so great. Plus, there are almost certainly more wars ahead." Scott glanced at Sam. He and Joe never talked about the future in any detail in front of her. "That'll mean more vets in need of us for many years to come. I'm glad you guys are young."

"Right," Joe said. "So, that means we're going to need even more barracks and individual houses for these people. It's all coming. We just wanted to let you know."

Scott had learned to keep his emotions in check. There hadn't been room for too many feelings in this life he had chosen for himself. Still, a growing sense of satisfaction spread through him. He looked toward the setting sun and said, "Man, I'm glad I wasn't ten seconds later getting back to the Dakota that night, or none of this would have happened."

JOE AND SAM'S PLANS for the adjacent twenty acres proceeded apace. No project that large ever happened quickly, but by 2001, the ground had been broken and once again new buildings were taking place.

When Scott was a year shy of the day he had died in his longest life, he went to the doctor to be tested. Sure enough, they found the earliest stages of prostate cancer. With the early discovery, it was treated and Scott was declared cancer free.

Scott hadn't shared with anyone what the day was that he had died in that previous life, but as it approached, he felt the old stirring to be on the road again. He borrowed one of the Oasis's vehicles and drove west to the Oregon coast. As the sun set on what had once been the last day of his life, he sat on a rock, staring out at the frothing Pacific Ocean.

Happy emancipation day to me. When I go to sleep tonight, that will be it. I won't have any idea what's coming next. No idea what technological advance or earth shaking news is ahead.

He took a deep breath of the immaculate ocean air and held it deep in his lungs.

And that's a wonderful thing.

Chapter Sixty-Two

The end of Scott McKenzie's life was quiet and drama-free, especially when compared to the events that had transpired earlier.

The older Scott grew, the more the violence and uncertainty of that part of his life faded into the background.

The last twenty-four years of his life were spent in service to others. In many ways, he became the patron saint of *The Rodrigo Hart Oasis for Veterans.* He was the constant face of the Oasis, walking the trails with his weather-beaten jo, beating newcomers at pool and rummy, and always having an ear to listen to anyone.

In early 2018, cancer returned to him, this time in a different form. He cooperated with the treatments for a few months because he was enjoying his life so much and didn't want it to end any sooner than it had to. Scott had little reason to fear death, although he had many questions about what might happen if he died of natural causes.

He got the chance to find out in the third week of September. The new *Scott McKenzie Hospital Oasis for Veterans* had been open and helping veterans for more than a decade. It was where he drew his last breath.

Scott was seventy years old and was surrounded by so many whose lives he had touched. His sister Cheryl, who he had once done his best to protect from the storms of their childhoods. Jerry and Lynn Werbeloff, who had been his constant friends for more than four decades. Joe and Samantha Hart, no longer young themselves, but still healthy and vibrant.

In addition, word had spread through the internet that the man once called *The Angel* was in his last days. Hundreds of veterans, many in a much-better place in their lives than they had been when they met him, came to pay their respects.

It meant everything to Scott to have a last chance to see so many of them, but it made it hard for him to focus on the job at hand, which was to die.

Finally, in the early morning of Friday, September 21, 2018, the ward was quiet. Machines hummed around Scott and his room was lit only by the green lights of the machines constantly taking his vitals.

Now is a good time. I'm tired of the pain and ready to leave.

He took a deep breath and slowly let it out.

It's been a good life.

Postscript

Scott McKenzie opened his eyes, mostly expecting to see his grandparents' old house in Evansville.

Instead, he was in an all-white room. Everything around him was blindingly white—the walls, the ceilings, the benches.

"Hello, Scott, my name is Shamus. Take a moment and get acclimated. When you're ready to talk, let me know."

Scott rolled his shoulders, flexed his legs. The pain that had been with him since the moment he had been shot in Vietnam was gone. He felt young and vital again.

He kept his own counsel for a few minutes, breathing in and out, peering around at the endless white.

Finally, he said, "Where am I?"

The disembodied voice said, "You are in the Universal Life Center. This is where all new transfers from Earth start out."

In a blink, a man sat beside Scott. He was slightly round, bald, and had the most devilishly sly eyes Scott had ever seen. Nonetheless, his face was split with a kind smile.

"It's a bit of a bear, this initial adjustment. I remember."

"So, you woke up here, too?"

"Oh, yes, we all did, at one time or another."

"We?"

"The Agents of Karma. We all work for the Karma Delivery Service. We've watched your life carefully. I'm here to offer you a position, if you want it."

Agents of Karma #1, available 2019.

The next book in the Middle Falls Time Travel series will be *The Reset Life of Cassandra Collins.* It is available for preorder here.[1]

Cassandra Collins is born into a privileged life as the youngest daughter of the wealthiest family in Middle Falls, Oregon. She finds there is a price to pay for privilege and safety, though. At the end of her life, she wishes that she had chosen another path.

When she dies, she wakes up in her eighteen year old body in 1968, able to make exactly that choice again. As in all Middle Falls stories, Cassandra's choices don't necessarily bring her the hoped-for results.

1. https://amzn.to/2D39mYG

The Reset Life of Cassandra Collins

Available December, 2018

THE
RESET
LIFE OF
CASSANDRA
COLLINS
A Middle Falls Time Travel Story
SHAWN INMON

1

Author's Note

One of my goals in writing The Middle Falls Time Travel series is to not get into too much of a rut. I don't ever want to repeat the same story. Yes, all of the Middle Falls stories have common elements—death and reawakening in a younger self, and redemption. But, the *stories* are all different, from Michael Hollister's redemption from being a cold blooded killer, to the lessons Nathaniel Moon still needed to learn, to the many choices Veronica McAllister had to make to find her own emancipation.

In that vein, *The Vigilante Life of Scott McKenzie* is once again a new kind of story. In reviewing the first six books in the series, one thing I had noticed was that there wasn't a lot of "action sequences." You know, car chases, or physical altercations and the like. I thought it was time to remedy that. So, we have a book that's relatively chock-full of those elements. It's important to me to not neglect the most important parts of the story, though—the emotional arc of Scott McKenzie, in particular.

If you've been reading these books in sequence, you might remember that after the last book—*The Changing Lives of Joe Hart*—I had announced I was going to take a break from writing more Middle Falls books for a while. That lasted all of about ten days, as Scott McKenzie kept banging on my brain, asking me to tell his story. That hadn't happened since I tried to kill of Michael Hollister at the end of the very first book. I turned out to love Michael's story, so I decided to listen to Scott. I'm glad I did.

It was a challenge to write Scott's character and have him come off to the reader the way I saw him—as a man conflicted by his natural tendencies of non-violence, but needing to embrace violence to fulfill his destiny. I worked hard to present him as a real person, warts and all, but show that ultimately, he was a good, and kind man.

---

1. https://amzn.to/2D39mYG

Did I get there? Only you can decide that. That's the great thing about our relationship. I do my best to write a good story, but it doesn't come to life until you put the words into your head.

Bestselling author Terry Schott once again was my alpha reader. He reads each of my books in ten-thousand word chunks and provides insight and incredible advice on the fly. He made some terrific suggestions and had a number of keen insights into what would make this book work. I appreciate him endlessly.

Once again, Linda Boulanger from TreasureLine Books handled the cover duties. This cover came together faster than any project we've ever worked on, and Linda's been doing my books since 2012. As soon as I saw the dirty, menacing face of Scott McKenzie, I knew she had captured the vibe I wanted perfectly.

Dan Hilton of Hilton Editing and Proofreading, once again had the editing reins. Dan is exceptionally busy and talented, but somehow he manages to find a way things done, always before the deadline. Dan made this book better, and I owe him a great deal of gratitude.

Mark Sturgell and Debra Galvan served as my 1-2 proofreading punch once again. Speaking of tight deadlines, I put them to the test with this book and they both did an outstanding job of catching my errant hyphens and commas. I believe if we didn't have hyphens in the English language, it would eliminate 80% of the mistakes I make.

Because this book contained some elements I am not familiar with, I consulted with two experts. Jerry Weible has been my best friend since third grade. He and his lovely wife Lynn are also the inspiration for Jerry and Lynn Werbeloff in this story. Jerry has been studying martial arts since 1974. He assisted me in making sure the fight scenes were believable. He also turned me on to the deadly karambit that Scott McKenzie used to great effect in the book.

Also, my brother-in-law, Brian Decker, helped me on many aspects of the book. Brian has been in law enforcement since the seventies and explained many things I was previously unaware of. One of those things, unfortunately, is that the collapsing baton that Scott uses throughout this book is illegal in many jurisdictions, and would have been difficult for Scott to obtain in the early seventies. Since I had already written that Scott had used that weapon in the last book in the series, I couldn't change it for this one, so I took a small literary license and left it in. Mea culpa.

Many thanks to both Jerry and Brian for their invaluable advice and assistance. All remaining errors in fact are mine alone.

Finally, I would like to thank my Constant Readers who make up my *Shawn Inmon's Advance Readers* group on Facebook. They read the story in its roughest form and give me a push in the right direction every time. If you are interested in volunteering to be one of my Advance Readers, drop me a line at shawninmon@gmail.com.

I want you to know how grateful I am that you choose to read my stories. You are the reason I write them.

Shawn Inmon
Seaview, WA
September 2018

Other Books by Shawn Inmon

The Unusual Second Life of Thomas Weaver[1] – Book one of the Middle Falls Time Travel Series. Thomas Weaver led a wasted life, but divine intervention gives him a chance to do it all over again. What would you do, if you could do it all again?

The Redemption of Michael Hollister[2] — Book two of the Middle Falls Time Travel Series. Michael Hollister was evil in Thomas Weaver's story. Is it possible for a murderer to find true redemption?

The Death and Life of Dominick Davidner[3] – Book Three of the Middle Falls Time Travel Series. When Dominick is murdered, he awakens back in his eight year old body with one thought: how to find Emily, the love of his life.

The Final Life of Nathaniel Moon[4] – Book Four of the Middle Falls Time Travel Series. Nathaniel Moon gains perfect consciousness in the womb, but when he tries to use his miraculous powers to do good, difficulties follow.

The Emancipation of Veronica McAllister[5] – Book Five of the Middle Falls Time Travel Series. Veronica McAllister said she was no good at life. When she dies and wakes up back in 1958, though, she has a second chance.

The Changing Lives of Joe Hart[6] – Book Six of the Middle Falls Time Travel Series. Joe Hart dies in 2004, but wakes up in his eighteen year old body and decides to change the world. As always, that isn't easy.

Feels Like the First Time[7] – Shawn's first book, his true story of falling in love with the girl next door in the 1970's, losing her for 30 years, and miraculously find-

---

1. *https://www.amazon.com/Unusual-Second-Life-Thomas-Weaver-ebook/dp/B01J8FBONO*
2. *http://amzn.to/2wyUfCH*
3. *http://amzn.to/2yTgHnk*
4. *https://www.amazon.com/gp/product/B078H3376R*
5. *http://amzn.to/2HkHegL*
6. *https://amzn.to/2rYBqVh*
7. *https://www.amazon.com/Feels-Like-First-Time-Story-ebook/dp/B00961VIIM*

ing her again. It is filled with nostalgia for a bygone era of high school dances, first love, and making out in the backseat of a Chevy Vega.

Both Sides Now[8] – It's the same true story as *Feels Like the First Time,* but told from Dawn's perspective. It will surprise no one that first love and loss feels very different to a young girl than it did for a young boy.

Rock 'n Roll Heaven[9] – Small-time guitarist Jimmy "Guitar" Velvet dies and ends up in Rock 'n Roll Heaven, where he meets Elvis Presley, Buddy Holly, Jim Morrison, and many other icons. To his great surprise, he learns that heaven might need him more than he needs it.

Second Chance Love[10] – Steve and Elizabeth were best friends in high school and college, but were separated by a family tragedy before either could confess that they were in love with the other. A chance meeting on a Christmas tree lot twenty years later gives them a second chance.

Life is Short[11] – A collection of all of Shawn's short writings. Thirteen stories, ranging from short memoirs about summers in Alaska, to the satire of obsessed fans.

A Lap Around America[12] – Shawn and Dawn quit good jobs and set out to see America. They saved you a spot in the car, so come along and visit national parks, tourist traps, and more than 13,000 miles of the back roads of America, all without leaving your easy chair.

A Lap Around Alaska[13] – Have you ever wanted to drive the Alaska Highway across Canada, then make a lap around central Alaska? Here's your chance! Includes 100 photographs!

---

8. *https://www.amazon.com/Both-Sides-Now-True-Story-ebook/dp/B00DV5GQ54*
9. *https://www.amazon.com/Rock-Roll-Heaven-Shawn-Inmon-ebook/dp/B00J9T1GQA*
10. *https://www.amazon.com/Second-Chance-Love-Shawn-Inmon-ebook/dp/B00T6MU7AQ*
11. *https://www.amazon.com/Life-Short-Collected-Fiction-Shawn-ebook/dp/B01MRCXNS3*
12. *https://www.amazon.com/Lap-Around-America-ebook/dp/B06XY9GSWC*
13. *https://www.amazon.com/Lap-Around-Alaska-AlCan-Adventure-ebook/dp/B0744CVWT4/ref=sr_1_4?s=digital-text&ie=UTF8&qid=1506966654&sr=1-4&keywords=shawn+inmon+kindle+books*

Made in the USA
Lexington, KY
07 July 2019